STARS' END

Other books by Glen Cook

STARS' END

THE STARFISHERS TRILOGY
VOLUME THREE

GLEN COOK

NIGHT SHADE BOOKS
SAN FRANCISCO

First Edition

ISBN: 978-1-59780-169-0

Printed In Canada

Night Shade Books
Please visit us on the web at
http://www.nightshadebooks.com

This one is for you,
Sherry Lynne Manes.
Without your help no deadlines would be met.

BOOK ONE
THE HIGH SEINERS

ONE: 3049 AD
The Main Sequence

The death cry of an exploding sun illuminated a starfleet the likes of which few men had ever seen. There were six great starships in the convoy. The smallest was forty kilometers long.

No drive glow enveloped those ships. No ion wake marked their passing. They were drifting. But they met the flash front of the nova with an inherent velocity approaching three-tenths the velocity of light.

Each of those starships looked like a mobile created by a sculptor, looked like someone had visited a planetary junkyard, had welded scraps together, and then had flung the results at the farthest star. Those ships were all angles, tubes and planes, globes, cubes, and what appeared to be silver sails. Whole forests of antennae bristled on the humped mountains of their backs.

Random chunks of debris accompanied the ships, thrown out from jagged wounds in their flanks. Wisps of atmosphere leaked from those great rents, twinkling in the nova light. Smaller ships, like blowflies, fluttered around the rawest injuries.

There had been a battle. A battle at Stars' End. Its fury and magnitude would have beggared the imagination of men who hadn't ever been out among the stars.

These limping, crippled starships were the survivors.

The great lens of the Milky Way sprawled before the starships, cold and silver and bright. Their noses were aimed toward its heart. Like a dying man crossing a desert, the starfleet was dragging itself toward healthier climes.

A patch on the smallest ship began to glow, throwing color back into the ocean of night. It was not a happy color. It was the dull, dark red of venous blood, the red of senescent suns. It brightened, became more intense.

The other ships drifted away. Fate had overtaken their little sister. She was about to lose control of her fusion plant. They did not want to be too close to the explosion. The smaller blowfly-vessels flitted away, carrying evacuees.

For a moment the smaller starship yielded a light which rivalled that of the nearby nova. Fragments as big as pyramids hurtled outward, adding to the clutter traveling with the fleet. The remainder of the ship began tumbling slowly, now little more than a disemboweled corpse. The little ships darted in again, swarmed around the remains. Signals leapt across the ether. Any survivors? Anyone at all? There was no answer from the wreck. But the little ships went in anyway.

Moyshe benRabi slapped the withdrawal switch beneath his left hand.

Agony smashed into his head. A demon slapped a pair of icehooks into his temples and yanked. He screamed. "Clara! Shot!"

He did not feel the needle bite his arm. Its prick was too tiny a pain. He knew it had happened only because blessed relief hit him seconds later.

Hans pulled his helmet. The youngster's face was drawn. Clara patted sweat from his face with a towel. "Bad, Moyshe?" she asked.

"The worst. I can't reach him anymore. He's out there without protection... And we just lost *Jariel*. They couldn't contain the anti-matter leak. The Service Ships went back... I don't think they'll find anybody to evacuate."

Hans asked, "Drink, Moyshe?" The youth's voice was tremulous. He had had a sister on *Jariel*.

"Something. Please. I must have sweated a couple of liters. They get through to Gruber yet?"

Clara shrugged. "I haven't heard." She was a plump, grandmotherly, greying woman with rosy cheeks. Her appearance reflected her personality. She was a book which could be read by its cover. BenRabi was in love with her, in a filial way.

"We've got to have help. We can't hide in this nova storm forever. The particle wave is on its way. It'll shred our screens."

"Payne says we're going out. Soon as *Jariel* is evacuated. The sharks will have to take their chances."

"Oh, damn."

"What do the starfish say?" Hans asked, returning with a fruit drink. He was putting on a brave face. He had been in the fleet long enough to learn how to wait for good news or bad. They would let him know about his sister.

BenRabi swung his feet to the deck. "Like I said. I couldn't get through. Too far."

"Maybe somebody else did."

"Somebody with more experience? I don't think so."

Hans was just nineteen, hardly out of creche. He had not yet hardened to all the realities of the harvestfleet.

"Well just have to do it Payne's way. Fight our way through." BenRabi began shuddering as his body reacted to the massive dosage of anti-pain drug. Clara swept a blanket around his shoulders. It did not lessen the chills.

They still did not know for certain that they had won the battle of Stars' End. They knew only that Payne's Fleet had held the battle space, had survived, and had begun making its way home. They had not been attacked again, yet, but it was only a matter of time till the struggle resumed.

"Look at me," benRabi whispered. "I can't stop shaking."

"Go home," Clara told him. "Get some sleep."

"We might break through. They might need me to go on mind-drive. Just let me stretch my legs." He picked at his arm where the needle had broken his skin. The strain of the emergency had begun to show on his flesh. He was getting tracks.

He collapsed when he tried to stand.

"Take him home, Hans," Clara told the youth. "Lester. Help

Hans load Moyshe onto a scooter, will you?"

"What's going on?" benRabi demanded as Hans halted the flatbed electric truck outside his quarters. For a moment he did not know where he was. "Why did you?..."

"What happened?" a woman demanded. Worry strangled her voice.

"He passed out," Hans replied. "Just needs rest."

"I told him..."A thin, pale, nervous face outlined by short blonde hair entered Moyshe's vision, peered down into his eyes. "What's the matter with you, Moyshe? You think you're a superman? Give me a hand with him, Hans. I'll tie him in bed if I have to."

"Somebody's got to..." benRabi protested.

"You aren't the only somebody on *Danion*. There's nobody like a new convert. I love him, but sometimes he drives me up the wall."

"Take care of him, Amy."

"Don't worry. I've got too much invested in this idiot."

They dropped benRabi into his bed. It surrounded him with a womblike comfort. He felt vaguely guilty. He shouldn't be sleeping while other mindtechs were still trying to make contact.

Amy sat on the edge of the bed. He was asleep long before she finished cussing him out for not taking better care of himself.

She was still hovering around when, six hours later, the cabin comm buzzed. She answered, "Amy Coleridge, Security."

A grey-framed face appeared in the little screen. "Good morning, Lieutenant. Is benRabi there?"

"Commander. Sir. Yes sir." Her voice dropped an octave and seemed to snap to attention. "He's sleeping, sir. But I can wake him if you really need him."

"No. Don't. I wanted to speak to you, Lieutenant. I'm on my way down to see you."

Two minutes later there was a knock on the cabin door. The Commander must have been on the way when he'd called her.

"I've just read your report on benRabi."

"You did? Why? It was just a routine report."

The Commander brushed her question aside. "We may need him for something more than Contact. Coleridge, I want to ask you a question. I want a considered answer."

"Sir?"

"Is your report honest? Did you let your feelings affect it?"

"No sir. Yes sir. I mean, it's honest, sir."

"You're sure he's become a Seiner without reservation?"

"He has a few. He grew up different. But he's committed, sir. Almost too much. That's the way he is."

"Will he stay committed? Under pressure? He's changed allegiances before."

"Before? When, sir?"

"When he left Old Earth."

"That's not the same thing. Earth is part of Confederation. He just joined the Navy."

Danion's commander reflected. "True. But, considering the way Old Earthers look at these things, it indicates a flighty nature. All right. Enough about benRabi. What about his cohort?"

Amy's colorless eyebrows crinkled over her pale blue eyes. "That's more difficult, sir. Mouse is more complicated."

"Are you sure you're not projecting a lack of understanding? His psych profiles make him look pretty simple. Almost black and white. He seems to have hung his whole existence on his hatred for the Sangaree."

"Then why did he stay here? He could've gone back to Confederation with the others. He can't fight Sangaree out here."

"I've been wondering. That's why I asked."

"I can't tell you, sir. He's all facade to me. All charm and silliness. I can't tell when he's serious and when he's joking. The only feeling I get is that the man I'm seeing isn't the real Masato Storm."

"Are you involved with him, too, Lieutenant?"

"Sir!"

"Answer me."

"No, sir! I am not involved with Mr. Storm."

"Makes you part of a vanishing breed, then. Seems he's bedded half the single women on *Danion*."

"He attracts a certain kind of woman."

"Oh?" The caller smiled. "But not you?"

She was a long time answering. "The temptation is there. He

has an animal magnetism. There's curiosity about what everyone else sees in him. But nothing is going to happen. I don't like him very much."

Her answer seemed to satisfy the Commander.

"We're entering a new era, Lieutenant. A time of changes. Our isolationism is under attack. The sharks are wearing us down. The Stars' End idea was a debacle. We're going to have to adjust. Either that or bend over and kiss our tails good-bye. Those two might be useful. They have unusual backgrounds. We don't have a secret service to speak of. They could build one. But that would mean trusting them. And they weren't born Starfishers."

"A lot of us weren't, somewhere along the line. My father…"

"I know. We're all refugees. Thank you, Lieutenant. Consider this discussion exclusive. Don't mention it to anybody. And if you learn anything that might have a bearing on the matter, call my office. I'll have your name red-tagged to my personal recorder. I'll call you back."

"Yes sir."

The Commander left as quickly as he'd arrived. Amy sat and stared into the shadows of the room.

After a while she lifted her thin frame and drifted into the room where benRabi was sleeping. She stared down at him with an expression approaching awe.

She had never seen or met the Ship's Commander before, except in public address announcements.

Her Moyshe, her last chance man… He might amount to something after all.

She would not have become involved with the foreigner at all had her self-image not been pit-deep. She could not make herself believe that she deserved a good man, a real Starfisher. She had expected to watch her life drift away from the foot of a social and career ladder.

The Commander's call changed everything. She would have to get Moyshe moving. And make sure his friend Mouse did not lead him astray.

The differences between the Confederated life that benRabi had chosen to leave and the lives of the Starfishers were deep.

The Starfishers, the High Seiners, spent their adult lives aboard these vast harvestships, drifting the deep-space hydrogen streams, gleaning the droppings of an almost intangible spacebeast they called a starfish. A whole ecology existed in the interstellar rivers. It was vast and slow, in keeping with the low random collision of the molecules from which their type of life had gradually evolved. That life was invisible to the eye or radar. The atoms constituting the "bodies" of the interstellar creatures could be scattered over cubic kilometers.

Starfish were more vast than harvestships, yet the matter in them could be compressed into a volume smaller than that occupied by the body of a ten-year-old. The atoms were as much foci for forces as part of the life process itself. And most of the creatures of the ecology existed, in part, in hyperspace and another, congruent universe.

At the starfish's heart a tiny fusion flame burned.

Starfish swept up hydrogen and random molecules and occasionally passed a node of hard waste. The nodes were incalculably precious.

The Starfishers called them ambergris. Ambergris was the foundation of their economy.

The nodes were used in instel communicators. There was no substitute. The Seiners controlled the only supply, and, consequently, the market and price.

Countless were the organizations which would pay almost any price for near instantaneous communication across interstellar distance.

Moyshe benRabi and Masato Storm had been sent among the Seiners to try to find a way for their employers, Confederation Navy, to seize the harvestships and ambergris industry. They had succeeded and failed. They had found the information…

And had elected to become Starfishers themselves.

The hydrogen streams boasted a complex ecology. It included the predatory "shark," which subsisted principally upon starfish. Evolution had equipped starfish with only one truly credible defensive weapon. Intellect.

Deep-space evolution had begun eons before the condensation of Old Earth's sun. The modern starfish species had a remembered history spanning billions of years. They had seen countless planet-born races come and go. They knew the value of their waste.

Over the past thousand Terran years, an eye's blink in the life of a starfish, shark numbers had exploded insanely. A new species was coming into being. It reasoned feebly, bred obsessively, and hunted in cooperative packs which now, sometimes, numbered as many as a thousand predators. The survival of the starfish species had come into sudden doubt.

Their Old Ones had deliberated with almost immoderate haste. A decision had been reached. They turned their intelligence to finding a means of contacting the tiny, hard, warm creatures who lived in the metal shells questing around their wakes.

They had struck a bargain with the original Starfishers. Ambergris in return for the protection of human weapons. It had been a good bargain. The sharks had been kept at bay for two hundred years.

Another mere blink of Time's eye.

Then the ever more numerous sharks had developed the tactic of assailing the protectors before the protected.

Danion had enlisted landsmen as emergency replacements for heavy casualties suffered during one such attack. Her leaders had hoped to draw high quality technicians who might be seduced away from their lives in Confederation. Instead, they had attracted scores of spies sent in hopes of capturing control of a harvestfleet. Confederation's Bureau of Naval Intelligence had sent senior field agents Moyshe benRabi and Masato Igarashi Storm.

The two had found what promised to be a home.

Sirens wailed throughout *Danion.*

Amy jerked out of her seat. "Moyshe! Battle stations! We must be coming out of the flash wave."

BenRabi surged out of the bedroom, climbing into his jumpsuit as he came. "Let's go, honey." He dragged her into the passageway outside, where a pair of electric scooters nursed charger sockets. He seized one, she the other. "See you, love," he said as he sailed away.

He pulled to the center of the passage and opened the scooter up. The walls blurred past. People were running in the pedestrian lanes. Scooters hurtled at him from the opposite direction. There were near collisions at every cross corridor. A voice like that of a god kept booming, "Battle stations. Battle station."

Damn, damn, damn, Moyshe thought. I shouldn't be going back under so soon.

Five vast and tangled ships began nosing out of the intense nova light. The blowfly vessels still swarmed around their wounds, and between them and the derelict tumbling along in their midst, guarded by their shell of fire. One by one, the five great ships rolled to present their heaviest weapons outward from a common center.

TWO: 3049 AD
The Contemporary Scene

A ship came into being slightly below the surface of a dust lake rilling a crater on a nameless moon circling a world far in toward the center of the galaxy. The most centerward world of Ulant lay a thousand light years rimward. No human being had traveled this part of space before.

Astronomers on the primary, had they been watching, would have been astonished by the geyser which exploded from the crater's flat dust face.

No astronomers were watching. They, like soldiers, wives, derelicts, and children… like everyone who lived on that world, were engaged in a death struggle so demanding they had ceased caring whether their satellite existed.

The ship that bobbed to the dust's surface looked like a giant doughnut with a beer can shoved through the hole and held in place by thin straws. One tall vane, like a shark's fin, rose from the torus, leaning away from the cylinder. A globe surmounted it.

The whole vessel was dead black. Not even a hull number broke its lack of color.

It was a tiny ship. The beer can was just sixty meters tall. The outer diameter of the doughnut barely spanned sixty-five meters. The curves of the vessel were broken only by a handful of antennae, two missile launch bays, and the snouts of laser and graser batteries. She was a deadly little beast, designed solely to kill.

She was a museum piece. Literally. And the nastiest little shark of a warship ever conceived by the mind of Man.

She was a Climber left over from the Ulantonid War. She had been dragged from the War Museum at Luna Command and reactivated especially for this mission.

She was the first Climber to space since the war's most desperate days—because Climbers were almost as deadly to their crews as to the enemies they stalked. Only the absolute imperative of racial survival would see them used in combat again.

Luna Command had that much heart. The Climber Fleets had been too destructive of the minds and bodies of their crews.

The little ambushers had changed the course of the Ulantonid War. And had filled the sanitariums of Confederation with walking wounded, the few survivors of service within their sanity-devouring fields of concealment.

The Climber generated a field in her torus which drove her into a dimension beyond hyper-space, called Null, where she remained virtually undetectable till she returned to Hyper or Norm to attack.

Climbers in schools had destroyed whole Ulantonid fleets.

This Climber had the most remarkable crew of any Navy had ever spaced.

Her Ship's Commander was Manfred, Fleet Admiral Graf von Staufenberg, First Deputy Chief of Staff of Confederation Navy. He had seen Climber duty toward the end of the war. The ship's First Watch Officer was Melene Telle-eych Cath, Defender Prime of Ulant, or Minister of Defense. Her Operations Officer was Ulant's Principal Peacemaker, or Chief of the General Staff, Turone Wahl-chyst Forse. Her Gunnery Officer and his leading mates were Star Lords of the Toke. One was the Star Lord who commanded Confederation's Marine Toke Legion. The others ranked him in the Caste of Warriors.

There was no man or woman aboard, of any five races, who ranked below the equivalent of Admiral or General, and none of them were not decision-makers.

A well-placed missile could have crippled the defenses of humanity and all its neighbors.

Admiral Wildblood, the lady who directed Navy's Bureau of Naval Intelligence, and Admiral Beckhart, who ran her department of dirty tricks, had two of the more menial assignments in Operations. One watched the hyper detection gear, the other the passive radar scans.

Star Lords and all, they slept in hammocks slung from the Climber's central structural member, or "keel." They shared the one toilet and did without the shower that had never existed. In Climb they used portable chamberpots and smelled one another's stinks as had the Climbermen of an age gone by.

One and all, they had come to see for themselves the growing disaster Ulantonid explorers had been bemoaning for years.

They had seen film. They had questioned witnesses. In some cases they had begun to act. But they had had to see with their own eyes before they could finally believe.

They had to watch the war going on below. On the primary of the moon.

A race from farther in toward the galactic core was systematically exterminating every sentient creature it encountered. The natives of this world were their latest victims.

The people aboard the Climber came of races which had fought bitterly in the past. There was little love among some of them now. But never, in the most desperate, heated days of their contention, had any considered eradicating their enemies. Their wars had been tests of racial wills, with territorial causes.

This world was the fourth assailed by the centerward race since its discovery by Ulantonid explorers. The first three worlds were lifeless now. The aggressors even shunned their use as bases.

Even the Warriors of Toke could not comprehend the destruction of intelligent life simply because it was intelligent.

The Warriors believed battle to be a crucible for purification of the soul, a road to honor and glory, grimly majestic and godlike. For them combat was almost an end in itself. They fought one another when there were no outsiders.

They were perfectly aware of the distinction between victory and obliteration. They were as appalled by the excesses of the centerward race as were any of their shipmates.

They had come to see for themselves. And the grim truth burned in the Climber's display tank.

The world's atmosphere was alive with spiderwebs of coherent light. Energy and particle beams hacked air and space like the flailing swords of a thousand ancient armies. The planet people had the technological edge. The exterminators had the numbers and determination. Their ships clouded the stars.

They had overwhelmed the world's off-planet protection months ago. Now they were pounding the on-world defenses, and were making their initial landings.

Star-bright, short-lived pinpoints speckled the world's surface.

"They're using nuclears!" Ulant's Defender growled. Even during their war's bitterest hour, neither human nor Ulantonid had violated each other's worlds with nuclear weapons. By tacit agreement those had been confined to vacuum.

"They know we're here," Beckhart called out. "Seven destroyer displacement ships are headed this way."

"Very well," Graf von Staufenberg replied. "Melene, most of that looks like it's happening in the troposphere. They're probably not pushing one in a thousand warheads through to the surface."

The Star Lord who commanded all Star Lords boomed, "Every one through destroys. The defense net weakness. Soon it will be two of a thousand. Then four."

"Not to mention what the radioactivity will do in the long run. Makes you wonder why they're forcing it with landings. Here. This south tropic archipelago. They've punched an open corridor down there."

"Hell of a defense," someone muttered. "Damn near as tough as Stars' End. I wouldn't want to try breaking it."

"How long till those destroyers are pushing us?" von Staufenberg asked.

"They're humping it in Norm. Four or five minutes for the closest. Looks like some other stuff starting to move, too."

"Can't we do anything?" the D.N.I. demanded.

Von Staufenberg replied, "We could bloody a few noses. It wouldn't change anything. We couldn't do that with a hundred

Climbers. There're just too damned many of them. Okay, let's give the people in the other compartments a look. I want everybody to see it. We'll have some decision to make on our way home."

"The Warriors have decided," said the Star Lord of the Marine Toke Legion.

"He speaks for Toke," his non-Service superior added. "For Toke there can be but one decision. We will come to them here. Alone if we have to."

"It's not that easy for me, Manfred," Melene said. "We're an adventurous species but I'm handicapped by democratic traditions and faith in peace. We don't organize quickly or well."

Von Staufenberg chuckled. "You did before."

The Defender was older than he. She had been a soldier throughout the Ulantonid War.

"I expect we will again. We can do anything when we decide to pull together. It's the decision process that's so abominably slow."

"Your decisions were made years ago, Melene," Beckhart growled from his radar boards. "Don't try to snow us. I can give you the names and hull numbers of a hundred new construction ships you've got tucked away in places you never thought we'd look."

"Admiral Beckhart?" von Staufenberg queried.

"I have my sources, sir. They're rearming as fast as their ship-building industry can space hulls. They come off the line looking like commercial ships, only they've got drive potential up the yang-yang, and they never get delivered to any of the transport outfits. They disappear for a while, then turn up somewhere else with guns dripping off them."

"Why wasn't High Command informed of this, Beckhart?"

"Because my sources are in the Defender's office. And I knew why they were rearming. You wouldn't have bought it. Half of High Command is still trying to refight the Ulantonid War. I let it go on playing that game because people were seeing enough of those new ships to get nervous and start us a secret building program of our own. So we're on our way too."

"Beckhart... Your logic baffles me. Totally baffles me. I have the distinct feeling that you'll have to explain it to a Board of

Inquiry. What else have you hidden from us?"

"You want an honest answer, or one that will please you?" Beckhart did not make many friends. He retained his position principally because no one else could do his job as well.

"Beckhart!"

"Several things, sir. Ongoing operations. If they work out, we'll be in good shape for meeting these monsters."

"Monsters?" Melene demanded. "There's no evidence…"

"Melene, the Admiral is a xenophobe. In fact, he doesn't like people very much. Tell me what you're doing, Beckhart."

"There's a chance I'm on the threshold to the solution of the Sangaree problem. Some new data was on its way in before we left. I'll probably want to borrow von Drachau again."

"What else?"

"Still too tentative for discussion. A possible breakthrough in communications and weapons technologies. I won't discuss it now. Not here."

"Beckhart…"

"Security privilege. Sir. Log it if you like."

Von Staufenberg wheeled on the Director of Naval Intelligence. She shrugged. "You won't get anything from me, either, Manfred."

"Damn! All right, let's get moving. Time's running out, and everybody's got to have a look at this."

Climbers were the most cramped vessels since Gemini. Circulating the forty-odd beings aboard was a slow, uncomfortable process.

"She's about to start shooting," Beckhart said of the nearest destroyer. "She has. Missile swarm. We have four minutes to hide."

"How do you like that? Didn't even try to find out who we were or what we wanted."

"This is the Ship's Commander," von Staufenberg said into the public address system. "We're under fire. Engineering, stand by to go Null." Thirty seconds before the swarm arrived, he ordered, "Take her up to ten Bev. First Watch Officer, a gesture is in order. Program me an attack approach on the vessel shooting at us."

The Ulantonid's feathery antennae stirred, quivered. The action was comparable to a human's pleased chuckle.

The Star Lords were in Weapons Department already, hoping they would be allowed to play with their deadly toys.

"One missile," said von Staufenberg. "Right up her wake."

It was the classic Climber attack strategy. Drives were a warship's soft spot. They simply could not be designed so that thrust apertures could be shielded as well as the remainder of the vessel.

The dust in the crater flowed together suddenly, smashing in like the Red Sea on Pharaoh's chariots. The doughnut ship had vanished.

"Take her all the way to forty Bev," von Staufenberg ordered. "I doubt they know enough to look for our Hawking Point, but let's get that cross-section down anyway." One of the curiosities about the Climber was that no other race known to humanity had ever developed it. And for humans it had been an accidental by-product of other research.

Twenty-three minutes passed before the First Watch Officer reported, "Attack position, Commander."

"Weapons, Ship's Commander. One missile. Stand by. Detection, when we go down I want you to get the ranges and vectors on everything you can see. We'll do what we can. And I want the tape rolling. Ship's Services, vent heat while we're Norm. All right. Everybody ready? Take her down, Engineering."

Heat accumulation was the biggest weakness of the Climber. There was no way to shed heat in Null. And a Climber often had to stay up for days while enemy warships hunted her.

The Climber was no warship in the slug-it-out sense. She was a hit-and-run fighter dependent on surprise for her effectiveness.

The Defender Prime brought them down just four kilometers behind the destroyer. The Climber rocked. The missile accelerated at 100 g. It arrived before the destroyer knew it was coming.

"One for the good guys," Beckhart grumped as the Climber went up again.

"What was that?" von Staufenberg demanded.

"Admiral, you're giving them valuable information just by blowing them out of space. You're telling them we can do it.

You'll get them wondering how. Head home before we give them any hard data. Let's save the surprises for when they'll do some good."

Von Staufenberg reddened. There was no love lost between him and Beckhart.

"He's right, Manfred," the Defender Prime interjected. "You almost wasted the Climber advantage by committing them piecemeal during the war. They would have more effective if whole fleets had appeared suddenly. We would not have had time to adapt."

"Of course. Of course. I was thinking with my guts. Program a course for the mother, Melene."

Climbers did not have a long range. A mother ship awaited this one a hundred light-years homeward. A small armada protected her.

This Climber's crew regarded themselves highly.

THREE: 3049 AD
The Main Sequence

BenRabi slammed his scooter through the entrance to Control Sector. Seconds later the massive shield doors rumbled shut behind him. The section was totally self-contained now. No one could come in or leave till those doors lifted.

Moyshe stopped in a long, squealing slide. He jumped off, slammed the charger plug into a socket, ran through the hatch to Contact.

"You made it," Clara said. "We didn't think you would. You live so far away. Here. Catch your breath."

"My scooter was smoking. Better have it checked, Hans." He settled onto a fitted couch.

"Ready?" Clara asked.

"No."

She smiled at him. Hans started massaging an odorless paste into his scalp. Clara slipped her fingers inside what looked like a hairnet.

"You never are. I thought you liked Chub."

BenRabi chuckled. "Chub, I like fine. He's good people. But I'd like him a lot better if he could walk in the door, stick out a hand, and say, 'Hey, Moyshe, let's go grab a couple of beers.'"

Chub was the starfish with whom benRabi usually linked.

"Xenophobe."

"Crap. It's not him. It's that out-of-body feeling…"

"Wrong, Moyshe. You can't fool old Clara. I was babying mindtechs before you were born. And you're all alike. You don't want to go out because it hurts so much to come back."

"Yeah?"

"Ready," Hans said.

Clara slid the net onto Moyshe's head. Her fingertips were soft and warm. They lingered on his cheeks. Momentary concern clouded her smile.

"Don't push yourself, Moyshe. Get out if it gets rough. You haven't had enough rest."

"Since Stars' End there isn't any rest. For anybody."

"We won," Hans reminded.

"The cost was too high."

"It was cheaper than losing."

BenRabi shrugged. "I guess you people see things different. I never would have gone in the first place."

"You took your whippings and smiled, back in Confederation?" Hans asked. "I never heard of that."

"No. We calculated the odds. We picked the right time. Then we ganged up. We didn't just go storming around like a rogue elephant, getting hurt as much as we did hurt."

"Oriflamme," Hans countered.

"What?"

"That's what they call Payne sometimes. It's something from olden times that has to do with not taking prisoners."

"Oh. The oriflamme. It was a special pennon that belonged to the King of France. If he raised it, it meant take no prisoners. It had a way of backfiring on him."

"Hans," Clara said, "Moyshe is an Academy man. He can probably tell you how many spokes in the wheel of a Roman war chariot."

"Take Poitiers, for instance…"

"Who?"

"It's a place. In France, which is on Old Earth…"

"I know where France is, Moyshe."

"All right. One of the big battles of the Hundred Years War

was fought there. And you could say that the French lost because of the oriflamme. See, they caught the English in a bad spot. Outnumbered them like ten to one. The Black Prince decided to surrender. But the French raised the oriflamme. Which pissed the English, so they proceeded to kick ass all over the countryside. When the dust settled, the French were wiped out and Louis was in chains. There's a lesson in there somewhere, if you want to look. Namely, don't ever push anybody into a corner where he can't get out."

"You see what he's doing, Hans?" Clara asked.

"You mean trying to educate us until the all-clear comes through? You're out of luck, Moyshe. Lift your head so I can put your helmet on."

BenRabi raised his head.

His scalp began tingling under the hairnet device. The helmet devoured his head, stealing the light. He fought the panic that always hit before he went under.

Hans strapped him in and adjusted the bio-monitor's pickups.

"Can you hear me, Moyshe?" Clara asked through the helmet's earphones.

He raised a hand. Then spoke: "Coming through clear."

"Got you too. Your boards look good. Blood pressure is up, but that's normal for you. Take a minute in TSD. Relax. Go when you want."

His, "I don't want," remained unspoken.

He depressed the switch beneath his right hand one click.

The only senses left him were internal. Total Sensory Deprivation left him only his aches and pains, the taste in his mouth, and the rush of blood. Once the field took hold, even those would go.

In small doses it *was* relaxing. But too much could drive a man insane.

He flicked his right hand again.

A universe took form around him. He was its center, its lord, its creator... There was no pain in that universe, nor much unhappiness. Too many wonders burned there, within the bounds of his mind.

It was a universe of colors both pastel and crisp. Every star was a blazing jewel, proclaiming its individual hue. The oncoming storm of the nova's solar wind was a rioting, psychedelic cloud that seemed to have as much substance as an Old Earth thunderhead. Opposite it, the pale pink glimmer of a hydrogen stream meandered off toward the heart of the galaxy. The surrounding harvestships were patches of iridescent gold.

A score of golden Chinese dragons drifted with the fleet, straining toward it, yet held away by the light pressure of the dying star. Starfish!

BenRabi's sourness gave way to elation. There would be contact this time.

He reached toward them with his thoughts. "Chub? Are you out there, my friend?" For a time there was nothing.

Then a warm glow enveloped him like some sudden outbreak of good cheer.

"Moyshe man-friend, hello. I see you. Coming out of the light, hello. One ship is gone."

"*Jariel.* They're still evacuating."

"Sad."

Chub did not seem sad. This fish, benRabi thought, is constitutionally incapable of anything but joy.

"Not so, Moyshe man-friend. I mourn with the herd the sorrows of Stars' End. Yet I must laugh with my man-friends over the joys of what was won."

"The ships-that-kill weren't all destroyed, Chub. The Sangaree carry their grudges forever."

"Ha! They are a tear in the eye of eternity. They will die. Their sun will die. And still there will be starfish to swim the rivers of the night."

"You've been puttering around in the back rooms of my mind again. You're stealing my images and shooting them back at me."

"You have an intriguing mind, Moyshe man-friend. A clouded, boxy mind, cobwebby, atticy, full of trap doors…"

"What would you know about trap doors?"

"Only what I relive through your memories, Moyshe man-friend."

Chub teased and giggled like an adolescent lover.

By starfish reckoning he *was* a child. He had not yet seen his millionth year.

BenRabi simply avoided thinking about starfish time spans. A life measured in millions of years was utterly beyond his ken. He only mourned the fact that those incredible spans could never touch upon worlds where beings of a biochemical nature lived. The stories they could have told! The historical mysteries they could have illuminated!

But starfish dared not get too near major gravitational or magnetic sources. Even the gravity of the larger harvestships felt to a starfish much as rheumatism to a human being.

They were terribly fragile creatures.

While Chub teased and enthused, Moyshe turned a part of his mind to his private universe again.

Red torpedoes idled along far away, across the pink river, against the galaxy.

"Yes," Chub said. "Sharks. Survivors of Stars' End called them here. They will attack. They starve. Another feast for the scavenger things."

Smaller ghosts in a mix of colors shadowed both dragons and torpedoes. They were Chub's scavengers.

The great slow ecology of the hydrogen streams had niches for creatures of most life-functions, though their definition in human terms was seldom more than an approximation. A convenient labeling.

Moyshe yielded to nervousness. Chub reached into his mind, calming him…

"I'm learning, Chub. I can see the river this time. I can see the particle storm coming from the sick sun."

"Very good, Moyshe man-friend. You relax now. Sharks come soon. You watch scavenger things instead. They tell when sharks can't wait anymore. They get dancey."

Moyshe laughed into his secret universe. Starfish believed in doing things with deliberation, as might be expected of creatures with vast life spans. Young starfish tended to be restless and excitable. They were prone to flutter impatiently in the presence of their elders. The Old Ones called it "getting dancey."

Chub was dancey most of the time.

The Old Ones considered him the herd idiot. Chub said they regretted exposing him to human hasty-think while he was still young and impressionable.

"Is a joke, Moyshe man-friend. Is a good joke? Yes?"

"Yes. Very funny." For a starfish. The Old Ones had to be the most phlegmatic, humorless, pragmatic intelligences in all creation. They couldn't even grasp the concept of a joke. With the exception of Chub, benRabi found them a depressing mob.

"I was lucky to become your mind-mate, Chub. Very lucky."

He meant it. He had linked with Old Ones. He compared it to making love to his grandmother bare-assed on an iceberg, with a crowd watching. Drawing Chub was the best thing that had happened to him in years.

"Yes. We half-wits stick together. Venceremos, Comrade Moyshe."

BenRabi filled the universe with laughter. "Where the hell did you get that?"

"Your mind full of cobwebby memories, Moyshe man-friend. One time you play revolutionary on hard matter place called Dustball."

"Yeah. I did. About two weeks. Then it was duck bullets all the way back to the Embassy."

"You live much in few years, Moyshe man-friend. Ten times anyone else linked by starfish Chub. Many adventures. Think Chub would make good spy?"

"Who would you spy on?"

"Yes. Problem. Very difficult to disguise as shark."

"That's another joke, isn't it?"

"Yes. You still spying, Moyshe man-friend?"

"Not anymore. I'm not Thomas McClennon anymore. I'm Moyshe benRabi. I've found me a home, Chub. These are my people now. You can't spy on your own people."

"Oh. Saw shadows in your mind. Thought maybe secret spy-stuff lurked. So. Hey! Maybe someday you go spy on hard matter place people? Be double spy."

"Double agent?"

"Oh. Yes. That right words."

"No more spying, Chub. I'm going to be a mindtech."

"Dangerous."

"So is spying. In more ways than you'll ever understand."

"Hurts-of-the-heart dangers, you mean?"

"I don't know why they tell you you're stupid. You're a lot smarter in a lot of ways than most people I know. You see things without having to have them explained."

"Helps, being starfish. People can't look inside, Moyshe man-friend. You have to tell. You have to show. You not the kind of man to do that."

"Yeah. Let's talk about something else, huh?"

"Running out of talk time, Moyshe man-friend. Scavenger creatures getting dancey. You not paying attention?"

"I still haven't got the hang of seeing everything at once."

That was one of the beauties of the mindtech's linked universe. He was not subject to the limitations of binocular vision. But he did have to unlearn its habits.

Blind people made better techs faster. They had no habits to unlearn, no preoccupations to overcome. But blind people who suffered from classical migraine were scarce.

Scarlet torpedoes edged toward the fleet. They were not yet wholly committed. Hunger still had not banished good sense.

Sharks were slow of wit, but they knew they had to get past the harvestships to reach their prey.

That was the whole point of the starfish-Starfisher alliance.

"Can't visit anymore, Chub. We're not going on mind-drive, so I'll have to help fight."

"Oh, yes, Moyshe man-friend. Shoot straight. I help, putting right vectors in your brain."

"All right." Aloud, into his helmet, benRabi said, "Gun Control."

A second later his earphones crackled. "Gun Control, aye."

"Mindtech. In link and free to assume control of a sector battery. Sharks will attack. Repeat, will attack."

"Shit. All right, buddy. But never mind the sector battery. Master Gunner says he wants you to feed the main battle tank. Think you and your link can give us good realtime input?"

"Yes," Chub murmured deep in benRabi's hindbrain.

"Yes," Moyshe said. And wondered why. It was not something

he had ever tried.

"Monitor?"

"All go, Gun Control," Clara's voice interjected. "Green boards all across. I've just keyed the translator. You can bring the computer on-line whenever you're ready."

"Stand by for draw, Linker."

"Moyshe," said Clara, "don't take any chances. Key out if it gets rough."

"Drawing, Linker."

For an instant benRabi felt as though some intangible vacuum were sucking his mind away. A smatter of panic quickly yielded to Chub's soothing.

Moyshe relaxed, became a conduit. He became an almost disinterested observer.

The scavengers suddenly grew dancey with a vengeance.

"Attack imminent," benRabi muttered.

Those pilot fish were excited because they would feast no matter what the outcome of battle. They would be perfectly content nibbling dead shark or dead starfish.

A dozen crimson torpedoes suddenly misted, stretched into long, fuzzy lines, and solidified again near the starfish herd.

A hundred swords of light started carving them into scavenger food. Sharks were easy meat for particle beams.

"Teach them to try end run through hyper," Chub whispered.

The starfish herd had not bothered to dodge. They would not begin maneuvering till the protection of the human ships began breaking down.

It might not hold, benRabi reflected. Five vessels could not establish a sound fire pattern. There would be blind spots. Big holes. To fill them would mean risking hitting your own people.

The shark packs milled. They had not yet found workable tactics for assailing a fleet of harvestships.

Their intellectual slowness was the only hope for starfish and Starfishers alike. Something had happened to the sharks. Their numbers were expanding almost exponentially. They were becoming ever more desperate in their quest for something to eat.

Their prey, historically, had been the stragglers of the great starfish herds. The feeble and injured and careless. But now they assaulted the strong and healthy as well, and had even begun turning on their own injured. Even the firepower of a harvestship could not hold the massed packs at bay when hunger heterodyned into a berserk killing rage.

"Not look so promising as you thought, Moyshe man-friend. All going to come at once, from everywhere, crazy. Just killing and dying."

There was dread in Chub's thought. Moyshe was dismayed. Even in the hell that had been the battle at Stars' End the starfish had not lost his good cheer.

The starfish's prediction proved correct. The red torpedoes suddenly exploded in every direction. Moyshe had seen the same reaction among humans. The first had been by a band of fair-weather revolutionaries who had heard the police were coming. Another time, a terrorist had lobbed a hand grenade into a crowded theater.

But the sharks were not fleeing. The instant-insanity had seized them. They were spreading out to attack.

They arrowed in on the harvestfleet. Laser and particle beam swords stabbed.

Danion's fire was deadly. The realtime simulation from the minds of a man and a starfish linked gave the weapons people a fractional second's advantage over their brethren in ships relying on normal detection systems.

The shark wave rolled round *Danion* like a breaker around a granite promontory.

They could have worn her down in time, had they had the patience of the sea, and the sea's resources for endlessly sending in another wave. They had hurt her bad at Stars' End. It only took one shark getting through, with its multi-dimensional fires, to ravage a whole section of ship. But this horde was more limited in its numbers and more driven by hunger.

"Oh, Christ," benRabi swore as an explosion ripped a huge chunk from a sister ship. A shark had gotten through there. The service ships, still evacuating *Jariel* and trying to plug the holes in the fire pattern, swarmed toward the fragment. Clouds of frozen water vapor boiled round it as atmosphere poured out.

A shark flung itself into the starfish herd.

The great night beasts were not defenseless. One burped a ball of the nuclear fire that burned in its "gut," flung it with Robin Hood accuracy. The shark perished in the fading flash of a hydrogen bomb.

One predator was gone. And one starfish was disarmed for hours. It took the creatures a long time to revitalize their internal fires.

BenRabi had seen the peaceable starfish use the same weapon against Sangaree raidships at Stars' End.

"Fur is flying now, Moyshe man-friend." Chub was straining for humor. "We doing all right, you and me. Maybe your Old Ones decide you not stupid after all." Left unthought was Chub's hope for the same reaction from his own Old Ones.

By way of support benRabi replied, "This is a new era, Chub. It's going to take hastiness and danciness to survive."

"Sharks coming again."

Once more *Danion*'s weaponry scarred the long night. Moyshe wondered what some alien would think if he happened on its unconcealable mark, a thousand years from now, a thousand light-years away.

Both sides had used retrospective observation techniques during the Ulantonid War. A battle's outcome might be fixed, but it could be studied over and over from every possible angle.

The second assault was more furious than the first. BenRabi stopped trying to think. He had to give his whole attention over to following the situation.

More sharks dropped hyper, drawn by no known means. The rage took them, too. They attacked everything, including wounded brethren floundering around the battle region.

This was the root of Chub's fear. That more and more sharks would be drawn till they simply overwhelmed everything.

It was the future foreseen by both starfish and Starfishers. The terror that herd after herd and harvestship after harvestship would be consumed was the force that had driven the maverick commander of this fleet to hazard the defenses of Stars' End.

The arrivals slowed to a trickle. Chub thought, "We going to win again, Moyshe man-friend. See the pattern? The glorious pattern. They waste their might devouring their own injured."

BenRabi searched his kaleidoscopic mind-link universe. He saw nothing but chaos. This, he reflected, is the sort of thing Czyzew-ski was thinking about when he wrote *The Old God*. So much of Czyzewski's poetry seemed reflective of recent events. Had the man been prescient?

No. He was far gone on stardust when he did the cycle including *The Old God*. The drug killed him less than a month after he finished the poem. The images were just the flaming madness of the drug burning through.

"Don't you get tired of being right?" he asked when the first sharks fled.

"Never, Moyshe man-friend. But learned long ago to wait till event is certain, predestined, to make observation. Error is painful. The scorn of Old Ones is like the fire of a thousand stars."

"I know the feeling." For some reason the face of Admiral Beckhart, his one-time commander, drifted through his universe. Here on the galactic rim, fighting for his life against creatures he had not suspected existed two years earlier, his previous career seemed as remote as that of another man. Of another incarnation, or something he had read about.

The assault collapsed once the first few well-fed sharks fled.

The starfish had suffered far less than their inedible guardians. Not one dragon was missing from the golden herd defended by the harvestships. But another ship had been injured severely.

A traitorous thought stole across Moyshe's mind on mouse-soft feet.

Chub was less indignant than he expected.

On a strictly pragmatic level, the starfish agreed that getting out of the interstellar rivers would be the best way to conserve Starfisher ships and lives.

"They'll never go, Chub. The harvestfleets are their nations. Their homelands. They're proud, stubborn people. They'll keep fighting and hoping."

"I know, Moyshe man-friend. It saddens the herd. And makes the Old Ones proud that they forged their alliance so well. But why do you say 'they'?"

"We, then. Part of the time... *Most* of the time I'm an outsider here. They do things differently than what I learned…"

"Sometimes you miss your old life, Moyshe man-friend."

"Sometimes. Not often, and not much, though. I'd better tend to business." He had to focus his attention to force his physical voice to croak, "Gun Control, Mindlink. The sharks are going. They've given up. You can secure when the last leaves firing range."

"You sure, Linker? Don't look like it in the display tank."

"I'm sure. Let me know when I can stop realtiming. This is my second link in eight hours."

"Right. Will do." The man on the far end seemed impressed.

Clara's voice broke in. "Are you all right, Moyshe? The strain getting heavy? We can bring you out."

"I'm okay. For a while. I remember what I am. Just be ready to hit me with that needle."

At Stars' End *Danion* had lost half her native, trained mindtechs because they had stayed in link too long, or had been mindburned by sharks breaking through the defensive fire screen. The best guess was that the former had become lost in the special interior universe of the linker. Dozens occupied a special hospital ward where doctors and nurses had to handle them like newly born babies.

Their bodies lived on. Their minds, it was hoped, might sometime be retrieved.

In all the history of the High Seiners no lost linker ever had been recalled.

The Starfishers were living on hopes these days. Stars' End had been one, for weapons capable of shattering shark tides.

BenRabi did not understand how the Seiners had hoped to accomplish what generations of madmen, fools, and geniuses had failed to do. Stars' End was a fortress unvanquishable.

It was a whole world, Earth-sized, that was a fortress. Or planetary battleship. Or whatever. It could be approached by nothing. The technologies of its defenses were beyond the imaginations of any of the races aware of its existence. Its builders had long since vanished into the abyss of time.

Generations of men had lusted after the weapons of Stars' End. Thousands had died trying to obtain them. And the fortress world remained inviolate.

Why had the Seiners been convinced that they would have better luck?

"You were right, Linker. Computer says they're pulling out. Going to let you off realtime now. We can handle it from here without."

"Thank you, Gun Control."

The sense of drain stopped abruptly. BenRabi's universe reeled. Chub reached in and steadied him. "Time to break, Moyshe man-friend. You losing sense of reality and orientation in space-time."

"I'm not lost yet, Chub."

"You all say so. No more you can do here, man-friend."

The crackle of reality beginning to fall into shards rose from benRabi's hindbrain. It pushed a wave of terror before it. Chub did nothing to soothe him.

"Clara! The needle. I'm coming out."

He slapped the switch beneath his left hand.

They were waiting for him. The agony persisted for only a few seconds.

That was bad enough. He screamed and screamed. It got worse every time.

FOUR: 3049 AD
The Main Sequence

They put him into Hospital Block this time. He was under sedation for three days.

Two people were at his bedside when the doctor came to bring him out. The thin, pale, blue-eyed woman with the nervous hands was Amy. The little Oriental with the presence of an iceberg was benRabi's friend Mouse.

Amy would sit for a minute, picking at her jumpsuit, shifting this way and that. She would cross and uncross her legs, then would rise and pace around for a minute before sitting again. She did not speak to Mouse. Most of the time she deliberately tried to distance Storm from herself and Moyshe. It was almost as if she saw Mouse as a competitor for benRabi's affection.

The men had shared missions under fire. Sometimes they did not like one another much. Their backgrounds were day and night. Centuries of prejudice had erected walls between them. Yet an indestructible bond had been forged and hammered on the anvils of shared peril. They had guarded one another's backs and saved one another's lives too often to let go.

Mouse waited without moving, with the patience of a samurai.

He was a dedicated Archaicist. He had just encountered his own ancient heritage and, in imagination, was trying the samurai role for size. The code and conduct suited the warrior within him.

But it did nothing for the libertine. And Mouse was a classic of that genre, at least with the opposite sex.

Masato Igarashi Storm did nothing by half measures.

The doctor coughed softly.

"Will he be all right?" Amy demanded. "He'll come out okay? I know what you told me, but…"

Mouse's facial muscles moved slightly. His wan expression spoke volumes about his disgust at her display.

The doctor was more patient. "Just an enforced rest, Miss. That's all it is. There's nothing wrong that rest can't cure. I hear he did a hell of a job feeding realtime to Weapons Control. He just pushed himself too far."

A look flickered across Mouse's stony face.

"What're *you* thinking?" Amy demanded.

"Just that he's not usually a pusher."

Amy was ready for a fight.

The doctor aborted it by giving benRabi an injection. He began to come around.

Mouse seemed indifferent to Amy's response. But not oblivious. He was an astute observer. He just did not care what she thought.

"Doc," he said, "is there any special reason for sticking with this kind of medical setup?"

The woman held benRabi's wrist, taking his pulse. "What do you mean?"

"It's primitive. Almost Archaicist obsolete. They had sonic sedation systems before I was born. Easier on the patient and staff both."

The doctor reddened. Mouse had been out of the hospital only a few weeks himself. He had spent a month recuperating from a severe wound received from a Sangaree agent who had tried to seize control of *Danion*. He was not pleased with the quality of medical care, and made no secret of it. But Mouse hated all doctors and hospitals. He could find fault with the finest.

BenRabi had tracked the Sangaree woman down, and had shot her…

Mouse had the nerve to stand toe-to-toe with the Devil and tell him to put it where the sun doesn't shine.

"We have to make do with what we can afford, Mr. Storm."

"So I've been told." Mouse did not pursue it, though he thought Seiners pleading poverty was on a par with Midas begging alms on a street corner.

BenRabi opened his eyes.

"How you doing, Moyshe?" Storm asked, trampling Amy's more dramatic opener. His presence there, betraying his concern, embarrassed him.

The fabric of centuries takes the stamp; they mark the children indelibly. Their legacy remains as invisible and irresistible as the secret coded in DNA. The young Mouse had learned that Old Earthers were pariahs.

Mouse's family had been in Service for three generations. They were part of Confederation's military aristocracy. BenRabi's forebears had been unemployed Social Insurees for centuries.

Neither man considered himself prejudiced. But false truths sown in the fallows of childhood, planted deep, continued to sprout unrealistic real-world responses.

BenRabi had begun bridling his prejudice early. He had to survive. There had been only two Old Earthers in his Academy battalion.

He needed a minute to get his bearings. "What am I doing here?" he demanded.

"You needed rest," Amy told him. "Lots of it. You overdid it this time."

"Come on. I can take care of myself. I know when…"

"Crap!" the doctor snapped. "Every mindtech thinks that. And then they turn up here, burned out. I change their diapers and spoon feed them. What is it with you people, benRabi? You all got egos two sizes too big for a small god."

Moyshe was fuzzy. He tried to say something flip. His tongue felt like it was wrapped in an old sock.

He saw tears in the doctor's eyes. "Did you lose someone at Stars' End?"

"My sister. She came out of creche just before you landsmen came aboard. She was only seventeen, benRabi."

"I'm sorry."

"No, you're not. You're a mindtech. Anyway, sorry doesn't help. Not when I have to take care of her every day. She was just like you, benRabi. She knew she could handle it. She wouldn't listen either. None of them would. Not even the controllers, who should've known better. They put her back in with only four hours' rest."

BenRabi kept his mouth shut. What could he say? He had been introduced to Contact during the battle at Stars' End. The main Contact room had been a shambles. Dozens of mindtechs had given everything to save *Danion*.

He never would have seen Contact, or even have discovered its existence, had those linker casualties not been cruel. In those days he had been a distrusted landsman, a convicted enemy spy who was screened from all Seiner secrets. They had drafted him into Contact only because he might give *Danion* a millimeter's better chance of surviving.

He had made his decision to cross over after Stars' End, virtually in the hatch of the ship designated to return the landsmen contractees to Confederation.

He had waited too long. Half of his personal possessions had departed with the ship. He had not recovered them. The service ship crew had gotten into a row with Customs. The bureaucrats had retaliated, seizing everything not bolted to the ship's frames.

BenRabi took Amy's thin, cool hand. "How've you been, darling? You look tired. How long has it been?" She felt so cold... She was a spooky woman. Why had he fallen in love with her?

He always fell for the strange ones, the neurotic and just plain rotten ones. Alyce, in Academy... What a loser she had turned out to be. And the Sangaree woman, Marya, who had been a vampire in the midst of his last two missions.

"I'm all right now that I know you'll be okay. Moyshe, please be more careful."

She seemed unusually remote. BenRabi glanced at her, at Mouse, and back again. More problems with Mouse? Her dislike for his friend had taken a quantum leap recently.

Mouse did not talk much. The inevitable chess board had

accompanied him, but he did not offer to play. Amy's presence restrained him. Chess was one of his great passions, rivaling his passion for seducing a parade of beautiful women.

"Hey, Mouse. Ever wonder what Max is doing these days?" Referring to someone they had known before coming out here was the only way he could think of to pull his friend into the conversation.

"Probably getting richer and wondering why we don't come into her shop anymore. I don't think Beckhart will bother giving her our new address."

"Yeah." BenRabi laughed. "He should have heard the news by now, don't you think? Or pretty soon. He'll foam at the mouth." For Amy's benefit, he explained, "Max was a friend of ours in Luna Command. She ran a stamp store."

"Best hobby shop in the moon," Mouse said.

Amy did not respond. She simply could not comprehend what these two got out of accumulating small bits of paper that were ages old and required jeweler's grade care.

And stamps were not the only thing. Between them they seemed to collect everything. Coins. Stamps. All kinds of ancient miscellanea. Mouse had little wrought-iron trivets and other old-time dohickeys all over his quarters. The one collection she could appreciate was Moyshe's butterflies. He had a frame of exotics on his wall. They were incredibly beautiful.

The Seiner ships were ecologically sterile. Only their zoos contained nonhuman life, and that the large, well-known mammals.

Amy had no hobbies of her own. She read for relaxation. She had acquired the habit from her mother.

Mouse even managed passably with a clarinet, an antique woodwind seldom seen anymore. He claimed to have learned from his father.

"What about Greta?" Mouse asked. "You think the Department will take care of her?"

Amy jumped at the name. "You never did tell me about Greta, Moyshe."

"That was in another life."

They were lovers, but they did not know one another well.

BenRabi did not like stirring up the snake pit of people's pasts. There was too much chance of finding something nasty. It was there in every life.

But he answered Amy's question. "I told you before. She's a kid I met the last time I was on Old Earth. The last time I visited my mother. She wanted out. Her friends wouldn't let her go. I arranged it for her. And ended up sponsoring her."

"Sort of like being a foster parent," Mouse explained.

"Guess she'd be eighteen now. I haven't thought about her in ages. You shouldn't have mentioned her, Mouse. Now you've got me worried."

"Hey, don't. Max will look out for her."

"Maybe. But that's not right, putting it on somebody else. Is there any way I could send her a letter now and then, Amy? Just to let her know I'm all right and thinking about her? I'd let you or Jarl write it if you wanted. You could even run it through the crypto computer to make sure it's innocent."

"This's just a kid?" Amy demanded.

"Yeah. She reminded me a lot of me when I came off Old Earth. Awful lost. I thought I could help out by sponsoring her. And then I kind of ran out when the Bureau sent us out here. I told her we'd be back in a couple of months. It's been almost fourteen."

"I'll ask Jarl. He lets a little mail go out. Some of us have relatives outside. But it's slow."

"That doesn't matter. Amy, you're a jewel. I love you."

"Well, if you're going to get mushy," Mouse said, standing. "I've got to run. A citizenship class. It's from hunger, Moyshe. Me and Emily Hopkins and this fascist bastard of a teacher... Maybe I'll hurt the arm again. Get back in here so I can miss a few too. Behave. Do what the doctor lady says. Or I'll wring your neck." He made his exit before Moyshe could embarrass him with many thanks-for-comings.

"You're awful quiet today, honey," benRabi said after a while. Perhaps if the doctor had not been there...

"I'm just tired. We're still doing double shifts and barely keeping our heads above water. We're going to be in the Yards a long time. Assuming *Danion* doesn't fall apart before we get there.

Assuming the sharks don't knock us apart."

"You've mentioned these Yards about fifty times and wouldn't tell me about them. Do you trust me enough now?"

"They're what the name sounds like. Where we build and fix our ships. Moyshe, you're not going anywhere for a while. Tell me about you."

"What?"

"I met you the very first day. Way back on Carson's, when you signed your contract. We lived together for months before I even found out you've got a daughter. I don't know anything about you."

"Greta isn't my daughter, honey. I just helped a kid who needed somebody…"

"It's almost the same thing, isn't it?"

"Legally, I guess. On paper. They'd have trouble making it stand up in court."

"Tell me. Everything."

There was little else to do but talk. He talked.

The doctor, lurking in the background watching suspiciously, had made it clear that he would be stuck here for a while.

"All right. Let me know when it gets boring."

He had been born in North America on Old Earth, to Clarence Hardaway and Myra McClennon. He had hardly known his father. His mother, for reasons he still did not understand, had elected to raise him at home instead of burying him in the State Creche. Only a few Social Insurees raised their children.

His early years had been typical for home-raised S.I. children. Little supervision, little love, little education. He had been running with a kid gang before he was eight.

He had been nine when he had seen his first offworlders. Spikes, they had called them. These had been Navy men in crisp dress blacks diligently pursuing the arcane business of offworlders.

Those uniforms had captured his imagination. They had become an obsession. He had started keying information out of his mother's home data retrieval terminal. He had not had the education to decipher most of it. He had started teaching himself, building from the ground up toward the things he so desperately wanted to know.

At ten he had quit the gang so he would have more time to study. Halfway through his eleventh year the revelation had come. He *had* to get into space. He had approached a Navy recruiter clandestinely. The man had arranged for him to sneak through the Academy exams.

He never would have made it had there been no special standards and quotas for Old Earthers. He would have gotten skunked had he been in direct competition with carefully prepared Outworlders, many of whom had grown up in the military life. Half the officers in Service were the children of officers. Service was a complete sub-culture, and one that was becoming increasingly less connected with and controlled by the over-culture. He had had motivation.

At twelve he had run away from home, fleeing to Luna Command and Academy. In six years he had climbed from dead last to the 95th percentile in class standing. At graduation he had taken his Line option and been assigned to the Fleet. He had served aboard the destroyers *Aquitaine* and *Hesse,* and the attack cruiser *Tamerlane,* before requesting Intelligence training.

Following a year of schooling the Bureau had assigned him as Naval Attaché to the Embassy on Feldspar. He had had a half dozen similar assignments on as many worlds before his work attracted the attention of Admiral Beckhart, whose department handled dangerous operations, and tricks on the grey side of legal.

He had taken part in several tight missions, and had reencountered his former classmate, Mouse. They had shared several assignments, the last being to join the Starfishers to ferret out information that could be used to force the Seiners to enter the Confederation fold.

Some of it Amy had heard before. Some she had not. She was not satisfied. Her first comment was, "You didn't say anything about women."

"What do you mean? What's that got to do with anything?"

"Everything, as far as I'm concerned. I want to know who your lovers were and how come you broke up. What they were like…"

"You'll shit in your hand and carry it to China first, Lady."

He was still a little dopey. He did not realize that he had said it aloud till he began to wonder why she had shut up so suddenly.

After one stunned gasp Amy blew out of the room like a tornado looking for a town to wreck.

The lady doctor came out of the background, took his blood pressure. "She's pushy, isn't she?"

"I don't know what's got into her. She wasn't like that before."

"You've had an interesting life."

"Not really. I don't think I'd do it the same if I had it to do again."

"Well, you could, couldn't you?"

"I don't understand."

"Rejuvenation. I thought it was available to everybody landside."

"Oh. Yes. More or less. Some of the brass have been around since Noah landed the Ark. But Fate has a way of catching up with people who try to slide around it."

"Wish we had it out here."

"You don't look that old."

"I was thinking about my father. He's getting on now."

"I see. How soon can I leave?"

"Any time, really. But I wish you'd wait a couple hours. You'll be weak and dizzy."

"Mouse was right about sonic sedation."

"I know. But I don't write the medical budget. Good luck, Mr. benRabi. Try not to see me again."

"I hate hospitals, Doctor."

He did. His only stays had been at Bureau insistence, to modify him mentally or physically.

He did a few minor exercises before catching a public tram home.

Amy was waiting. "Oh, Moyshe. That was stupid of me. You were right. Those things aren't any of my business."

She had been crying. Her eyes were red.

"It's all right. I understand." But he did not. His cultural background had not prepared him for personal nosiness. In

Confederation people lived *now*. They did not consider the past.

"It's just that I feel... Well, everything's so chancy the way it is between us."

Here she comes, he thought. Hints about getting married.

Marriage was important to the Seiners. In Confederation it was more an amusing relic, an entertainment or daydream for the young and the romantic. He could not reconcile his attitudes with Seiner seriousness. Not yet.

The Starfishers had won his loyalty, but they could not make him a different man. They could not make him reflect themselves merely by adopting him.

Was Mouse having the same trouble? he wondered. Probably not. Mouse was a chameleon. He could adapt anywhere, vanish into any crowd.

"I have to go to work," Amy told him. Weariness seemed to be dragging her down.

"You'd better get some rest yourself, honey."

After she left he took out his stamp collection and turned the well-thumbed album pages. Mouse had opened a Pandora's box by mentioning Max and Greta. After a while he pushed the album aside and tried to compose a letter to the girl.

He could not think of much to say.

FIVE: 3049 AD
The Contemporary Scene

Admirals and generals did not have to endure the usual waiting and decontamination procedures getting into Luna Command. The security checks were abbreviated. No staff-grade officer had gone sour since Admiral McGraw had turned freebooter following the peace with Ulant. Admiral Beckhart entered his office just three hours after his personal shuttle berthed a little south of the Sea of Tranquility.

He had not spared the horses, in the vernacular of another age. The mother had dropped hyper midway between Luna and L-5. The first message he had received had been code-tagged, "Personal presence required immediately. Critical."

Either the bottom had dropped off of the universe or McClennon and Storm had come home with their saddlebags dripping delicious little secrets.

The Crew, as he called his hand-picked brain-trust, were in the office when he arrived.

He raised a hand. "As you were. What have we got?"

Jones asked, "You don't want to shower and change?"

Beckhart looked ragged. Almost seedy. Like a derelict costumed as an Admiral.

"You clowns sent a Personal Presence, Critical. If I've got time to shit, shower, and shave, you should've said it was urgent."

"Maybe we were hasty," Namaguchi admitted. "We'd just scanned the crypto breakdown. We were a little excited."

"Breakdown? What the hell's going on?" Beckhart tumbled into a huge chair behind a vast, gleaming wood desk. "Get to the point, Akido."

Namaguchi jerked out of his seat, flipped a square of manila across the gleaming desk.

"Numbers. Your handwriting hasn't improved."

"The Section's doing up a printout. That, sir, is what Storm had for us."

"Well?"

"Morgan Standard Coordinate Data, sir. A stellar designation. Took us two days to convert it from the Sangaree system."

"Sangaree?... Holy Christ! Is it?..."

"What we've been waiting for all our lives. Where to find their home star."

"Ah, god. Ah. It can't be. Two hundred years we've been looking. Cutting and dying and generally carrying on like a gang of fascist assholes. So it paid off. I bet my butt on a long shot and it paid off. Give me the comm. Somebody give me the goddamn comm."

Jones eased it across the desk. Beckhart punched furiously. "Beckhart. Priority. Hey! I don't give a damn if he's banging the Queen of Sheba. Personal, Critical, and I'm going to have your ass for breakfast if you don't... Excuse me, sir." His manners improved dramatically.

"Yes, sir, it is. I want a confirmation of our position on Memorandum of Permanent Policy and Procedure Number Four. Specifically, Paragraph Six."

A long silence ensued. Beckhart's cronies leaned closer and closer to their chief. The man on the other end finally said something.

"Yes, sir. Absolutely. I have the data in my hand, sir. Just decoded. Give me von Drachau and the First Fleet... Yes, sir. What I want is a blank check for a while. I can get started tomorrow."

More silence.

Then, "Yes, sir. I thought so, sir. I understand, sir. Thank you, sir." Beckhart broke the connection. "He wants to take it up with the Chiefs of Staff."

"They're going to back down now? After all the lives we've spent?"

"Commander Jones. Do you *realize* the enormity of what I just dumped on him? Let me draw you a picture. I interrupted him while von Staufenberg was briefing him on what we saw centerward. Which was about what we expected to see, and as pretty as a barge loaded with dead babies. Some psychopathic race is doing its damnedest to kill off anything sentient it can find. Then I horn in and ask for a confirm on Memo Four slash Six. Which is a vow to exterminate the Sangaree whenever we find out where the hell they're hiding their homeworld. We're supposed to be the good guys, Jones. The things he's looking at right now kind of tend to put the damper on the fires of that good old-time anti-Sangaree righteousness."

"I don't see the problem, sir."

"Pragmatically it doesn't exist. Having seen what's going on centerward, I'd say Four slash Six is a strategic imperative. We've got to get those bloodsuckers off our backs fast. They ate us alive during the wars with Ulant and Toke. Any time there's a dust-up between non-Confederation worlds they come on like jackals. Raidships in swarms... Not to mention the price we pay in stardust addiction. Hell, half the fleet is tied up protecting shipping. Four slash Six would free those ships. And if we burned the Sangaree, the McGraws would close up shop. Those are the arguments in favor. Akido. Take the Devil's advocate."

It was an old game. Namaguchi knew his commander well. "Sir. How in God's name can we go to the people of Confederation—not to mention our allies—with the news that we've destroyed a whole race? Just when we're about to pump them up with moral indignation so we can justify a preemptive strike against a species we claim is guilty of the identical sin? Let me understate, sir, and say that the positions are inconsistent. Let me say, sir, that we're on a quick slide down into a moral cesspool. We would, quite simply, be the biggest hypocrites this universe has ever seen."

"Shit," Jones responded with no great force. "There isn't one in a thousand of them would ever see the inconsistency. They'll cheer about the Sangaree going down, then go sign up for the war against these centerward creeps. Akido, you're giving Mr. Average Man too much credit. He can't even follow his credit balance, let alone weigh a moral one."

"Charlie, that attitude is going to destroy Luna Command. And when we go, Confederation goes. When Confederation goes, the barbarians come in. In the words of the Roman Centurion Publius Minutius, speaking of the legions, 'We *are* the Empire.'"

"Just a minute," Beckhart interjected. "Akido. Come over here." He pushed the comm across the desk. "Punch up the library and get me an abstract on this Minutius."

"Uh…"

"I thought so. Another one of your out-of-the-dark authorities."

Namaguchi chuckled. It was a favorite trick. His boss was the only man who caught him every time. "Actually, old Publius probably said something more like, 'Which way to the nearest whorehouse, buddy?' But I'll stake my reputation on the fact that some Roman soldier said it somewhere along the way. It was true. The army *was* the Empire."

"You don't have any reputation to stake, Akido," Jones quipped.

"The army got a lot of help from the fact that everybody in the provinces went along with a lot of tacit rules, Akido," Beckhart remarked. "We're getting off the subject. What about McClennon's report?"

"They're still working on it. First abstracts should be up any time now. The key thing we've gotten is that the Starfishers did go after Stars' End. So you guessed right on that one, too."

"I didn't guess. I had inside information."

"Whatever. That's where Storm came up with the Sangaree data. Raidships hit the harvestfleet there. They came out on the short end. The point is, the Seiners were sure they could pull it off. The battering the Sangaree gave them is what kept them from trying."

"How soon will those boys be done debriefing? I want to see them."

Silence hit that room like a cat jumping on a mouse. It stretched till it became an embarrassment.

"Well?"

"Uh…"

"Not one of your more endearing traits, Akido. I don't need protecting. Out with it. Who got hurt? How bad was it?"

"It's not that. Sir, they didn't come back."

"They're dead? How did they?…"

"They're alive. But they crossed over."

"They what?"

"Remember, McClennon was programmed for it."

"I know that. It was my idea. But he wasn't supposed to make a career out of it. He didn't de-program? What the hell was wrong with Storm? What's his story? Why didn't he bring Thomas out?"

"We're working on it, sir. Interrogating returnees. When we can lay hands on them. They scattered after they hit Carson's, before we knew we had a problem. Near as we can tell, Storm stayed behind because he didn't want to leave McClennon there alone. The programming must have broken down. McClennon asked to stay. They kept Storm from bringing him out."

"I see. That would be like Mouse. Don't leave your wounded behind. He's too much like his father. I knew Gneaus Storm. When you get to the bottom line, it was his sense of honor that got him killed. Well, I've got my honor too, even if it's a little discolored around the edges. I don't leave my wounded behind either. Akido, I want those boys brought out."

Jones snorted.

"Charles? What's biting your ass?"

"I was just thinking that anybody who cared as much about his troops as you put on wouldn't have thrown them back in the furnace before they'd cooled off from The Broken Wings. And you hit them with that one before they'd cooled off from…"

"Hey! Charlie, it's my conscience. I'm the one who's got to live with it."

"Storm could handle it. He didn't get the deep Psych-briefings. But McClennon… You probably overloaded the poor bastard. He was goofy at his best times."

"That's enough. Right now, right here, we finish crying about

Storm and McClennon. That understood? We start figuring out how to get them back. And in our spare time we worry about the Four slash Six. And come bedtime, if you get tempted to waste time sleeping, start figuring how we're going to get a hammerlock on the Starfishers before they get their hands on Stars' End."

"Sir?" Namaguchi inquired.

"One of you clowns told me they were sure they could get in. You know what happens if they do?"

"Sir?"

"We bend over and kiss our asses good-bye. Because we're dead. We can hope, but we'll still be in the line to the showers."

"I don't follow your reasoning this time."

"You're not looking at the whole picture, that's why. The gestalt, if that's the right word. Look. If they get those weapons before we do, they can tell us to go pound sand and make it stick. We won't get control of ambergris production, meaning the Fleet will have to do without adequate instel communications, meaning its chances against those centerward things will go down to zit. They aren't your candy-ass Ulantonids, planning to give us a fair shake after they whip us."

"On the other hand," Namaguchi suggested, "if we get the Fishers under the gun in time, we'll not only be able to equip the Fleet, we'll have the potential of the Stars' End weaponry. Assuming it's adaptable."

"There," Beckhart told the others. "You see why Akido is the Crown Prince around here. You take a stick and whack on him long enough and he actually starts thinking. Let's do a little brainstorming, gentlemen. Along the lines of turning our liabilities into assets."

Jones suggested, "Regarding the Four slash Six paradox. The right leak of the right info at the right time at the right place might give Luna Command a public opinion base that would make the kill a matter of popular demand. There are some real pros in the Public Information Office. They've done a hell of a job creating a climate of trepidation with hints about trouble in the March. Suppose they let a little truth wriggle out now? Just enough so people start asking what kind of horror we're covering up by giving our friends from Ulant a bad press. There isn't anything the public won't swallow quicker than a good conspiracy theory. Especially a cover-up conspiracy."

Beckhart chuckled. "What is this? Two brains working in one room? At the same time? Gentlemen, that's a first. So. We've got a couple of things to work on. Will they let us orchestrate the show?"

"Why don't we just do it? It wouldn't be the first time."

"But it could be the last. We've reached a crossroads. We—and I mean everybody in Luna Command—are going to have to fine-tune the Luna Command machine. It won't have the internal tolerance for playing games with each other. We don't have much time to get ready for this centerward race… That plan is simple. We're going to hit them first, hit them hard, and keep hitting them with everything we've got."

"The way Ulant did us?"

"Exactly. The Prime Defender's General Staff is doing the planning, based on their intelligence. She'll modify it daily, keeping as close to the realtime situation as she can. We come up with something, it'll be programmed in. If the centerward crowd do something unexpected, that'll go in too. They've sent out a whole fleet of self-destruct equipped, instelled scout ships to keep track of what's happening."

"Sir, that strategy didn't work for Ulant before."

"It may not work this time, but it's the best shot we've got. Ulant's intelligence analyses paint a pretty grim picture. The numbers… You'll see the tapes. While you're watching, remember that you're only seeing one battle fleet. Ulant has identified another four. They just seem to skip from star to star behind a swarm of scouts, coming out the Arm, scouring every inhabited world of any sentient life." The comm hummed. Beckhart stabbed it with one finger. "Beckhart. Yes, sir."

The sound was uni-directional, the picture flat-faced television. The others could not hear, nor could they identify the caller. After listening awhile, Beckhart said, "Very well, sir," in an unhappy tone. He punched out.

"That was the C.S.N. They've decided to go with Four slash Six. But they're not going to let us run it. He said they'll use von Drachau, but R and D will have operational control."

"R and D? What the hell?"

"What have they got going over there? What don't we know?"

The comm hummed again. Beckhart answered, said, "This one's for you, Charlie."

Jones sat on the edge of the vast desk, turned the comm his way. "Go ahead." In a few seconds his tall, lean, black frame began quivering with excitement. "Good. All right. Thank you."

"Well?" Beckhart growled.

"One of my Electronic Intercept people. They just picked up a message from the Starfisher Council to Confederation Senate. Routine request for clearance to hold an ambergris auction. They asked for The Broken Wings. Usual rules and mutual obligations. The same request they send whenever they hold auction on a Confederation world."

"The Broken Wings is close to Stars' End. Any other reason to be excited?"

"Payne's Fleet is going to sponsor."

Beckhart stared at his hands for more than a minute. When he looked up his expression had become beatific. "Gentlemen, the gods love us after all. Cancel all leaves. Cancel any computation capacity loans we have out. Pass the word that we're going on overtime. Everybody, including the janitors and shredder opera-tors. I've got a feeling we'll find a rose in this dungheap yet." He laughed demoniacally. "Eyes open and ears to the ground, gentlemen. Everything that comes in from now on—and I mean *everything*—goes into the master program for correlation. And have the programming teams start working backward. I want the biggest and best goddamned model outside the High Command Strategic Analysis. Let's see if we can't do this all up in one big, pretty package."

Beckhart departed his desk and unlocked his personal bar. He took out glasses and the half gallon of genuine Old Earth Scotch he saved for occasions of millennial significance. "A toast to successes and victories. Hopefully ours." He poured doubles.

SIX: 3049 AD
The Main Sequence

The five great harvestships barely moved. Their velocity relative to the debris was a scant three kilometers per hour. Gnatlike service ships flitted before the head and flanks of their line, nudging any flying mountain that threatened collision.

It was almost an embarrassment, the way those swift monsters of the spatial deeps had to crawl. Elsewhere they could have sprinted off and left light lagging like a toddler behind an Olympic runner. Here they could not match the pace of a lazily strolling old man.

Those battered survivors of Payne's Fleet had been making the passage for a week.

The dense boulder screen gave way to a less crowded region occupied principally by asteroidal chunks the size of small moons. The harvestfleet accelerated. The line dispersed.

"Well, you kept asking about the Yards," Amy told benRabi. "We're there." She indicated the viewscreen they had been watching.

"Yes, but…" All Moyshe saw was a big asteroid illuminated by *Danion*'s powerful lights. A few smaller boulders drifted around it. Not one star was visible in the background. All outside light was screened by the dust of the nebula.

Danion seemed to be stalking that big asteroid.

"But what?"

"There's nothing here. We're in the tail end of nowhere. I expected a hidden planet. Maybe even Osiris. Something First Expansion. Strange cities, drydocks…"

"Planetary docks? How could we take *Danion* into atmosphere? Or lift her out of a gravity well? Most of your Navy ships wouldn't try that."

"But you'd have to have thousands of people to work on a ship this big. Tens of thousands. Not to mention a hell of an industrial base, and one all-time grandfather of a drydock."

"The dock's right in front of you."

"What? Where?"

"Watch and see."

He watched. And he saw.

A gargantuan piece of rock began separating from the asteroid. In time it exposed a brightly lit interior vast enough to accept a harvestship. Diminutive tugs swarmed out. Some pushed the cork. Some hurried toward *Danion* like eager bees to a clover patch.

BenRabi saw a glow in the remote distance. Another asteroid was opening its stone mouth.

"We're going inside?"

"You got it. You catch on quick, don't you?"

"Smart mouth."

"They'll lock the door behind us. Then they'll flood the chamber with air. The work goes faster that way. And the dock will hide us from any snoopers who wander by."

"Who would come poking around in a mess like this? That would be asking to get fine-ground between those flying millstones."

BenRabi was less surprised by the existence of the nebula than by the Seiners' willingness to hazard it. Similar asteroidal shoals existed inside several dust nebulae.

"But they come anyway. Moyshe, this's the Three Sky Nebula."

"No. Not really? Yes. I guess you're serious."

One of the most dramatic actions of the Ulantonid War had

occurred in the outer shoals of the Three Sky Nebula. After the war, the repatriated human survivors had circulated stories of having seen abandoned alien ships there. Some had been wrecks, some had appeared to be intact.

Three Sky had won an immediate reputation as a Sargasso of space. The treasure-seekers, xeno-archaeologists, and official investigators who went there hunting the alien ships were seldom seen again.

"The expeditions… There must have been fifteen or twenty that disappeared. What happened to them?"

"We interned them before they could stumble onto something and run home to report it. They're doing what they came to do. They just can't go home."

"Why risk setting up here if the traffic gets so heavy?"

"The risk isn't that big. We don't have visitors very often. Not when they always disappear. And, of course, it's such an unlikely place to look for us."

"Still… There's been talk at Luna Command, off and on, about sending a squadron to back up an investigation. In case it's McGraws or Sangaree that have been getting the others."

"If that happened, we'd fight. And we'd win. Only a fool would attack what we've made out of Three Sky. We've been here since before the Ulantonid War. That's a lot of time to get ready. It'd be almost like guerrilla warfare. We think we can hold off Confederation if we ever have to."

"I think you're a little over-optimistic. For people who don't have the muscle to duke it out with the sharks. I'll let you know for sure after I've looked things over."

"Why do you say that?"

"Because I haven't met a Seiner yet who had the least idea of just how big and strong Confederation is. Or how tough Luna Command can be when they put their minds to it. Or that your weapons systems are prehistoric relics. *Danion*'s got a ton of firepower, but one Empire Class battleship could carve this whole harvestfleet up like a side of beef and never get in a sweat."

"I think you're probably too impressed with your Navy. Our shortcomings were calculated into our defense plans."

BenRabi decided not to argue. Each of them was telling the truth as he or she knew it. "Are the creches here?"

"Some. All of them will be someday. It's a big job, civilizing a nebula."

"Mainly an engineering problem, I'd think."

"Yes. But it takes time and money. Especially money. We have to buy everything we can't manufacture ourselves. Which means we have to wait for the auctions because our credit is pretty slim."

"Ah. I begin to see why the good doctor was making do with primitive equipment."

"We've colonized more than seven thousand asteroids, Moyshe," Amy proudly declared. "But we've only just begun. They're all cramped. The harvestships are cramped. Our other hidden places are overcrowded. We've been taking in Confederation's dropouts for two hundred years. The ones who didn't become McGraws or run away to the outworlds."

Outworlds was a word as relative as *yonder*. For benRabi, born an Old Earther, it meant anything off Old Earth. Around Luna Command it meant any planet not one of the original seven founders of Confederation. Those seven usually called themselves The Inner Worlds. But out on the fringes of Confederation outworlds were human planets not signatory to the federal pact. BenRabi was unsure which meaning Amy wanted to convey.

"You didn't answer my question," he said. "Why here?"

"Because of the industrial advantages. The stories those internees took back were true. There's a lot of salvageable stuff here. We've identified over thirty thousand wrecks and abandoned ships. Built by seven different races."

"Really?" He ticked fingers. He could name five, not counting humanity. Six if he counted the prehistoric race that had built Stars' End. "I'll give you human and Ulantonid. From the war. Who were the others?"

"I thought you'd wonder why they'd be here."

He frowned at her. Was she trying to bait him by showing off her superior knowledge? Savoring one minuscule advantage? He knew more than she about almost everything and she seemed to take it as a personal affront.

"I imagine because it's a good place to lay an ambush. That's why *Carolingian* came here during the war."

Her smile shrank. "Yeah. And because it's close to the obvious space lanes. Moyshe, there've been battles here for ages. Probably for millions of years. Or even billions. Except for the wrecks from the Ulantonid war, which I didn't even count, none of the ships here were built by any race we've ever met. They were all extinct before man ever left Old Earth. Or at least they were gone from this part of the galaxy. They all predate any of the races we have encountered."

"Ask the starfish about them."

"We did. We're not stupid. But they don't have much to tell. They don't pay any more attention to hard matter races than we do to bacteria. Less, really, because we're curious and they aren't. We're pretty sure one bunch of ships, though, belonged to a race that moved the ancestors of the Sangaree from Earth to wherever it is their homeworld is."

"Ah? Don't let Mouse know about that. He'll drive you crazy trying to get to them."

Only in this century had geneticists surrendered to the popular notion that Human and Sangaree sprang from the same root stock. The man in the street would not believe in a parallel evolution so similar that it could produce a being indistinguishable from himself. Scientists had demurred, citing no evidence on Old Earth for extraterrestrial intervention.

Then the abandoned alien base beneath the moon's dark side had been discovered. Some major rethinking had been necessary. Then had come confirmation of reports that the human female could, occasionally, be impregnated by the Sangaree male.

The most famous—or infamous—of Sangaree agents, Michael Dee, had been half human.

"Mouse will be protected from himself."

BenRabi studied her. She wore an oddly ferocious expression.

"Amy, I've been here almost fourteen months and you're still springing surprises on me. When are you going to run out?" He stared into the hollow asteroid and awaited her response.

"Moyshe, what happened to the people who built Stars' End?"

"We'll probably never know. Unless somebody cracks its defenses."

"We'll do that. We're going back. That was a rhetorical question."

"Wait a sec. Back? To Stars' End? After what happened? You're out of your minds. You're all raving lunatics."

She laughed. "Moyshe, they left their ships behind when they disappeared. Right here. God knows how many of them there are. Three Sky occupies a cubic light-year. We haven't explored a tenth of it. They had their yards and secret places too. Most of the ships we find were theirs. They were the people who transported the Sangaree, we think. We have explorers who don't do anything but hunt for their hideouts. Every one we find is one we don't have to build for ourselves."

He spoke to the engulfing maw in the viewscreen. "She's serious."

"Absolutely, darling. Absolutely. Oh, we're not really *sure* that it was the same race that did all three things. But the computers go with the probability. See, these are mostly good ships, Moyshe. They aren't derelicts. Some of them still have a little emergency power left. They try to scare us off with mind noises the way Stars' End does. And they have parts missing. Somebody took off all their weapons. I wish we had a whole army of xeno-archaeologists and anthropologists. It's really interesting. I always go see what they're working on whenever we come in. The scientists don't go very fast. They're mostly ones we captured, so they aren't real enthusiastic about helping us out. They train some of our people as aides, sometimes. Old folks and birth defect types who can't do much else."

"That don't make sense. People don't abandon good ships, Amy. Where did they go? Why? How? And if they did build Stars' End, *why*?"

She shrugged. "They weren't people, Moyshe. Not our kind. Don't judge their motives by ours."

"I wouldn't... though some ideas would seem universal. Just thinking questions out loud."

"The questions are why I wish we had more scientists." She switched the viewscreen over to a stern camera. *Danion* was well into the asteroid's interior. "They could be the same creatures that did the tunneling at Luna Command. But were they really? Is there a connection between the moon and Three Sky and Stars' End? Were we meant to find Stars' End and Three Sky? Is it all some kind of big puzzle that we're supposed to figure out? Is it a test?"

"You think they were planning to come back?"

"Who knows? The questions are all a hundred years old. The answers haven't been born. And if we ever do answer any of them, then right away we're going to ask three more.

"Anyway, those old ships are our main reason for being here. Some we fix up and use. They make good service ships. If they can be adapted. We scavenge some for materials to build harvestships. We only buy outside if we have to. Usually the Freehaulers make our purchases landside, for a commission, and make delivery to an asteroid at the edge of the nebula. They think it's just a way station. They don't ask questions. Too many questions is bad for business. They don't try very hard to follow us around, either. They're good people."

"Is that a cut?"

"If you think so."

"I suspected the Freehaulers. I know they had something to do with me and Mouse getting caught. How's chances of me getting to look at one of those ships? I know a little about xeno-archaeology."

A girl's face crossed his mind. Alyce. She had been his Academy love. She had been a recorder at the alien digs in the moon. She had taught him a little, and the Bureau had taught him more.

Sooner or later, the Bureau touched every base.

"You'll have to ask Jarl. I don't think he'll let you, though. We're going to be awful busy repairing *Danion*. Plus you've got your citizenship classes and your beer nights with Mouse."

"Now don't start that again. He's my friend, and that's the way it's going to stay. It don't hurt for him and me to play a couple of games of chess once in a while. You can come keep an eye on us if you think we're cooking up a plot against the Greater Seiner Empire, Lieutenant."

She ignored his sarcasm. "I don't feel like it. I always…" She stopped before she began waving the red flag. Their positions were inflexible. Argument would be pointless. "Moyshe, we've got to get *Danion* whipped into shape fast. The fleets are coming in. As soon as they're all here we're leaving for auction and another crack at Stars' End."

"Stars' End. Stars' End. That's all I hear anymore. And it's completely insane. We can't stick our necks in that noose again, Amy. Look what it cost last time. And remember, I was there too. I was outside with the starfish. I know what that planet can do."

"We've got to have those weapons, Moyshe. You saw the casualty reports. You saw the extrapolations. What the sharks are doing now is going to look pacifistic in ten years. We're talking survival, Love. And you're still thinking power politics."

"You'll just get yourselves killed."

"Either way, then. But we'll handle Stars' End. Honest. The fish really do know how to open the way. They found the key while we were there before."

"Huh?" He had not caught a hint from Chub. "The Sangaree, or Confederation…"

"They'd better come toting their guns if they want to steal it from us, Moyshe. Because they'll have a hell of a fight on their hands. There's a lot of us, honey. And we're looking for a fight. People have been pushing us ever since I can remember. We're tired of it. Once we get those weapons…"

"And sharks, darling. Don't forget the sharks. Oh, it's bound to be a gay party. How do I get transferred to a ground job?"

"You don't." She laughed. "I just heard a couple hours ago. You're going to be transferred to Security for the auction project."

She did not tell him that the auction project would be a pilot for a more ambitious program. If he and Storm performed well and faithfully they would be given joint chieftainship of their own espionage outfit. She did not think her own boss, Jarl Kindervoort, knew yet. The Ship's Commander seemed reluctant to discuss it with the man.

"Auction? That's Mouse's special haunt. How'd he get stuck with it, anyway?"

"It's going to be yours, too. Our new mindtechs will start

coming aboard in a couple of days. And you'll move over to the project."

"Why?"

"Because you know The Broken Wings."

"Yeah. And I want to forget it." His previous mission, as a Bureau agent, had taken him to The Broken Wings. It had been a nasty affair.

"That's where the auction's going to be held. They already sent the permission request. It's just form from here on."

"Form? What you want to bet the place is crawling with Confies and Sangaree? You people stirred up some bad feelings…"

"She hit you pretty hard, eh?"

"What?"

"The woman. The Sangaree woman. That Marya Strehlts-weiter."

"What? How did you?… Mouse. Shooting off his mouth."

"He didn't exactly volunteer it. And he told Jarl, not me. I found out when I was looking through the files for something else."

"All right." His heart hammered for no reason he could justify to himself. So he had gotten involved with the woman. He had not known she was Sangaree then. "It's over."

"I know. I knew that a long time ago. Mouse wrote that report after you shot her. I guess he thought it was important for Jarl to understand what you were going through."

That did not sound like Mouse. "She would've killed all of us. Sooner or later. I had to do it. I never shot anybody before."

"Especially somebody you still halfway cared about, eh?"

"Yeah. Can we drop it?"

"Did Mouse really do that? Inject her children with star-dust?"

"Yes. Mouse plays for keeps. He doesn't have trouble with his conscience. Not the way I do."

"You really think the Sangaree will be at the auction?"

"They'll be there. They hold a grudge the way Mouse does. Amy, I don't want to get involved in that. I'm happy where I'm at. I like linking. Chub is a good friend. I was just scared there at first. I've been getting to know the other members of the herd… Hell, sometimes I go in just to bullshit with Chub."

BenRabi could relax with the starfish as he could with no human. He did not feel naked when he let the starfish see what he really felt and thought. Chub made no value judgments. His values were not human. He had, in fact, helped Moyshe make some small peace within himself.

Parts of his mind remained inaccessible to the starfish. Whole sections were hidden behind rigid walls. Moyshe could not guess what might lie there. He could sense nothing missing from his past.

Seiner life was changing Mouse, too, he reflected. Storm was becoming even more sure of himself, more bigger-than-life than he had always been. BenRabi could not pin it down. One or two nights a week playing chess together was not the same as sharing a minute to minute life under fire.

Mouse was an operative born. He had changed allegiance, but not professions. He had become part of Jarl Kindervoort's staff.

Flying easy. That was what benRabi had been doing since his release from the hospital. The only pressure he faced was Amy's near-militance in hinting about their getting married. Under Chub's ministrations his neuroses were scaling away. He had come to the Seiners with a great many.

"Not much more to see," Amy told him. The rearmost cameras were inside the asteroid. The tugs were guiding the cork back toward the entrance.

"What? Oh. I'd better go say good-bye to Chub."

He reached Contact almost as quickly as he had the day of the last battle. "Clara. Where's Hans?"

"He's off. We don't have anything going."

"I want to go in. They're telling me I'm going to be transferred."

"You can't. We're closed down, Moyshe. They'll be cutting power in a minute. Heck, the herd should be out of range by now."

"Clara, I probably won't ever get another chance."

"Ah, Moyshe. It's silly. But all right. Get on the couch." She prepared his scalp and the hairnet device in seconds. The helmet devoured his head almost before he could catch his breath.

He shifted to TSD, then onward.

The colors of the nebula were incredible. It was a dreary place to the eye, completely dark unless illuminated artificially. In this internal universe Moyshe could reach out and touch all the specks of it, the clouds of luminescent dust, the glowing asteroids majestically circling the nebula's center in their million-year orbits. He could even sense the protostar down in the nebula's heart, lying patiently in its time-womb, gathering the sustenance it would need to blaze for eons.

"Chub!" his mind shouted into the color storm. "Are you there? Can you hear me?"

For a time he thought there would be no answer. The herd lay far off the bounds of the nebula, beyond the pain threshold of its diminutive gravitation.

Then, "Moyshe man-friend? What is happening?"

The link was tenuous. He could barely discern the starfish's thoughts. He could not locate the creature with his inner sight.

"I came to say good-bye, Chub. They say I'm not going to be a mindtech anymore. You were right. They want me to go back to being what I was."

"Ah. I am saddened, Moyshe man-friend. I am saddened because you are sad. We have been good friends. I am pleased that you thought it important to let me know. So many linkers just disappear. Perhaps this last time we can break through those barriers, Moyshe man-friend."

But those corners of benRabi's mind would not yield.

"Moyshe." Clara's voice seemed to come from kilometers away. "They're going to shut the power off. You've got to come out."

"Farewell, Moyshe man-friend." BenRabi could feel the sadness in the starfish.

"Go softly, golden dragon," he whispered. "My heart flies with you down the long dark journey."

Chub's sadness welled up. Moyshe could not stand it. He pounded the switch beneath his left hand.

There was very little pain. He had not been under long. "I don't need it, Clara." He pushed the needle away.

"Moyshe. You're crying."

"No."

"But…"

"No. Just leave me alone."

"All right."

He heard the hurt in her voice. He struggled off of the couch, pulled her to him. "I'm sorry. Clara, I haven't known you very long. But you've been a good friend. I'll miss you. And Hans, too. Tell him to behave."

"I see that he does. He's my grandson."

"Oh. I didn't know." What had he heard about Hans's sister? Or was it mother? She had been lost with *Jariel.* Clara had never let on.

"There're a lot of things you don't know, Moyshe benRabi. About people. Because you never get around to asking."

"Clara… Clara, come visit. Will you?"

"Yes."

"Promise? Amy would love to meet you."

"I promise. Now get out of here before somebody calls the boss and wants to know what the hell's going on up here."

"Thanks, Clara. Thanks a lot. For everything."

His return trip was less precipitous. He was not eager to get home. Amy was bound to be waiting with some unimaginative new approach to the subject of marriage.

SEVEN: 3049 AD
The Main Sequence

"What's the occasion?" benRabi asked. He had come home to find Amy clad only in a negligee. She had been playing body games all week. He supposed she was holding out in hopes lust would make him propose. She was going to be disappointed. He was not seventeen.

The tactic did not bode well for their relationship. There was no future in any relationship where one party practiced extortion upon the other. No one endured that for long. And benRabi had had his fill of it from Alyce, way back when.

Was this why he was so reluctant? Because Amy came on like a spoiled child?

Why *did* he resist it? If he was to make a life here he had to surrender to the culture. This one had scant tolerance for prolonged bachelorhoods.

Older singles tended to get shoved beyond the social fringes. He was out there now. And Mouse, for all the charm he exuded, was slipping too. The ladies were not buzzing round so much anymore. He had made it too clear that he was available for good times only, not for long times and old-style fidelity.

If Amy was the best available, why not?

Part of it was habit. He had been a loner for too long, caught

63

up in a profession where responsibilities to anyone else made a deadly liability. That was why, through mission after mission, he had fought his growing friendship for Mouse.

He had failed at that, and Mouse had too. They saw so little of one another nowadays… That was a pity. Just when they had given in to it, life had taken a twist and spun them along separate paths.

That would end with his transfer to Security, wouldn't it?

"There's a bright side to everything, I guess," he murmured.

Thinking about Mouse, he remembered their last evening together. He could have sworn Mouse had been hinting that he should do something about Amy. It was a damned conspiracy!

Why the hell would Mouse want him married? Mouse did not believe in the institution.

He should take the plunge. But not too soon. He could not let Amy get the idea that she could manipulate him.

He sat with his head in his hands, scurrying around the slot-tracks of an uncertain mind. The tracks did not always follow sane routes. There were moments when he did not know who or where he was. Sometimes he did not understand what was happening, or why. Sometimes he woke up thinking he was back on The Broken Wings, or in Luna Command. There had been a night when he had called Amy Max while they were making love… And a time when he had thought she was Greta… Frightening though they were, those had been isolated incidents. So far.

He and Amy made love fiercely, desperately.

She started getting dressed immediately afterward. "What's going on?" he asked.

"You forgot? We're supposed to have supper with the Sheik and his harem."

"One thing I'm going to tell you right now, woman. And you better understand it. That man's my friend. Learn to fly with it." He had forgotten the dinner. Completely. There wasn't a ghost of memory to be found anywhere in his head.

They joined Mouse and his shrinking clutch of dollies an hour later. BenRabi found his eye roving. Mouse had several honeys he would not mind topping himself. He dared not let Amy notice him looking. Any woman who got that jealous of a male friend...

This affair is headed for trouble, he thought.

Kindervoort appeared suddenly.

Jarl Kindervoort was a tall, lean man who reminded benRabi of Don Quixote, or the Pale Imperator in Czyzewski's novel, *His Banners Bright and Golden*. Like Amy, and most *Danion* Seiners, he was pale, blond, and blue-eyed. BenRabi liked him as a person and found him physically repulsive. It was a combination he did not comprehend.

He did not quite understand Kindervoort's position in the *Danion* scheme either. Kindervoort was, apparently, Amy's immediate superior. Amy was only a Lieutenant, a low-grade officer, yet her boss seemed to speak for *Danion*'s whole Security force. The ship had a population matching that of a fair-sized city. Could the police force be that small?

Kindervoort had high cheekbones and a lantern jaw. They gave him a death's head look. His pale eyes were seldom happy. He could have given Mouse lessons in cold stares. Yet he was a genuinely warm and caring person. He asked, "May I join you?"

"Sure, Jarl," Mouse said. "Glad to have you." Amy and benRabi nodded. Kindervoort settled down, plunged into his meal tray. He did not join the table banter. Neither did benRabi, though Amy brightened for a while and kept up with Mouse in a thrust and parry duel of the risqué and outré.

During his dessert Kindervoort asked, "You told him yet?"

"What? Oh. I forgot," Amy replied.

"Told me what?" benRabi asked.

"We're moving you to Security. Starting tomorrow. For the auction project."

"Oh. That. I know."

"Who told you?"

"I'm not stupid, Jarl. I may act it, but I'm a trained professional. I can see the signs and add the numbers."

"Ah. Exactly. That's why we want you on the auction thing. You're a professional. And you know The Broken Wings. Payne's Fleet has gotten the shove into the barrel this time. Payne thinks *Danion* should provide the protection for our auction crew. Off the record, I'd guess we get the auction because Gruber doesn't want any Payne people with him at Stars' End."

"What? Stars' End? Christ! I'm starting to hope a rogue singularity comes romping around and gobbles up that goddamned gun-runner's pyramid like a big fat chocolate cherry."

"Moyshe! What in the name of…"

"Jarl, you people are crazy. Every last one of you. I won't stand around on the steps of the Senate screaming 'Beware the Ides of March!' but only because none of you whackos have got the sense to listen. It's going to kill you. Can't you get that through your thick heads? But what do I care? You're only taking me down with you. All right. What do you want me on The Broken Wings for?"

"Security shift leader down in Angel City. Night shift. I picked your men already. I want you to start drilling them tomorrow. The feedback we get says it might get hairy."

"What'd I tell you?" benRabi told Amy. To Kindervoort, "At the risk of sounding inane, why me?"

"You and Mouse both. Because you know the city."

"Yeah. And he gets stuck with the other shift? Twelve hours at a crack. Wait. It's only nine on The Broken Wings, but that's bad enough, watch and watch with some guy around every corner waiting to burn you. You know what you're asking us to walk into?"

"What?" Kindervoort would not meet his eye. He knew.

"Mouse killed her kids. I shot her here. And you let her get away. She'll be there if she has to walk halfway across the galaxy. When she hears our fleet is going to handle it… It won't matter if she can get her people's okay. She'll come, Kindervoort. With every goddamned thing she can lay hands on. Come to think of it, the Heads will probably back her even if they don't like it. They're going to be damned hot about what happened to the raidfleet at Stars' End."

"Anything else bothering you, Moyshe?"

"What?"

"I'd like to hear all your objections now. So we can get them out of the way ahead of time."

"All right. Why trust me? I'm the man you caught leading Navy ships to your herd, remember?"

"Three points. One, you're a convert. I saw your test results. Two, the Ship's Commander recommended you. And the third I'd rather keep to myself."

BenRabi tried to remember all the tests he had taken, both before and after deciding to remain with the Starfishers. They had seemed standard, but he might have missed something. "Typical security-type job? Three hours' sleep and ten minutes for personals every day? Need them or not?"

"Probably." Kindervoort smiled.

His smile did not have the desired effect on benRabi. Moyshe saw it as grim, not friendly.

"Then I'd better settle my affairs. Because I don't expect to get through this one alive. I was going to put this off a few days. Mouse, want to be best man? Jarl, you can stand witness. Everybody's invited. I'll put on a party in my room afterwards. If we can come up with anything drinkable."

Nobody said anything for several seconds. Mouse stared blankly. Kindervoort managed to appear both surprised and amused. Mouse's girls just looked puzzled.

Amy showed a half dozen quick reactions. Lack of comprehension. Stunned disbelief. Shock. Distress that threatened to become anger. "It isn't fair," she murmured. She wanted a pompous, ostentatious Archaicist affair with all the splendor of old-time royal weddings. "You're making fun of me." Their friends knew how badly she wanted him to propose.

He had to reassure her quickly.

"Jarl, can we get it done now?"

"We could start in ten minutes if you're serious."

"Go ahead."

"Moyshe, that isn't fair!" Amy cried. "You never even asked me! And I'm not dressed for it and I haven't got anything to wear and..." She had a whole list of ands and buts. BenRabi and Kindervoort waited till she got them out of her system.

"Do I call or not, Amy?" Kindervoort asked.

"Oh!" She hit the table with her fists. "Yes! Yes, dammit! Call him. Moyshe benRabi, you are the meanest, connivingest man I've ever known. How can you do this to me?"

"Hey! You've been all over me about it…"

"Isn't love wonderful?" Mouse asked the air. Amy stopped bitching. Mouse had given her a look which warned her that she was pushing her luck.

The ceremony was not what she wanted. Moyshe kissed her and whispered, "If I get out alive, you'll have the real thing. The big one you want. That's a promise."

After the reception began, Kindervoort pulled Mouse and benRabi aside. "Finally got some word on that failsafer."

Back when the landside contractees had been boarding the service ship for return to Confederation a man had tried to kill them when it had become obvious that they were staying behind. He had suicided after missing. They had assumed he was a Bureau agent failsafing them.

"The autopsy finally got done," Kindervoort said. "He was Sangaree."

"Sangaree!" Mouse said it as if it were a swear word.

"Yes. And he did commit suicide. He was wearing a poison ring."

"Nobody killed him? There wasn't a second failsafer?" BenRabi shook his head. "That doesn't make sense."

"It didn't make sense when we thought there were two of them, and one got away," Mouse said. "Looks to me like he was Strehltsweiter's man, not the Admiral's. Makes sense in that context. She wanted us pretty bad."

"That's the way I figured it," Kindervoort said. "Till now I half-way thought it might have been a setup. To make you look more palatable. It doesn't look that obvious anymore. I'm confused, though. She was in intensive care all the time. Isolated. How did she make contact? How did she relay the order, even assuming the failsafer was pre-programmed? If you come up with any theories, let me know. I'd hate to think my own people helped her."

"Uhm." BenRabi glanced at Mouse.

Mouse shrugged. "I was sure he was Beckhart's."

"Ever heard of a Sangaree suiciding?"

"It happens. Borroway."

"Those were kids. They didn't have any other way out, and they knew too much."

"He had to be programmed."

"What's going on?" Amy demanded. "Consoling the victim, Mouse? You look like your best friend just died."

"We'll talk it out later, Mouse. No, we were just talking about something Jarl brought up. Sort of a puzzle. Let's dance, honey."

It was a zestless party. It did not last long. Neither did the honeymoon. Mouse dragged benRabi out early next morning.

"Hey. I'm supposed to be a newlywed."

"Come on. You been tapping it for eight months. Getting married didn't make it new. Jarl wants us. Time to go into training."

BenRabi spent the next fourteen hours talking about Angel City, studying maps, teaching the use of small arms in a coliseum cube that had been commandeered for the purpose.

His group consisted of twenty-five people. Mouse had another the same size. Mouse drilled his mercilessly in unarmed combat. His was the easier task. His students at least had some idea of what he was talking about.

BenRabi worked at it, but thought the Seiners were taking everything too damned seriously—despite his own admonition about how rough it could get.

He vacillated between a belief that they would find The Broken Wings hip deep in Sangaree and the opposing view, that Navy Security would be so tight that not one unfriendly would get through.

His fourth morning of teaching was interrupted by Kindervoort. "Moyshe. Sorry. Got to take you off this today. They've got a tour planned for citizenship applicants."

"Can't it wait? This auction won't, and these clowns are so bad they couldn't hurt themselves."

"I argued. I got shouted down. I guess they think it's important that you know what you're fighting for."

"Yeah? I never did before, and I did my job…"

"Oh. You're bitter today."

"Just frustrated. The more I see, the worse it looks. We're going to get hurt if this thing goes Roman candle, Jarl. We won't be ready."

"Do the best you can. That's all you can ever do, Moyshe."

"Sometimes that's not enough, Jarl. I want to do enough."

"Make a vacation out of today. Just relax. I don't think it's that important. They're supposed to show you what life's like for Starfishers who don't live on harvestships. Probably do you good to get away from Amy, too. I don't know what's the matter with her. She's even bitchy around the office anymore."

"You've known her longer than I have. You figure it out. You tell me."

Mouse stalked in. "You ready, Moyshe? I scrounged a scooter. Let's go before somebody liberates it back."

EIGHT: 3049 AD
The Contemporary Scene

Hel did not belong. It was a Pluto-sized twerp of a straggler planet which, like an orphaned puppy, had taken up with the first warm body it had come across. When it did so, it set up for business too far from the unstable Cepheid it adopted. Even at perihelion in its lazy, eggy orbit it did not receive enough warmth to melt carbon dioxide.

Hel was a black eight ball of a world silver-chased by ice lying in the canyons of its wrinkled carcass. Its sun was but the brightest of the stars in its sky. No one would expect such a planet to exist, and no one would want to visit it if a suspicion of its existence arose.

Those were the reasons Confederation's Navy Bureau of Research and Development considered Hel the perfect site for a bizarre, dangerous, and ultra-secret research project.

Hel Station lay buried in a mountain like a clam in sand. Its appendages reached the surface at just two points.

The Station was not meant to be found.

"Ion?"

Marescu was a sight. His waistcoat was soiled, ragged, and wrinkled. His hose was bagged and falling. His wig was askew.

His facial makeup was caked and streaked.

"Ion?" Neidermeyer said a second time, catching his friend's elbow. "You hear the news? Von Drachau is coming here."

Marescu yanked his arm away. "Who?" At the moment he did not give a damn about anything, Paul's news included. The agony was too much for mortal man to bear. He yanked a grimy silk handkerchief from a pocket, cleared the water from his eyes. Paul should not see his tears.

"Von Drachau. Jupp von Drachau. The guy who pulled off that raid in the Hell Stars a couple of years back. You remember. The commentators called him High Command's fair-haired boy. They talked like he'd be Chief of Staff Navy someday."

"Oh. Another one of your militarist heroes." Marescu could set in abeyance the worst blues for a good fight about the Services. "Fascist lackey."

Paul grinned, refused the bait. "Not me, Ion. I know you too well."

No fight? Marescu faded off into his internal reality. Damn her eyes! How could she have done it? And with that… that *blackamoor*!

"Hey. Ion? Is something wrong?"

More than normal? Ion Marescu was Hel Station's resident crank and grouch, its leading Mr. Blues and Vinegar. Most people shunned him unless work forced contact. He had one real friend, astrophysicist Paul Neidermeyer, a lady love named Melanie Bounds, and managed a certain strained formality with his boss, Käthe the Eagle. Everybody else was fair game for his vituperation.

"Von Drachau? He's Line, isn't he? Why would they tell a Line officer about this place? They planning on locking him up?"

"Ion. Man, what's wrong? You look bad. Why don't we take you down and get you a shower and a clean jumper?"

One of the curiosities of Ion Marescu was that he appeared to change personalities with his clothing. When he wore standard Navy work clothing he was almost tolerable. When he donned his Archaicist costume he became arrogant, argumentative, viper-tongued, and abnormally misty, as if half the time half of him truly did exist in eighteenth-century England.

Marescu paused before a mirror inset in the passage wall, ignoring the people trying to pass. "I do look a little ragged, don't I?" he muttered. He adjusted his wig, straightened the ruffles at his throat, thought, I wish this *were* Georgian England. I could call the bastard out. Settle this crap with steel.

But you would not have done that with a Negro, would you? You'd have gotten some friends together and played dangle the darky from a tree limb. If you could have stood the shame of confessing to your friends.

Marescu was not one of Hel Station's more polished Archaicists. The others had brought their costumes and research materials with them. He had taken up the hobby only after the isolation had begun to grind him down. He had sewn his own costume, with Melanie's help.

He was more devoted than most Station Archaicists. He prided himself on that, as he prided himself on his contrariness, his crotchets, and the perfection of his work with the test programs. He liked to think that he was the best at whatever he did—including at making himself obnoxious. He seldom noticed the compensatory sloppiness he expressed in his personal habits and hobby.

He had not researched his period thoroughly. He winged most of it. His hobby-era values and beliefs were based on hearsay.

There were those who thought the dichotomy between a perfectionist work life and slovenly play life, taken far too seriously, was indicative of deep disturbance. Admiral Adler disagreed. She felt Marescu was all showoff.

Marescu started walking. He had forgotten Paul. Neidermeyer seized his arm again. "Ion, if I can't help, who can? We've been friends for years."

"It's not something anybody can help with, Paul. It's Melanie. I got off shift early. The quark tube was acting up. The strange positives and bottom negs were coming off almost a milli-degree out of track. They couldn't inject them into their orbital shells… They shut down. She had Mitchell with her."

Neidermeyer murmured an insincere, "I'm sorry." He thought, so what? and wondered if Marescu was not getting a little too far out of touch. Maybe the staff psychologists should hear about this.

A man who started confusing the mores of now with those of his hobby period was more than a little unstable.

Ion always had been neurotic. Now he seemed to have become marginally psychotic.

"How could she do it, Paul?"

"Calm down. You're shaking. Follow me, my son. What you need is a little firewater to settle the old nerves. Eh! None of that, now. Doctor's orders. Drink up, then tell me about it and we'll scope something out."

"Yeah. A drink. Okay." Marescu decided to get blotted. "Tell me about this von Dago."

"Von Drachau. Rhymes with Cracow, like in Poland."

"Poland? Where the hell is Poland?"

"Where they raise the Chinese pigs." Neidermeyer grinned.

Marescu stopped walking. His thin little face puckered into a baffled squint. Seconds passed before the intuition that made him one of Confederation's better test programmers clicked. "The non sequitur game? We haven't played in ages, have we? Poland. Chinese pigs. Poland China hogs... Isn't that the strain they were talking about on that ag show the other day? They want to breed back to something extinct?"

"I don't know what they smell like."

"Okay, Paul. I'm all right now. Ease up. That was a weak one, anyway. Just give me the story on your mercenary hero."

Neidermeyer refused the challenge. "I don't know much. It's just something I overheard at Security. They were chasing their tails getting ready. Guess it took them by surprise. We're here. What're you drinking?"

They stepped off the escalator into soft luminescence just bright enough to prevent stumbling over furniture.

The lounge had been designed to give an impression of being open to Hel's surface. Its protective dome was undetectable. The lighting was too diffuse to glare off the glassteel. The dome itself pimpled from the flank of a mountain, overlooking dark peaks and cruel gorges. The Milky Way burned above, a billion-jeweled expanse of glory.

"Ever notice how it seems colder up here?" Marescu asked, for at least the hundredth time in their acquaintance. He stared out at the poorly illuminated skin of the dead world. The inconstant Cepheid sun hung behind a peak, limning it with a trace of gold. In its off moments that sun was little more noticeable than the brighter neighboring stars. "You pick it, Paul. I'm not particular today. But build it big."

Neidermeyer collected brandy and glasses from behind the bar. "Francis must have gone down for the Security festival," he said. A Marine with an unpronounceable Old Earther name, dubbed Francis Bacon by the research staff, usually tended bar. Security had very little to do most of the time, so filled time by trying to make the Station more endurable for everyone.

People came to Hel on a one-way ticket. Only the Director of Research and Chief of Security ever ventured off world. For security reasons there was no instel comm system available. Isolation was absolute.

"Brandy?" Marescu asked, startled. Paul was a whisky man.

"Old Earth's best, Ion. Almost makes being here worthwhile."

Marescu downed half a snifter at a gulp. "They ought to turn us loose now, Paul. We built their damned bombs. All we're doing now is piddling around with make-work."

"They won't, though. Security. Won't be any leaks as long as they keep us here."

"Paul, how could she?"

"You knew she was…"

"When I got involved? I know. I keep telling myself. But that doesn't make it hurt any less, Paul."

"What can I tell you?"

Marescu stared into his empty snifter.

"Ion… Maybe you ought to ease up on the Archaicist thing. Try to get your perspective back."

"The modern perspective sucks, Paul. You know that? There's no humanity in it. You probably laugh at me because of this outfit. It's a symbol, Paul. It's a symbol of times when people did have real feelings. When they cared."

"I've got feelings, Ion. I care about you. You're my friend."

"You don't. Not really. You're just here because having feelings bothers you."

Neidermeyer glared. There were times when being Ion's friend was work. Marescu refused to apologize. Paul took his brandy to the side of the dome. He stared at the indistinct hide of Hel. The critical question glared back from the serpent eyes of his own weak reflection.

Should Marescu be reported? Was he that far gone?

Nobody wanted to turn in a friend. The Psych people could lock him up forever. Their zoo of Hel-born mental mutations was a blue-chip growth industry.

The project was too delicate to risk its compromise by the unbalanced.

But the production team needed Ion. Nobody had his sure, delicate touch with the test systems. Best let it ride and hope he would come around. This thing with Melanie could be a positive if it jarred him back to reality.

Paul turned. He looked at a thin, short, weary little man who had a thousand years etched into his face and a million agonies flaring from his narrow little black eyes. Right decision? Those eyes were lamps of torment backfired by incipient madness.

Something rattled the foundations of the universe.

The snowy landscape glowed a deep, bloody red. The glow faded quickly.

Marescu turned an ashen color. He stumbled to the dome face, caressed it with shaking fingers. "Paul... That was damned close. They could have destabilized one of the test cores. We'd have been blown into the next universe."

Fear had drained Neidermeyer's face too. He mumbled, "But nothing happened."

"I'm complaining anyway. They ought to have better sense." Feeling the breath of the angel on his neck had snapped his streak of self-pity.

He stared into the darkness outside. A pale new light had begun etching the shadows more deeply. One brilliant point of light slid across the screen of fixed stars, growing more intense.

"They're coming in fast."

Hel's surface was screaming under a storm of violet-white light when the dome polarized. The glass continued to respond to the light beating against it, its inner surface crawling with an iridescence like that of oil on water.

"Doctor Neidermeyer? Mister Marescu? Excuse me a moment."

They turned. Marine Major Gottfried Feuchtmayer stood at the escalator's head. He was Deputy Chief of Security, and a man who appeared to have just stepped out of a recruiting commercial. He was the quintessential Marine.

"Bet he wakes up looking like that," Marescu muttered.

"What is it, Major?" Neidermeyer asked.

"We need your assistance in the arsenal. We need two devices for shipboard installation."

Marescu's stomach went fluttery. The butterflies donned Alpine boots and started dancing. "Major…"

"Briefing in Final Process in fifteen minutes, gentlemen. Thank you."

Neidermeyer nodded. The Major descended the escalator.

"So," Marescu snapped. "They'll never use it, eh? You're a fool, Paul."

"Maybe they won't. You don't know… Maybe it's a field test of some kind."

"Don't lie to yourself. No more than you already are. The damned bomb doesn't need testing. I already tested it. They're going to blow up a sun, Paul!" Ion's mouth worked faster and faster. His voice rose toward a squeak. "Not some star, Paul. A sun. Somebody's sun. The goddamned murdering fascists are going to wipe out a whole solar system."

"Calm down, Ion."

"Calm down? I can't. I won't! How many lives, Paul? How many lives are going to be blasted away by those firecrackers we've given them? They've made bloody fools of us, haven't they? They suckered us. Smug little purblind fools that we are, we made ourselves believe that it would never go that far. But we were lying to ourselves. We knew. They always use the weapon, no matter how horrible it is."

Paul did not respond. Marescu was reacting without all the facts. And saying things everyone else thought but did not say.

For the research staff, service at Hel Station had been a deal with the devil. Each scientist had traded physical freedom and talent for unlimited funding and support for a pet line of research. The Station was ultra-secret, but the knowledge it produced was reshaping modern science. The place seethed with new discoveries.

All Navy had asked for its money was a weapon capable of making a sun go nova.

Navy had its weapon now. The scientists had scrounged around and found a few Hawking Holes left over from the Big Bang, had pulled a few mega-trillion quarks out of a linear accelerator which circumscribed Hel itself, had sorted them, had stacked them in orbital shells around the mini-singularities, and had installed these "cores" in a delivery system. The carrier missile would perish in the fires of a star, but the core itself would sink to the star's heart before the quark shells collapsed, mixing positives and negatives in a tremendous energy yield which would ignite a swift and savage helium fusion process.

Navy had its weapon. And now, apparently, a target for it.

"What have you done, Paul?"

"I don't know, Ion. God help me if you're right."

The passageways were a-crawl with Marines. Marescu swore. "I didn't realize there were so many of the bastards. They been breeding on us? Where's everybody else?" The usual back and forth of technical and scientific staffs had ceased. Civilians were scarce.

At Final Process they were told to report to the arsenal instead.

They found three civilians waiting outside the scarlet door. The Director, though, was an R & D admiral in civilian disguise.

"This's a farce," Marescu growled at her. "Two hundred comic opera soldiers…"

"Can it, Ion," Paul whispered.

The Director did not bat an eye. "They're watching you, Ion. They don't like your mouth."

Marescu was startled. Ordinarily, even the Eagle did not bite back.

"What's going on, Käthe?" Neidermeyer asked.

Marescu grinned. Käthe Adler. Käthe the Eagle. It was one of those nasty little jokes that drift around behind an unpopular superior's back. Admiral Adler had a thin wedge of a face, an all-time beak of a nose, and a receding hairline. Never had a birthname fit its bearer so well.

"They're taking delivery on the product, Paul. I want you to work with their science officers. Ion, you'll prepare a test program for their shipboard computers."

"They're going to use it, aren't they?" Marescu demanded.

"I hope not. We all hope not, Ion."

"Shit. I believe that like I believe in the Tooth Fairy." He glanced at Paul. Neidermeyer was trying to believe. He was like all the science staff. Keeping himself fed on lies.

"Ship's down, Major," a Marine Lieutenant announced.

"Very well," Feuchtmayer replied.

"We'd better get lined out," the Director said. "Paul, pick whomever you want to help. Ion, you'll have to visit the ship to see what you'll be working with. I want your preliminary brief as soon as you can write it. Josip, get with their Weapons officers and draw up the preparatory specs for carrying mounts and launch systems. Have the people in the shops drop everything else."

Josip asked, "We have to build it all here?"

"From scratch. Orders."

"But…"

"Gentlemen, they're in a hurry. I suggest you get started."

"They brought the whole ship down?" Paul asked. Ships seldom made planetary landings.

"That's right. They don't want to waste time working from orbit. That would take an extra month."

"But…" That was dangerous business. The ship's crew would stay crazy-busy balancing her gravity fields with the planet's. If they made one mistake the vessel would be torn apart.

"It shouldn't take more than twelve days this way," Admiral Adler speculated. "Assuming we hit no snags. Let's go." She pushed through the red door.

The completed weapons had a sharkish, deadly look, looking nothing like bombs. The four devices were spaced around the arsenal floor. Each was a lean needle of black a hundred meters long and ten in diameter. They were longer than the shuttle craft intended to lift them to orbit. Antennae and the snouts of nasty defensive weapons sprouted from their dark skins like scrub brush from an old, burned slope.

They were fully automated little warships. The essentials of the nova bomb occupied space that would have been given over to crew in manned vessels. They were fast and shielded heavily enough to punch through a powerful defense.

The weapon remained largely theoretical. But the men who had created it were confident it would function.

Neidemeyer whispered to Marescu as they donned working suits, trying to convince his friend, and himself, that they were just gearing up for a field test. "I'm sure the money people just want to see if they're getting any return on their investment," he insisted. "You can't blame them for wanting to try their new toy."

"Yeah. Our hero von Drachau is going to take potshots at a couple of insignificant stars. Right?"

"Right."

"You're a fool, Paul."

A band of strangers entered the arsenal. They stared at the four dark needles, clearly awed and a little frightened.

"That's von Drachau on the right," Paul whispered. "I recognize him from the holo. Only he looks a lot older."

"Looks a little grey around the gills, I'd say."

Von Drachau did look depressed. He spoke with the Major and Käthe Adler. Käthe led his party around one of the missiles. Von Drachau became more impressed.

There was something about the big, terrible ones that excited a resonance in the soul. It was almost a siren call. Marescu felt it himself each time he touched one of the monsters. He was ashamed of himself when he did.

"Little boys play with firecrackers, and big boys play with bombs," he muttered.

"Ease up. Käthe meant it when she said they're watching you. Feuchtmayer isn't one of your big fans, Ion."

"I'll stay out of his way."

The days whipped past. Technicians swarmed over the pair of weapons von Drachau selected. Marescu tested systems and supervised the installation of special shipping aids. Josip brought the missiles' computation systems into communion with the battle computers aboard von Drachau's ship. Technicians designed and installed adapters and links that would fit the securing rings and launch vanes going onto the belly of the warship.

Neidermeyer prepared a manual for the science officers responsible for arming the sunkiller and monitoring its gluon pulse in passage, watching for that tiny anomaly that might forecast the expansion of a quark shell into disaster.

Marescu could not believe there was so much to do. His shifts were long and demanding. He felt a lot of sympathy for Paul, whose personal research project seemed threatened with death by inattention.

Neidermeyer watched his friend more closely than he did the gluon pulse, hunting some telltale psychological anomaly. Marescu seemed almost too much in control, and had thrown himself into his work with a near-fanaticism that bespoke a very fragile stability fighting its last stand. Yet there were positive signs. Ion had shed the filthy Archaicist outfit. He had begun devoting more time to his personal appearance...

Then it was over.

Käthe Adler joined them in the lounge. "Let the firewater flow," she proclaimed. "It's time to say the hell with it and turn loose of the brass ring for a while."

Marescu gave her an odd look.

The celebration became a premature New Year's bash.

The pressure was off. The antagonisms went on the shelf for the day. Guilts got tucked away. Scientists and technicians made shows of comradeship with the Marines. A handful of von Drachau's officers joined in, drinking lightly, listening to the jokes but seldom laughing.

"For them it's just begun," Ion murmured. He glanced around. No one had heard him.

Von Drachau was a focus of brooding gloom. He seemed to have sunk two-thirds into another universe. Ion watched him glare at Paul as if Neidermeyer were some small, venomous insect when Paul tried to strike up a conversation about the raid in the Hell Stars. Von Drachau disappeared only minutes later.

"Don't think you made an impression, my friend," Ion said.

Käthe agreed. "He's sensitive about it, Paul. He's a strange one. You should have heard the row he and Ion had."

Marescu met Paul's gaze. "It wasn't any big thing. I came on a little too strong, that's all."

"What was it?" Neidermeyer asked.

"About the morality of using the weapon," Käthe said. "Von Drachau is damned near a pacifist. Ion was pretty shook when he found out the man could adapt his convictions enough to let him use the weapon."

"Ion's problem is that he's an absolutist. He's got to have everything black or white. And he's getting worse. Is there any way we can get him into therapy without having him committed?"

"You think there's a reason to worry? His profiles keep coming up off-center, but they never show any danger."

"Sometimes. Lately... He's got a creepy feeling to him. Except for that argument with von Drachau, he's swung too far away from what he was. I'm nervous about the backswing. Like I can hear the timer clicking. He might break loose going the other way."

They had begun talking about Marescu as if he were not around for the very good reason that he was not, though neither of them had consciously marked his departure.

Käthe Adler had called von Drachau a crypto-pacifist, and Marescu had seen red. Literally. The dome and people went raggedly, liquid, and red. Then it was all clear. All perfectly clear. He had to go see Melanie and explain.

He was walking down a passageway. Time seemed to have passed. He had the distinct feeling that his head was on sideways. That mercenary von Drachau... The man had kicked the foundations out from under him. A flexible morality? How could there be such a thing? A thing was either right, or it wasn't. The nova bomb was the most evil thing yet conceived by the military mind. And he had helped midwife that evil into this universe. He had allowed himself to be seduced... He had whored himself...

There had to be a way to show them what they were doing.

He shook his head violently. Things were foggy. A band seemed to be tightening around his temples. There was something wrong.

He could not force his thoughts into a straight line.

For an instant he considered finding a Psych officer.

Von Drachau seemed to laugh at him again.

"You fascist bastard!"

Christ! Some Torquemada had taken another turn on the strap. His skull was creaking with the pressure.

"Where am I?" he blurted. His feet had been moving without conscious direction. He tried to concentrate on his surroundings. "What am I doing here?"

He wanted to turn and go back. His feet kept going in the direction he was headed. His hand pushed on Melanie's door.

He was an alien, a passenger aboard a body under another's control. He was a slightly panicky observer of actions being carried out by another creature.

The little gasps and grunts lashed that devil, punishing it like a wizard's curse. He stared at the eight-limbed, twenty-toed beast. It heaved and lunged. Its four blind eyes rolled swiftly. Its three uncontrolled mouths made wet, hungry sounds.

The Ion of him silently screamed and turned inward, refusing to see any more. A darkness closed round it.

A clumsy puppeteer jerked him around, dragged him out the door and down the passageway with jerky, meandering, drunken steps. When next the Ion rider surfaced it found its steed in the arsenal, clad in its Georgian, bent over the computer board in the heavily shielded test control kiosk. The clock claimed that hours had vanished from his life. His hands and fingers were flying, a pair of pale white dancing spiders.

They were doing something dreadful. He did not know what, and they would not stop when he commanded them. He watched them like a baffled child watching slow death.

An image here, an image there, surged into his mind, playing back fragments of the missing hours. Ion Marescu crawled over a long black needle. Ion Marescu crouched beneath the needle, connecting the heavy cables that ran to the test station. Ion Marescu squeezed through the cramped interior of the black ship, removing safety chips...

"Ion?"

Paul's voice barely penetrated the thick stressglass of the booth's walls. He was screaming. Ion realized the yelling had been going on for a while. He glanced at Paul puzzledly, barely recognizing him. He did not stop working. This was the most important test he had ever run. For the first time in his life he was doing something of real worth. He had found himself a holy mission.

What was it? He shook his head, tried to clear the mists. They would not go.

His hands danced.

Käthe Adler joined Paul. They pounded the unbreakable glass with their fists. Then the woman fled. Paul grabbed a fire axe and swung away.

When Ion next glanced up, the vast arsenal floor was a-crawl with Marines. Major Feuchtmayer had his pale face pressed against the glass directly in front of him. His lips writhed obscenely. He was screaming something. Ion had no time to listen. He had to hurry.

What the hell was going on out there? the observer part of him wondered.

He finished programming the test sequences.

Each weapon had to be run through a simulated plunge into Hel's own sun. Ion usually performed the test series on a system-by-system basis, with the drive never operational and the safety chips preventing the weapon from going active. "How do we know the drive will work?" Marescu muttered. "We just take their word for it?"

Paul and the Marines stopped trying to break the glass with hand tools. Ion saw the Major laying a sticky grey rope of something round the door frame.

"Plastic explosives? My God! What are those madmen trying to do?"

His right hand depressed the big black palm switch that opened the arsenal's huge exit doors. It was through those very doors that that hired assassin von Drachau had moved his two missiles to his ship.

People flung in all directions as the arsenal air burst into Hel's eternal night. Baffled, Marescu watched their broken doll figures tumble and bloat.

His left hand danced, initiating the test sequences. The arsenal drowned in intense light. The stressglass of the booth polarized, but could not block it all. The sabotaged holding blocks fell away from the number four weapon. It dragged itself forward, off its dolly. It flung off clouds of sparks and gouged its spoor deep into the concrete floor.

"Wait a minute," Ion said. "Wait a minute. There's something wrong. It's not supposed to do that. Paul? Where did you go, Paul?" Paud did not answer.

The black needle, its tail a stinger of white-hot light, lanced into the night, dwindled. The little star of it drifted to one side and downward as its homing systems turned its nose toward the target.

"What's happening?" Marescu asked plaintively. "Paul? What went wrong?"

The eye of the black needle fixed itself on Hel's sun. It accelerated at 100 g.

And in the booth, where the atmospheric pressure had begun to fall, Ion Marescu realized the enormity of what he had done. With a shaking hand he took a suggestion form from a drawer and began composing a recommendation that, in future, all test programs be cross-programmed in such a way that the activation of any one would automatically lock out the others.

"We have influence, Commander," Lieutenant Callaway reported.

"Take hyper," von Drachau replied. "And destroy that Hel astrogational cassette as soon as you have her in the hyper arc. For the record, gentlemen, we've never heard of this place. We don't know anything about it and we've never been here."

He stared into a viewscreen, slumped, wondering what he was, what he was doing, and whether or not he had been told the whole truth. The screen went kaleidoscopic at the instant of hyper-take, then blanked.

Seventeen minutes and twenty-one seconds later the sun of the world he had just fled felt the first touch of a black needle. The little manmade gamete fertilized the great hydrogen ovum. In a few hours the nova chain would begin.

There would be no survivors. Security allowed no ships to

remain on Hel. The Station personnel could do nothing but await their fate.

And nowhere else did there exist one scrap of information on the magnificent, deadly weapon created at Hel Station. That, too, had been a Security-decreed precaution.

NINE: 3049 AD
The Main Sequence

Mouse drove down to the same departure station that had witnessed the Sangaree failsafer's suicide. A half dozen bewildered former landsmen were there already. He and benRabi were last to arrive. All but one of the others were women.

"They haven't shown yet, Ellen?" Mouse asked.

"No. Did you hear anything? You know what it's about?"

"Not really."

BenRabi tuned them out. He walked through those last few minutes before Kindervoort's men had come to disarm Mouse and he had walked into the failsafer's line of fire. He went to the spot where he had been standing, turned slowly.

"Jarl was here. Mouse was there. Bunch of people were there... They brought Marya's intensive care unit down that way, before Jarl showed, and took her right into the service ship."

He walked through it three times. He could not recall anything new. He had been distracted at the time. He had believed that Mouse was shanghaiing him, and had not wanted to leave. Then Jarl had distracted him...

"Hey, Mouse. Walk through this with me. Maybe you can think of something."

A scooter rolled into the bay. A pair of unfamiliar Starfishers dismounted. "You the citizenship class?" the woman asked.

"Hello there," Mouse said, like a man who had just crossed a ridgeline and spied all seven cities of Cibola.

The woman stepped back, her eyes widening.

"Must be Storm," the man said. "My wife, Mister Storm."

"Well… You win some, lose some. You don't know till you try."

"I suppose not. All right. Let's check the roll, then get started. Looks like we're good. We've got the right number of heads. All right. What we're going to do is leave the ship through the personnel lock and line over to one of the work bays on one of the mooring stays. There's zero gravity in the work area so you don't have to worry about falling. Follow me."

He went to a hatchway, opened it, stepped through. The future Seiner citizens followed.

Mouse tried hanging back, to get nearer to the woman.

BenRabi gouged his ribs. "Come on. Let her alone."

"Moyshe, she's driving me crazy."

"She's prime. Yes. And married, and we don't need any more enemies."

"Hey. It isn't sex. I mean, she's fine. Like you say, prime stuff. What I'm saying, though, is this is our shot at somebody from outside."

"What're you talking about?"

"She's not from *Danion*."

"How the hell do you know that?" BenRabi ducked through the third of the lock doors. "You've maybe been around the world here, but I don't think you've gotten to them all. Not yet. We haven't run into a hundredth of *Danion*'s people."

"But the ones we have all came from the same mold. Oh, Christ!"

BenRabi slithered out of the ship. He stood on her skin, offering Mouse a hand. In both directions, as far as he could see, were tubes, cubes, spars, bars… Hectare on hectare of abused metal. Overhead, the laser-polished stone of the asteroid arched in an almost indiscernible bow. *Danion*'s outermost extremities cleared it by a scant hundred meters.

Those hundred meters had Mouse petrified.

Mouse was scared to death of falling. The phobia usually manifested itself during a liftoff or landing, when up and down had a more definite meaning.

"You all right?"

Storm was shaking. Sweat beaded his face. He shoved a hand out the hatch, twice, like a drowning man clawing for a lifeline.

The others were hand-over-handing it along a cable spanning the gap between ship and asteroid.

"Come on, Mouse. It won't be that bad." How the hell had he gotten through all the e.v.a. exercises and small boat drills they had had to endure in Academy?

Mouse's phobia perpetually astonished benRabi. Nothing else fazed the man. Whining bullets and crackling lasers simply created the background noises of his work...

His work!

"Assassin's mind, Mouse. Go into assassin's mind." The state approximated a meditational trance, except that while he was in it Mouse was one of the most deadly men who ever lived.

Was he too much out of practice?

Mouse's shaking slowly subsided. His eyes became glassy.

"All right," benRabi said. "Come on. Slow. Take the handholds and work your way over to the line. That's good. Good. Now across to the balcony."

Moyshe spoke softly, without inflection. In this state Mouse had to be handled gently. Anything could set him off. Anyone not programmed in as Friendly could get broken up pretty bad.

The woman instructor overtook benRabi on the line. "What's wrong with your friend?"

"He's an acrophobe."

"A Navy man?"

"I know. Be real careful for a few minutes. Keep the group away. He's not very stable right now."

He got Mouse onto the balcony, with his back to the vast mass of the ship, and talked him down. In five minutes Storm was asking, "You ever meet anyone on *Danion* who wasn't blond with blue eyes?"

"Some. Not many."

"Anybody with black blood?"

"No."

"I rest my case." Mouse surveyed the harvestship. "Damn, she took a beating."

"Huh?"

"Different perspective, Moyshe. It's not up and down from here."

BenRabi scanned the battered ship. "Mouse, I think we've been set up."

"What?"

"I thought it was a little weird, coming out the way we did. I was going to ask the lady why they didn't have something better." He pointed with his chin.

A half kilometer away a telescoping tubeway connected the ship with the rock face. BenRabi soon indicated a half dozen more connections. Each was large enough to use to drive heavy equipment onto and off the harvestship.

"Think they're just working on you and me? Or the whole group?"

"Fly easy," benRabi suggested.

"It's my ass in a sling, Moyshe. I'll be your basic model of decorum."

"Are these two part of a plan?"

"Take it for granted. The question is, was it supposed to be obvious? Or are they just clumsy?"

"To quote a certain Admiral, who used to tell us what to do, 'Just lay back in the weeds and let them show their hand.' He was good at mixing metaphors."

"How's the writing going, Moyshe?"

They turned to follow the Seiner couple, who were shooing the others into a tunnel.

"I haven't written a page in months. I don't know why."

"Time?"

"That's part of it. But I always found time before."

Atop all his other hobbies, benRabi dabbled at writing short fiction. Traveling to Carson's from Luna Command, an eon ago, he had looked forward to the Starfisher mission as a vacation operation during which he could get a lot of work done. He had expected to stay a maximum of six weeks. The Admiral had promised... A year had passed, and he had completed one dreary story, the manuscript of which he had not seen in months.

Once they departed the central hollow of the asteroid they entered local artificial gravity. There was little visible difference between ship and shore.

"Oh, boy!" Mouse said. "More brand new same old thing. This is going to get boring in a few years, Moyshe."

"Sorry you decided to stay?"

Mouse eyed him momentarily. "No." His expression became a little strange, but benRabi paid it no attention.

"Look, Mouse. Kids. I haven't seen any kids since we left Luna Command."

"Hooray."

"Come on, man. Look at that. Must be some kind of class tour."

Twenty little girls around eight years old were giggling along behind an old man. The old man was explaining something in a crackling voice. Several of the girls were aping him behind his back. Some of the others were making faces at the mockers.

"Call me back in ten years," Mouse said. "I got no use for them till they get ripe."

"You have got to be the sourest..."

"It some kind of crime not to like kids? Speaking of which, I never saw you get along with any but Jupp's boy and that Greta. And she was sixteen going on twenty-six."

Jupp von Drachau had been their classmate in Academy. He was now High Command's special errand boy. He had helped with their operation on The Broken Wings. Later, it had been his assignment to provide the firepower when it had come time to seize Payne's Fleet. They had thought. His premature approach and detection had left them stranded for the full year they had contracted to work for the Seiners.

"Horst-Johann. I didn't see him last time we were in Luna Command. That's two years ago now. Damn, time flies. Bet he's grown half a meter."

Their male guide said, "People, we'll lunch in one of the worker's commons before we show you a typical creche. Don't be shy. Visit. People here are as curious about you as you are about them. We'd appreciate it if you'd stay close, though. If one of you gets lost, we'll both have trouble explaining."

"Great," Mouse said. "Still more brand new same old thing. Doesn't anybody ever eat anywhere but in these goddamned cafeterias? I'd sell my soul for a go at a decent kitchen on my own."

"You cook?"

"I'm a man of myriad talents, Moyshe. Think that's what I'll do when we hit The Broken Wings. Figure out how to make myself a home-cooked meal. And devour it in private. Not out in the middle of a goddamned football field with five thousand other people."

"You've got one classic case of the crankies this morning, my friend."

"I didn't get any last night. Besides, I'm not patient with crap, and this whole field trip is main course horseshit without the hollandaise."

The commons was as predictable as Mouse feared. So was the food. The conversation did not sparkle either, till Mouse took the offensive. "Grace, what's the point of this exercise?"

"I don't understand your question, Mister Storm."

Moyshe grinned behind his hand. The woman was sensitive to that overpowering Mouse charm. She had become as decorous as a schoolteacher by way of compensation.

"This bullshit exercise. You dragged us away from work we don't have time to get done right anyway. You run us out on a goddamned wire, then walk us all to hell and gone when we could have done the whole thing on a bus. You tell us we're going to see how Seiners live when they're not in the fleet, but you just show us the same old stuff. And since you've only kidnapped us for today, you're not really serious about showing us anything. I mean, an idiot would realize that it would take weeks just to skim the surface of a civilization like yours."

The woman's dusky face darkened with embarrassment.

"I mean, here we sit, eight former landsmen, all with that much figured out, and all of us on our best behavior figuring it's some kind of test or someone wants us off *Danion* for a while...

Whichever, it's dumb. You're wasting our time and yours."

"Mister Storm…"

"Don't mind him," Moyshe interjected. "It's old age creeping up on him. He's not as tolerant of games-playing as he used to be."

Mouse grinned and winked. BenRabi grinned back.

Their guides surveyed the other landsmen. They said nothing, but aggravated agreement marked each of their faces.

"There's no point in going ahead, then," the male guide said. "Your response is data enough. Finish your meals. I'll be right back." He disappeared.

"What *is* the point?" benRabi asked.

Grace shrugged. "I just work here."

"Psychologist?"

She was startled. "How did you know?"

"I can smell them. You really married to him?"

"No." She laughed weakly. "He's my brother."

"Ooh." Mouse said it softly. Only Moyshe heard.

"You swallow something radioactive, Mouse?"

"What?"

"You just started glowing."

The lady psychologist was not immune. Mouse wangled a date before her brother returned. BenRabi did not doubt that Mouse would make the date an interesting experience.

He could not fathom Mouse's method. Even knowing they were being manipulated, knowing Mouse's reputation, women walked right in. Indeed, Mouse's reputation seemed to make him more interesting.

Their guide returned. He deposited his half-finished tray on the conveyor to the sculleries. He waited impatiently while his flock followed suit. He scowled at Mouse, who had opened up with the big guns and had Grace laughing like a teenager at stories woollier than the mammoths they antedated.

"Style," benRabi told himself. "That's what he's got."

"Excuse me?" one of the ladies asked.

"Talking to myself, Ellen. It's the only way to hold an intelligent conversation."

"You think they'll be mad at us because of this?"

"Maybe. More likely at each other. Like Mouse said, it was a dumb idea, no matter what the point was."

"Unless it's a cover."

"That's a possibility."

The man had a bus waiting outside the cafeteria. In ten minutes it reached the departure bay they had left so laboriously earlier. By then Mouse was holding Grace's hand. He had her purring and almost unable to wait till he got off work.

"Come on, Storm," her brother snapped. "Back to your assigned department. The rest of you, go back to your jobs. Grace, for god's sake…"

"Oh, shut up, Burt."

"He's got a name," one of the ladies crowed. Mouse's mutinous attitude was catching. The Seiners had tried to put something over on the landsmen and they were responding with a mocking camaraderie.

"Come on, Mouse," Moyshe grumbled. "Let's don't start anything."

"Right. At eight, Grace? Bye." Storm bounced onto the scooter he had commandeered for the ride to the departure station. Moyshe took the seat behind him.

"New worlds to conquer, eh?"

"That's one way of looking at it, Moyshe. This old one is starting to wear. They must have some kind of open contract on me. Some kind of bounty for the girl who cons me into the 'I dos.' They won't take no for an answer. Not and stay friends. Weird people."

"What the hell are you doing here?" Kindervoort demanded when they strolled into the coliseum, where he was overseeing some especially poor marksmen.

"Surprise," Mouse crowed. "The game was called on account of rain."

"What's he talking about, Moyshe?"

"It was some kind of dumb exercise. I'm sure you know what it was all about."

"I told him it was stupid."

"Who?"

"The Ship's Commander. He's up to something with you two.

I don't know what."

"Remind him that one of the reasons I crossed over was because people wouldn't play games with me here. I'd have a job I knew what it was. I'd have a place in the scheme. Tell him that if the crap keeps up, I hike my ass back to Contact and chain me to a couch. He can put his auction project where the sun don't shine. It's a stupid operation too."

"Calm down, Moyshe. Just go back to your job."

When Kindervoort turned away, Mouse said, "Good to see you stand up on your hind legs, Moyshe."

"It takes me awhile to get fired up."

"Like the man said, let's go to work. We've got a long way to go with these clowns."

The next morning, whispering with motionless lips as they hurried along a crowded passageway, Mouse said, "They used the time to fix us up with a new set of bugs, Moyshe. Very good stuff. Better than anything Kindervoort stocks. The kind that hook into a stress analyzer. They're putting the big eye on us, Moyshe. From now on you'd better play safe, no matter where you are or who you're with."

"What would they be looking for? We don't have anything to hide."

"Who knows? But don't forget that they're looking."

TEN: 3049 AD
The Main Sequence

BenRabi was trying to clip a couple of stubborn, noxious-looking hairs out of his right ear. Amy called, "Ready yet, honey?"

"Half a minute." He had butterflies. He did not want to go. The stalls and arguments had run out, though. He had to meet Amy's family. Such as it was.

He was about to be exhibited to her mother. A prime trophy, he thought. Former landsman turned Seiner, on his way up. A prize for any single girl.

He had been getting that feeling from Amy. The new was wearing off. The magic was fading. He was becoming an object of value instead of one of emotion.

Was the problem his or hers? Was he reading her wrong? He always misinterpreted women.

"Moyshe, will you come on?"

He stepped out of the bathroom. "How do I look?"

"Perfect. Come on. We'll be late for the shuttle."

"I want to make a good impression."

"Stop worrying. Mom would be happy with a warthog, so long as I was married."

"Thanks a lot."

A flash of the old Amy returned. "Any time."

They rode a scooter out one of the connecting tubes, into the halls of the asteroid. Amy slowed to pass a series of doors with temporary plaques hung on them, reading names Moyshe found meaningless. "We're here."

The plaque said STAFINGLAS. Amy parked the scooter among a small herd nursing charger teats.

"What's that mean? Stafinglas?" Moyshe asked.

"I don't know. I think it's made up."

"That's where your mother lives?"

Amy nodded. "We've got to hurry. They'll start pumping the air out of the lock in a couple minutes. They won't let us board after they start."

Could he stall that long? He decided that would be a petty trick. Much as intuition warned him that the trip was a waste, it was important to Amy. The thing to do was grit his teeth and ride it out.

The shuttle was a small, boxy vessel useful for nothing but hauling passengers. The seats were full when Moyshe and Amy boarded. Dozens of people stood in the aisles. BenRabi recognized a few as *Danion* crewfolk.

"Lot of relatives of *Danion* people in this Stafinglas, eh?"

"Yes. The old harvestships are like family enterprises. Three or four generations have served in the same ship. It gets to be a tradition. Almost nobody ships outside their own fleet. They say that's why we're getting into this nationalistic competitiveness between fleets. There's talk about having a computer assign new crews by lot."

Moyshe smiled. "Bet that's a popular idea."

"Like the black plague."

His feet hurt and his back ached before the shuttle reached its destination. It was a six-hour passage. He spent every minute standing.

Stafinglas was exactly what Moyshe expected. An asteroid with kilometer upon kilometer of broad tunnels which served as residential streets. "I'm home," he told Amy. "It's just like Luna Command."

She gave him a funny look. "Really?"

"On a smaller scale." He wanted to tell her it was not a natural or comfortable way to live. Instead, he asked, "You ever been down on a planet?"

"No. Why?"

"Just curious." He could not explain. She did not have the experience to understand.

"Anything else I should know about your mother? I want to make a good impression."

"Stop saying that," Amy snapped. "Stick to literary things. You can't miss. Duck an argument. She's contrary as hell. She'll start a fight just to find out how stubborn somebody is."

He looked at her askance.

"We had some beauts when I was young. Nothing I did and nobody I knew was ever good enough. Talk libraries if you know anything about them. She's librarian for Stafinglas."

The more Amy talked about her mother the less he wanted to meet the woman. He had encountered dragons before. They rolled right over him.

"We're here." Amy stopped at a door, reluctant to take the last step.

"Well?"

Biting her lower lip, Amy knocked.

Four hours later they excused themselves to go out for lunch. Neither spoke till they had drawn their meal trays. As he settled at a table, Moyshe said, "Jesus, do I have a headache."

"Headache? Not here?"

"Tension headache. Not migraine." It had been bad. Much worse than he had expected. The woman was a classic. He glanced at Amy. Want to know what a woman will be like in twenty-five years? Have a good, long look at her mother.

"I'm sorry, Moyshe. I... I can't even make excuses for her. There isn't any excuse for that kind of behavior."

"Uhm. Maybe I'd better get used to it. Maybe she was just saying what a lot of people think. Me and Mouse and the others may have to live with that the rest of our lives."

"You should have fought back."

"Would that have changed anything? No. It would've kept her going that much longer."

Moyshe was still numb. As an Old Earther he had been fighting prejudice since entering the Navy. He had thought he possessed a thick hide. But never had he encountered anyone as virulent as Amy's mother. Outworlders went through the forms of equality, keeping their prejudices subtle and silent. Amy's mother was open and vicious and adamantine about hers. Neither suasion nor force would alter her thinking in the least.

She had disowned Amy before it was over.

"You want to try again?" Amy asked.

He was startled. "What?"

"She *is* my mother, Moyshe."

He reached across the table, took her hand for a second. "I know." She was doing her brave act to conceal her pain. "I know. I've got one too. And she isn't that much different."

"They want the best for you. And they think they're the ones to decide what's best." Amy gulped several mouthfuls. "Mother never was good at expressing feelings positively. Maybe that's why I'm a little weird. I spent a lot of time with her while I was growing up. She never qualified for fleet duty. That was the big disappointment of her life. Till we gave her something else to feel sorry for herself about."

Amy almost never mentioned her father. All Moyshe ever learned was his name and the fact that he had been killed in an accident here in the nebula. Apparently, despite protestations to the contrary, Amy's mother had found the accident convenient.

"We'd better not go back, Moyshe," Amy decided. "Not today. Let's give her a chance to calm down and get used to the idea."

"Okay."

They had to kill four hours before a shuttle became available. Moyshe thought Amy would use the time to visit old friends. She did not. She said all her real friends were aboard *Danion*. She became defensive. She did not want to face any more disapproval. The stay-at-home Seiners were, apparently, less cosmopolitan than the people of the harvestfleets.

Going back, Amy suggested, "If you want, tomorrow we can sneak over and see those alien ships. The research center isn't that far."

Moyshe perked up a little. "All right. That's a good idea. I've been looking forward to it. What do we do about our work assignments?"

"I'll take care of everything."

Amy took sleeping pills as soon as they reached their cabin. Despite a long, long day, Moyshe was not in the mood for bed. He strolled down the passageway and awakened Mouse.

"How'd the get-together go?" Mouse asked. And, without awaiting an answer, "That bad, eh?"

"It's a whole different world, Mouse. I thought I knew how to handle prejudice... I never saw anything like it. Her mother was the worst, but there was plenty everywhere else we went, too."

"I know. Grace took me for a little tour this morning."

"You guys got out of bed long enough?"

"Hey, you got to do something the other twenty-three hours of the day."

"So tell me. And where's the board? I've been here three minutes and I still haven't seen a chess board."

"Sorry." Mouse grinned. BenRabi had accused him of being unable to relate with the human male unless a chess board was interposed. "Guess I'm preoccupied."

"She show you anything interesting?"

"I'm not sure. You can't break the habits of trade-craft. So you look and you listen. But you don't find anything that gives you a handle on these people."

"Where'd you go?"

"To some kind of office complex first. Like a government and trade headquarters. We hunked around there for five hours. They had everything out in the open... You know, like no confidential files or anything, and nobody getting excited because you pick up a paper and read it. You take white. But there wasn't anything there. I mean, nothing anybody back home would give a damn about. I didn't see a damned thing worth remembering."

"What the hell kind of weird move is that?"

Mouse smiled. "Some Seiner pulled that on me the other day."

"And lost."

"Yeah. But I was better than him. Hey. You know what they're doing? They're getting ready to go back to Stars' End."

"That isn't any secret."

"No. But they're so damned serious. I mean, Grace and I went to this one asteroid they were making into a dry-dock. After we left the other place, I got to talking to this engineer. Her husband is on the team that's adapting a shuttle to piggyback the Stars' End weapons to orbit."

BenRabi raised his attention from the board. "Curious. Everywhere you go... They're so damned sure of themselves, aren't they?"

"Awfully. Maybe we're too sure they can't do it. Maybe they have an angle." Mouse's attention had left the board too. He seemed to have a question he was afraid to ask. Moyshe felt the intensity of it, boiling there behind his friend's eyes.

"I've got a hunch that they do. Through the starfish, somehow."

Mouse returned to the game. His unorthodox opening got him into trouble early. BenRabi had him on the ropes, but let him wriggle loose by making a too-eager move. It cost him a knight.

"You always did get too excited," Mouse observed. "How has your head been?"

"I had a headache today. Just tension, though. Why?"

"Just asking." A move later, "What I meant was that disorientation stuff you had because of the Psych program. Any trouble?"

"Not much. Not like it was. I have my moments. You know. Blanking out for a second, then coming back wondering where I am and who I am. They don't amount to anything. They don't last long enough for anybody to notice."

"Good. I was scared when you were doing that Contact stuff. Thought you might get mixed up while you were in, and come back somebody else permanently."

"You didn't, by chance, have anything to do with getting me transferred, did you?"

"I would have if I'd thought I had the drag. For your own good. But I didn't." Mouse rose, indicated that Moyshe should follow him. He stepped into the passageway, tapping his ear.

"What is it?"

"Don't want them to know I know this. The orders came from up top. Way up top. I know this woman who works in Communications. She told me a couple things she thought I already knew. Naturally, I played along."

"Naturally. If it's female, you'll go along with anything."

Mouse grinned. "One of these days I'll tell you about the Admiral sending me to pimp school. Whoring isn't the oldest profession. Pimping is. You'd be knocked on your ass if you saw what a really good pimp can do with women."

"He sent you to school?"

"Yeah. Hell, Moyshe, it's the oldest trick in the spy business. You teach a guy how to make a woman fall for him, then turn him loose on the women who work for the organization you want to penetrate."

"I thought it worked the other way around. Women seducing men."

"It's done. It doesn't work as well. Men don't respond the same to emotional blackmail."

"What did your friend have to say? We can't stay out here too long."

"Buddy, we're headed for the top. Somebody upstairs has decided we're the medicine Seiner foreign relations needs. This auction project is a test. If we come through, they'll give us a shot at setting up our own secret service."

BenRabi had had a few hints. He had formed a few suspicions. Still, he was not ready for the truth.

"A real fleetwide secret service. Inside and out. Intelligence and counter-intelligence. The works. For all the Starfishers. The way it sounds, they'll give us anything we want and turn us loose. They've got friends landside who try to keep them informed. The friends have fed them enough, the last couple of years, to get them worried about what's going on in Luna Command."

"Ah. I begin to smell the rat. We've got connections. We could turn a few of our old buddies."

"You've got it."

"How do you feel about it?"

"I was about to ask you, Moyshe."

"After you."

"All right."

"All right. It would be a challenge. We'd be going head to head with the Old Man. It would be a hell of a match-up."

BenRabi was not pleased. "I take it you're excited."

"Damned right I am. Not meaning to brag, but if we'd gone back, I'd have had Beckhart's job eventually. He said so himself. And you'd have become my Chief of Operations. He thought we had what it takes, Moyshe. You see what I'm driving at?"

"I think so." BenRabi was disappointed for a moment. There was not a shred of loyalty in Mouse. His attitude was wholly mercenary… What the hell am I crying about? he wondered. I started this side-changing stuff.

He cast Mouse a sharp glance. More and more, he suspected his partner had stayed here only because *he* had, not out of conviction. What did that mean when taken with this sudden enthusiasm for directing an organization targeted against their former employer? What had become of his obsession with destroying the Sangaree?

"So what I think you should maybe be thinking about," Mouse said, "is how we could set it up. Who we should use, where we should keep our eyes open, like that. And structure, too. You're more of a theorist than I am."

"Communications would be the big problem, Mouse." He tried not to take Mouse's chatter seriously. The obstacles to creating an effective Seiner secret service were insurmountable. "How do you run an S or K net without communications? See what I mean? We're out here and the targets are the hell and gone somewhere else. You and I were always where we could use a public comm if we had to. Or we could use the Navy nets. Say we got somebody into Luna Command. He finds out something we should know right now. What does he do? Run outside and yell real loud?"

"We'll figure it out, Moyshe. Don't worry about the details that way. Don't be so negative all the time. Instead of saying, 'It's impossible,' say, 'How can we do it?' Figure a way, then organize to fit it. Let's get back in there before they get too suspicious."

They exchanged a couple of moves. Moyshe said, "I yield. I would've had you this time except for that one stupid move."

"It was a bad opening. I deserved to get stomped. Another game?"

"Just one. Then I'd better turn in. Amy's sneaking me out for a look at their xeno-archaeological project tomorrow."

"Wish I could go. But Jarl will have fits enough about you."

The main research station was awesome.

"What they did," Amy explained, "was take over one of the drydock asteroids. So they could study the ships inside."

The planetoid was smaller than the one that had engulfed *Danion*, but still was vast. At least a hundred ships floated in its interior. Some were so alien their lines almost hurt the eye.

Around the inner face of the asteroid lay an office and laboratory level. It was roofed by a layer of glassteel. The researchers and their staffs could look up at the ships floating overhead. People in the bay could see what was going on in the offices and labs. The asteroid had been given spin along its longitudinal axis instead of using artificial gravity generators, which would have been in continuous imbalance by facing inward.

Moyshe and Amy entered through a lock in the asteroid's end, and observed briefly from a lookout there. Moyshe was impressed. The line of ships marched on till it vanished in the distance.

"They bring them in this end," Amy said. "They look them over, study them, and the ones that aren't useful they move up the line." She indicated a remote vessel. Tugs were guiding it away. "The far end is industrialized. The ships the scientists don't want they break up for raw materials or refit for us to use. Let's see if we can find a scooter."

An hour later Amy introduced him to a woman named Consuela el-Sanga. "Consuela is an old friend, Moyshe. Consuela, Moyshe might be able to give you an idea or two."

Consuela el-Sanga was a small, dusky woman in her early fifties. She bore the stamp of the preoccupied researcher, of a person who had devoted a lifetime to her curiosity. Moyshe liked her immediately, and as quickly felt a kinship. She was a shy, diffident individual in matters outside her expertise.

"Are you a xeno-archaeologist, Mister benRabi?"

"No. Amy's exaggerating. I'm not even a gifted amateur. My only claim is that I followed the Lunar digs close till a year ago. I had a friend on the project."

Darkness hit him. It had the impact of a physical blow. A woman's face floated before him. He had not seen that face in years. Alyce. Academy love. The girl who had worked at the Lunar digs…

"Moyshe!" Amy sounded frightened. "What's the matter? Are you all right?"

He held up a hand, patted at the air. "Okay. Okay. I'm okay." He shook his head violently. "Just a delayed reaction to the spin here," he lied. "I've never been in centrifugal gravity."

Inside, panic. What the hell was this? It had not happened for months. He realized he was talking, and talking fast. "I was at the digs a year and a half ago. They'd just opened a new chamber, in almost perfect condition. They thought some of the machinery might still work."

Amy and Consuela watched him carefully. "You sure you're all right?" Amy asked.

"Sure. Sure. Miss el-Sanga, what could I do to help?"

"I really don't know. We could walk you through one of the ships we think relates to the Lunar base, for a layman's opinion. We're sure there was a connection, but, because of politics, we can't work with the people there."

"It's a pity, too."

"Come along. We'll start with artifacts recovered from the ships. So you're married now, Amy."

BenRabi caught an odd note in what could have been either statement or question. He gave the women a closer look. There was a slight tenseness between them, as if there had been more to their relationship than friendship and shared interests. He filed it in the back of his mind.

"Took me long enough, didn't it?" Amy tried to sound light. She failed.

The moment of disorientation had turned something on inside Moyshe. His mind went to work agent-wise. The cameras rolled. The cross-reference computer clicked. His surroundings took on more depth, more meaning. They became brighter and more interesting. His movements became quicker and more assured.

"This is what we laughingly call the museum," Consuela el-Sanga said, pausing before opening a door. "It's not, really. It's just a storage room. Whoever those people were, they didn't leave much behind. Mostly just trash. But that's all archaeologists ever have to work with. Broken points, potsherds, and whatever else the ancients threw out behind their huts."

Moyshe moved up and down rows of metal shelves. They contained hundreds of items, each tagged with a date, ship number, inventory number, and brief guess as to what the object might be. Some were referenced to other inventory numbers.

Twice he paused, reexamined an item, said, "I saw something like this at the Lunar digs. I'd say there's a definite connection."

The second time, Consuela el-Sanga responded, "Not necessarily. Parallel function. Say a comb. Any creature with hair would invent a comb. Wouldn't you say? So the existence of a comb wouldn't prove anything but a common physical trait." And when Moyshe finished with the racks and shelves, she said, "Now into my office. I'll show you our two real treasures."

Moyshe and Amy followed her through another door.

"You haven't seen these either, Amy. We found them while you were out. They were both part of the same find."

Consuela El-Sanga took two plastic cases from her desk. She handled them with loving care.

Moyshe accepted one, Amy the other. The item benRabi held was a piece of paper that had been torn into small fragments. A very few faded marks were visible.

"Is it a photograph?" Amy asked.

"Good guess," Consuela said. "We had a hell of a time with them." Moyshe traded with Amy. The second object *was* an extremely faded, flat, two-dimensional photo. It had been torn in two.

Consuela continued, "First we pieced all the tears together. Then we did scans with low-intensity lasers and computer enhancements. We came up with these." The woman glowed with pride as she handed over reproductions of the items.

The photo, in color, was of a creature very similar to the Lunar dig reconstructions. BenRabi said as much. The other object appeared to be a handwritten letter.

"Any luck interpreting this?" Moyshe asked.

"No. We haven't even determined which direction it's supposed to be read."

"You haven't found any technical manuals or anything?"

"Not a speck. Just a few characters on nameplates, stuff like you'd find around instrumentation and doors on any ship. Any time there's more than three characters, they're arranged in matrices like these."

"Maybe they had a holographic system for reading."

"No. Doesn't go with a two-d photo. We don't think."

"Very interesting," Moyshe said, studying the picture again. "A Dear John letter? And the guy, or gal, gets mad and tears up the lover's letter and picture, but then can't bear to part with the pieces?"

"That's one of our hypotheses."

Moyshe scanned the letter. "Thirty-four different characters here. Some punctuation?"

"Don't try to figure it out in your head. Even the computers can't get a handle on it. Just think how hard it would be to break our language without a starting clue. Big letters, little letters, script, punctuation, spelling variations by dialect, different type faces, all the stylized lettering and special symbols we use for technical stuff... You see? We'd need a whole ship full of old letters, novels, and newspapers to break it. Not just a few plaques on an instrument panel."

"Don't worry, Consuela," Amy said. "We'll be into Stars' End soon. You'll find your answers there."

"If I'm lucky enough to go. They haven't picked the science team yet. I'm worried."

"You'll go. You're the best."

BenRabi looked at the woman and slowly shook his head. That Stars' End insanity again.

"I don't know what I'd do if they turned me down, Amy. It's my whole life. I'm not getting any younger. And they might use my age to keep me home."

"Don't worry. You know they can't leave you behind. There's

nobody better than you. And they know how much it means to you."

"How soon, Amy? Do you know?"

"It hasn't been decided yet. But it won't be long. A month or two."

Consuela brightened. "You're sure they'll send me?"

"Of course. Don't be silly."

"That's what I am, you know. A silly old woman."

Amy enfolded her in gentle arms. "No you're not. No you're not. Come on, now. Show us one of those ships."

Consuela el-Sanga led them to a little four-place air scooter, flew them out to a vessel. BenRabi felt lightheaded in the lack of gravity. "I feel like I could fall all the way to the end," he said, staring down the length of the hollow.

The ship was one of the least alien of those in the lineup. "Form follows function," Moyshe muttered, remembering the Luna Command constructs, which had very much resembled small human beings.

The ship's lock was open. Consuela made fast, led them inside. She was small, but even she had to stoop in the passageways.

Moyshe wandered around for an hour. He finally summed up his impressions by observing, "It's not that strange. Just kind of dollhouse. Like it was built for children. You can figure out what half the stuff is. It's just parked places we consider weird."

"You said it yourself, form follows function," Consuela replied. "We've done comparative studies between these, Sangaree, Ulantonid, and our own ships. The physical requirements of bipeds appear to be universal. Scales seem to be the most noticeable difference."

"That ship two ahead of this one. What built it? A giant slug?"

"We don't know. It's funny. There's something almost repulsive about it. You have to work yourself up to it if it's your turn to study it. It's like the alienness oozes out of the metal. It's more of a mystery than the other ships. It's almost contemporary, if our dating technique is valid. It shows battle damage. It's the only one of its kind we've ever located. It was as clean as these others. One of my colleagues believes the crew were forced to abandon ship after an accidental encounter during some crisis period, like the Ulantonid War, when everyone was shooting at anybody who didn't yell friend fast enough. Curiously, though, it was surrounded by a whole squadron of our little friends here."

"Enemies?"

Consuela shrugged. "Or purely chance. The ships aren't contemporary with one another. What were they doing together? There aren't enough books to write down all the questions, Mister benRabi. It gets frustrating sometimes."

"I can imagine. Could the crew have been studying the old ships when they were attacked by a third party?"

"That's a possibility we hadn't considered. I'll bring it up…"

"Consuela?" someone shouted into the vessel. "Is that you in there?"

"Yes, Robert. What is it?"

"Somebody's looking for those people who came to see you. A man named Kindervoort. He sounded pretty excited."

"Oh-oh," Amy said. "I'm in trouble now. I thought he wouldn't notice. Consuela, I'd better call him."

She placed the call from Consuela's office. Jarl foamed at the mouth and ordered them to return to *Danion*. Now. He snarled at benRabi, "Moyshe, I don't care if you cut those nitwit citizenship classes. They're a waste of time anyway. But you're not ducking out on the training schedule. Now come back here and get your men ready. You've got the rest of your life to look at old ships. The auction is now."

Amy was quiet throughout the return passage. Once she whispered, "He's really going to give it to me," and clutched Moyshe's hand. She was shaking.

"He's an amateur," benRabi told her. "You haven't been chewed out till you've taken it from Admiral Beckhart." A moment later he grinned and added, "But if it's private, he lets you yell back."

Soon after they returned they heard that another of the great harvestfleets was entering the nebula. The news generated a fresh air of excitement aboard *Danion*.

One by one, the harvestfleets came in. Scores of fresh, eager young faces appeared aboard *Danion* as graduates of Seiner technical schools filled the billets of people lost at Stars' End. The howl and hammer of repairs went on around the clock. The excitement and tension continued to mount.

They were going back. This time in full strength, and to stay. A prideful, nationalistic, bellicose mood gripped the fleets.

Moyshe benRabi and Masato Storm pursued their instruction of the teams they would direct on The Broken Wings. Their days were long and exhausting. Moyshe often tumbled into bed without enough energy left for a good-night kiss.

He began to feel the pressure. It started to intrude into his sleeping hours. He began to dream of the girl he had left behind, so long ago. He suffered more momentary lapses of attention while he was awake.

He began to grow frightened of what might be going on back in the nether reaches of his mind.

ELEVEN: CHRISTMAS 3049 AD
The Contemporary Scene

Tension gripped the bridge of the attack cruiser *Lepanto*. "One minute to drop," the astrogation officer announced.

Jupp von Drachau scanned his people. They were poised like runners in the blocks, awaiting the crack of the starter's pistol. They would have to grab an enormous fund of data in a few brief minutes.

Lepanto was coming up to an enemy star. There was no way of guessing what might be waiting. Detection gear would not work from hyper unless initial detection had been made in norm. The cruiser was going in blind.

No one knew the capabilities of the Sangaree detection systems. Operating from norm, they would not have the same handicap. A force might be moving toward the drop zone now.

"Thirty seconds."

"Stand by, Weapons," von Drachau ordered. "Button up, people." He sealed the faceplate of his own helmet.

One quick drop to get his bearings, then a short arc in to the fringes of the Sangaree sun...

"Five seconds. Four. Three."

The figures on the bridge hunched forward a centimeter more.

"One. Drop."

"Screens up."

"Commander, heavy vessels bearing..."

"Display active."

"Three ships bearing..."

"Range to star one point three two a.u..."

"We have a local inherent velocity of..."

"Attack missiles bearing..."

"Bridge. Weapons. Launching two salvos."

The vessel shuddered and rocked. Von Drachau stared at the display tank. Six red blips had come to life there. They sped along projected curves which would bring them within spitting distance of *Lepanto*. Tiny ruby pinpoints raced ahead, toward the cruiser.

"... time to intercept forty-seven seconds..."

The hyper alarm commenced its hooted warning to the crew. "Time to hyper one minute," a voice boomed.

Someone said, "Commander, we've located the planet."

"Bring me up a visual."

"Aye, sir."

Von Drachau's command screen came to life. For an instant it displayed a computer graphic of the local solar system. The schematic yielded to a visual from an external camera. It showed a white third-crescent. The amplification rose quickly, revealing a world heavy with clouds and seas. "Looks a lot like Old Earth," von Drachau murmured.

"Yes sir."

"Are you taping?"

"We're getting everything we can, sir."

"Twenty seconds to hyper."

Von Drachau glanced at the display tank. The missile salvos were driving closer. Weapons Department was not bothering with anything but defensive fire. Considering the nature of the mission, engaging a handful of raidships was pointless. "Anything near that sun?" he asked.

"No sir. We have a lot of activity near and on the planet."

That made sense. The Sangaree would be scrambling everything in fear that *Lepanto* might be the spearhead of a thrust against their Homeworld. That was the doom they had dreaded for centuries.

"Hyper in five seconds. Four."

Von Drachau did not think these picket ships would jump with him. They should await the rest of a suspected battle fleet.

"One. Taking."

The universe shifted. Screens went blank. The display tank, cued in norm, remained active. Von Drachau stared, willing the Sangaree raidships to remain where they were.

"One minute to drop." Astrogation had programmed a very short, slow arc.

Von Drachau reached back into his soul, searching for any wisp of feeling that might bear on the orders he had to give. He did not want to do this thing. Every cell of him protested. And yet... And yet he knew too much. He knew the critical importance of obtaining results. And he had his own orders.

"Special Weapons Party, stand by."

His orders would be a formality. The pre-launch program had begun an hour ago. The only significant command he could give now would be the abort.

He checked the tank again.

"Damn!" They were coming. Their detection gear was good. They knew no one else was coming in right away. "Looks like we knocked over a beehive," he said. The six raidships from the drop zone were being joined by a horde quartering in from the planet.

"Twenty seconds till drop."

It would be a narrow squeak, making the launch and getting clear in time. And some of them would chase him all the way home... "Astrogation, program your next jump for Carson's." He did not want to lead the pursuit too close to the action on The Broken Wings.

"Sir?"

"Pull the cassette and reprogram." An attack squadron would be on station near Carson's. He could scoot in and cling to its protective skirts.

"Yes sir."

"Drop."

"Special Weapons Party, launch when ready."

There. It was too late to take it back. Too late to keep from having to live with it the rest of his life.

"Special Weapons launch in three minutes, twelve seconds," launch party captain replied.

"What's the holdup? We've got Sangaree crawling up our backs."

"Sorry, sir. A coupling jammed."

"Long range hunter missiles bearing…"

"Visuals, please," von Drachau said. His screen came to life. "Show me the star."

In a second he was staring at an endless plain of fire. Broad continental reaches of darkness lay upon it. The star appeared to be passing through a period of heavy sunspotting. But, as he remembered it, the Sangaree home star was supposed to be highly active, with exceptionally intense solar winds.

"Two minutes to special launch."

Von Drachau checked the display tank. The Sangaree were coming on in a mob. They were not organized, but there were too many of them. *Lepanto* wouldn't have a prayer in a heads-up fight.

"Astrogation, how's your program coming?"

"Five minutes, sir."

"We don't have five minutes. Make it a basal arc that'll drop us in the neighborhood. Do your fine calculation during the fly."

"Yes sir."

"… to intercept fifty-two seconds."

Von Drachau glared at the tank. They would have missiles in their pockets by launch time. Power weapons would be pounding *Lepanto*'s energy screens. "Damn!"

It looked bad.

"Time to launch one minute."

The bridge watch took on that hunchbacked look of people anticipating the kiss of the whip. Sixty lousy seconds. That could make a damned short life. Mayflies lasted longer.

"… to intercept fourteen seconds."

That was close. And the next salvo would be closer.

"Astrogation. One millisecond free hyper straight linear," von Drachau snapped.

"Sir?"

"Do it!"

The alarm hooted as the ship lurched.

The Ship's Commander's screen returned to life. The Sangaree sun had moved. He could see a horizon line. It had no curvature.

Weapons Department howled. They had to reprogram.

"So do those boys over there. Special Weapons. Time to launch."

"Thirty-two seconds, sir."

"Missiles bearing two five-niner relative, one two degrees nadir. Time to intercept two six seconds."

Von Drachau sighed. That was right on the line. "Gentlemen, we're going to make it."

The bridge watch did not relax. They knew his remark was half prayer. The tank proclaimed that in its totally unambiguous display. A saturation barrage was hurtling toward them.

And it was a long, long run back to friendly space.

"Ten seconds to launch."

And there was the problem of the weapon safely reaching target. If the Sangaree sniped it, *Lepanto* would have to try again. A second pass could get hairy.

Lepanto shuddered and lurched. Someone yelled, "That was too goddamned close!"

"Two. One. Launch. Weapon away."

The warship lurched again. "One tenth second free hyper straight linear!" von Drachau ordered. "Detection, lock on that weapon. I want to know if it makes it."

The cruiser dodged. Von Drachau shifted attention between display tank and screen, following the weapon into the sun.

Sangaree missiles had no chance to catch it. Scores of laser and graser weapons probed for it, caressed it with their deadly tongues.

"Telemetry. How are its screens holding?"

"Perfectly, sir."

Lepanto rocked. Time was running out.

"She's in, sir. They can't stop her now. Her sun screens are stable."

"Astrogation, get us out of here."

"You still want an observation pass, sir?" R & D had asked them to hang around and study the results.

"The hell with that noise! Get out of here before they barbecue us."

The hyper alarm hooted. The ship twisted away into an alternate dimension. Von Drachau turned to the display tank.

"Some of them are good," he murmured. "Very good."

Four vessels had caught the trail already, and were coming hard.

"Drive. Run your influence factor to the red line."

"Sir!"

"You heard me. You'll take it over if you have to. Stand by for it."

"Yes sir."

Von Drachau glanced at the sun shape dwindling in the display tank. The weapon would be sinking toward its heart. The killing process would begin in a few hours. He turned into himself again, looking for his feelings. All he found was a big vacancy, an arid desert of the soul.

He did not think much of Jupp von Drachau just then.

BOOK TWO
THE BROKEN WINGS

TWELVE: 3050 AD
The Contemporary Scene

Lemuel Beckhart felt totally vulnerable while walking the streets of Angel City. The berg was domed, of course, but the glassteel arced too far overhead. He had been born in Luna Command and had spent most of his life there and in warships. He needed overheads, decks, and bulkheads close at hand before he felt comfortable.

Worlds with open skies were pure hell for him.

He shoved his hands into the pockets of the civilian trousers he wore. It was coming together. The timing looked good. The leaks had the commentators howling for blood.

Funny how they became raving patriots when it looked like their asses were going to go in the can too… Those people in Public Information knew their trade. They were keeping a fine balance. They were generating alarm without causing panic. They were stampeding legislative sessions hither and yon, herding them like unsuspecting cattle, getting everything Luna Command wanted. Confederation Senate was passing appropriations measures like the gold seam had no end.

The real victory was a stream of confederacy applications from outworlds that had remained stubbornly independent for generations. Well-tempered fear. That was the lever. Let them know Confederation would defend its own, and ignore the others when the hammer fell... Those cunning politicians. They were using the crisis too. Everybody was scoring on this one. Would the maneuvering and manipulation settle out in time? It was human nature to go on wasting energy on internal bickering when doom was closing in.

Those PI people... They were something. They still had not released anything concrete. The propaganda machine in high gear was a wonder to behold.

Beckhart was bemused by his own pleasure at observing a high level of professional competence in a department not under his own command.

His mood soured when he reflected on the latest news from his colleagues in Ulantonid intelligence. That centerward race... They seemed to draw some special, wholly inexplicable pleasure from killing.

The latest Ulantonid package had included tape taken on a world with a Bronze Age technology. It showed small, suited bipeds, built like a cross between orangutans and kangaroos, armed principally with small arms, systematically eradicating the natives. There was ample footage of shattered cities, burning villages, and murdered babies. Not to mention clips of cadavers of virtually every other mobile lifeform the planet boasted.

If it moved, the hopping, long-armed creatures shot it. If it did not, they dug it out of hiding and killed it anyway.

There had been no sky full of ships for this primitive world, just a stream of transports sending in troops, munitions, small flyers, and the equipment used to hunt down the wilder creatures of mountain and forest. The Ulantonid experts estimated a troop input approaching ten billion "soldiers."

Beckhart could not grasp that number. Ten billions. For one primitive world... Confederation and Ulant together had not had that many people under arms during the most savage years of their conflict.

"They've got to be crazy," he muttered.

He paused near the building where Thomas McClennon, now Moyshe benRabi, had kept the Sangaree woman distracted while Storm had torn the guts out of her Angel City operation. Christ, but hadn't those boys pulled a coup? And now they had come through again, giving him the Sangaree Homeworld.

He had to bring them out. Somehow. He refused to write men off while they lived.

He was determined. There had to be a way to apply enough leverage to force their release... If it came to that alone, and he could prise no better yield from the coming encounter, he would be satisfied.

The thing looked made to order for another coup. "Down, boy," he muttered. "First things first. You're here to get your boys back. Anything else comes second."

Still, it was coming together. The word was, the Sangaree wanted revenge. It was a good bet the Seiners would have another go at Stars' End. The rumors and leaks from Luna Command had everybody excited about an ambergris shortage. A lot of eyes would be staring down gun barrels at this end of the Arm.

He was pleased. He had choreographed it perfectly. Only he and High Command would be thinking about von Drachau. If von Drachau succeeded, the news would hit like the proverbial ton of bricks.

He strolled on to the warehouse that had headquartered the local Sangaree operation. It was a fire-blackened pile of rubble. The authorities had not cleared it yet.

"Sometimes, Lemuel, you're not a very nice person," he murmured.

He was repelled by some of the things he did. But he was sincere in his belief that they were necessary.

He was terrified of that centerward race. The hungry bunnies, he called them, for no truly good reason.

Ten billions for one world. Tens of thousands of ships.

How could they be stopped?

Why the hell were they so determined to kill? There was no logic to it.

Was there anything more he could do? Anything he had overlooked?

He lay awake nights trying to think of something. He suspected that everyone in High Command slept poorly of late, running the same perilous race courses in hopes of finding the key to escape from the nightmare.

His beeper squeaked. He raised it to his ear. "Hand delivery only, urgent, for Blackstone," a remote voice told him. He returned the beeper to his belt and walked briskly toward his headquarters.

The courier was a full Commander. He wore a side-arm, and carried the message in a tamperproof case that would destruct should anyone but Lemuel Beckhart attempt to open it. The case bore a High Command seal.

"Sit, Commander. What's the news from Luna Command?"

The Commander was a taciturn man. "We seem to be in for some excitement, sir."

"That's a fact. You came in with the squadrons taking station?" Three heavy squadrons had taken orbit around The Broken Wings. They were there at his request.

"Yes sir. Aboard *Assyrian*."

"Popanokulos still Ship's Commander?" Beckhart placed his thumbs at the proper points on the case. Something whirred. He prised it open with a fingernail.

"Yes sir."

"How is he? He was one of my students, years ago." He was reluctant to open the plain white envelope lying within the case.

"He's in excellent health, sir. He asked me to extend his best regards."

"Extend mine in return, Commander." He initialed a pink slip for the second time, indicating that the contents of the case had been received. He would have to do so twice more, indicating message read, then message destroyed.

The Commander moved slightly in his chair. He appeared impatient to return to *Assyrian*. Beckhart opened the envelope, removed what appeared to be a sheet of plain white paper. He pressed his thumbs against the bottom corners. Invisible microcircuitry read his prints. A handwritten message slowly took form, appearing at the rate it had been written.

L: All-time screw-up at R&D research facility. Cause unclear. System destroyed. Total loss. VD away with 2 apples. Public disclosure disaster unavoidable. M.

Beckhart laid the sheet on his desk, covered his face with the palms of his hands.

There went a key hope. Without telling his Ulantonid opposite number why, he had asked for additional deep probes toward galaxy center, hoping to locate homeworlds that could be shattered with the new weapon. He had hoped the grandeur and viciousness of the thing could be used to intimidate the centerward race into abandoning their insane crusade.

A total loss. All the info, both on the weapon itself and what had gone wrong. Damn it to hell, anyway!

He initialed the pink slip, burned the message, and initialed the slip again. "Thank you, Commander." He handed slip and case over. "There won't be a reply."

"Very well, sir. Have a nice day."

Beckhart wore a puzzled smile as the officer pushed out the door. A nice day? Not likely. He keyed a switch on his desk communicator. "I need Major Damon."

A few days later his comm whined at him. "Yes?"

"Communications, sir." The commtech sounded choked. "Signals from *Assyrian*, sir. The Starfishers are here. Just detected."

Beckhart felt a stir of excitement. He asked, "What's the problem?"

"Sir, I... Let me feed you the *Assyrian* data, sir."

Beckhart touched a button. The tiny screen on his comm crackled to life. A series of computer data began flashing across it. Then came a schematic of a ship.

He read the size figures three times before murmuring, "Holy shit." He leaned back, said, "Communications, keep running that till I say stop."

"Yes sir."

He watched the report three times through before he was satisfied.

So those were harvestships... They were self-contained worlds. If Navy could lay hands on a few of those, and arm them with Empire Class weaponry... "Communications, page Major Damon. Tell him to come to my office."

The commander of the Marine Military Police battalion reported only minutes later.

"Major, there'll be an adjustment in our plans. Watch this."
Beckhart ran the report from *Assyrian*. Damon was suitably
impressed.

"Major, sit. We're going to do some brainstorming."

The session lasted the day and the night and into the next day.
It ended when Communications interrupted. "Admiral, signals
from *Assyrian*. Sir, they've intercepted signals between the Seiner
ships. They thought you'd be interested."

"Of course I am. Give it to me."

The relay was not long. And it was both baffling and exciting.
The Starfishers were going to put his own boys in charge of their
auction security effort.

He had it run twice. Satisfied, he said, "Major, go get yourself
eight hours. Then get back here and we'll pick up where we left
off. This changes things again. We work it right, now, and we're
in the chips."

After the Major departed, he had *Assyrian* open an instel
link with Luna Command. He spent an hour in conference. He
broke off smiling a weak smile. This auction might be more than
serendipitous.

He dragged himself to his cot, hoping to catch a few hours,
but could not fall asleep.

His conscience kept nagging him. Once again he would have
to use men cruelly for the sake of the Services and Confederation.

He was so weary of that...

THIRTEEN: 3050 AD
The Main Sequence

Payne's Fleet dropped hyper a Sol System radius from The Broken Wings. *Danion* formed the point of the arrowhead of ships flashing toward the planet. Accompanying the harvestships were a hundred service ships borrowed from other fleets.

The Seiners wanted to make an impression. They believed this show of strength would rivet all eyes on The Broken Wings.

While the credit from the auction was important to them, distracting attention from Stars' End meant even more.

Almost all Seinerdom had taken hyper for the fortress world. The harvestfleets had gathered. A hundred harvestships, a thousand service ships, and untold millions of people would be involved in the effort to recover the citadel world's weapons. That gargantuan armada, bearing the hope of a nation, was avoiding traffic lanes, flying easy, awaiting word of the success of the auction diversion.

A confrontation with Confederation had to be avoided. The Seiner leadership understood the swift doom inherent in a two-front war.

A one-front war was a terrible enough hazard.

"We've got trouble," Jarl Kindervoort told his staff. "We've just received a scout report from Stars' End. The Sangaree have moved in there."

Mouse made a sound suspiciously like a purr. "Won't hurt my feelings if they get crunched again."

"Somebody's going to get crunched. The report says there're hundreds of raidships there."

Storm and benRabi became more attentive. Mouse asked, "Hundreds? That would take... Hell, the Families would all have to be working together. They don't do that."

Kindervoort replied, "They seem to have their hearts set on grabbing Stars' End."

"They aren't the only ones," benRabi muttered. He snorted in disgust, shook his head. "Who's fault is that, Jarl?"

"What do you mean, Moyshe?"

"Consider our last run-in. Consider one Maria Elana Gonzales, technician, alias Marya Strehltsweiter, Sangaree agent. Remember her? The lady who tried to kill *Danion*? I shot her and stopped her. And you nice people politely patched her up and sent her home with the other returning landsmen. Bet you she ran straight to her bosses and set this up. Nice doesn't pay, Jarl."

Mouse shifted his chair so he could stare at benRabi. He said nothing.

Once upon a time, on a faraway world called The Broken Wings, a partner of Mouse's, wearing the work-name Dr. Gundaker Niven, had stopped him from killing a Sangaree agent named Marya Strehltsweiter.

Moyshe reddened.

"Let's not cry about what we should have done," Kindervoort said. "We're here now. Let me have those situation reports, Amy."

Amy pushed a sheaf of flimsies across the tabletop. "Navy is damned interested in this end of the universe, too. Three heavy squadrons off The Broken Wings. Squadrons *Hapsburg*, *Prussian*, and *Assyrian*."

"Empire Class?" Mouse asked. "All of them? They mean business, don't they?"

"There're battle squadrons at Carson's and Sierra, too. Our friends the Freehaulers couldn't get close enough to identify them."

"And no telling what's in the bushes," benRabi mused.

"Moyshe?"

"They're playing poker, Jarl. They've shown us a couple of aces face up. What you have to worry about is their hole cards. What have they got cruising around a couple of light years away ready to jump in?"

"You think they'll try a power play?"

"No. Not like that. But it might behoove us to spend a little brain power figuring what they're up to. Navy doesn't put that much power together unless they're scared they'll have to use it. You hardly ever see a patrol of more than two ships."

"You know Service thinking better than me. Why're they so excited?"

"The dispositions look defensive," Moyshe said. "And that leads us to our lack of landside intelligence. What's the Planetary Defense Forces alert level in the Transverse? Have they activated any reserves? If so, which units? We could extrapolate their fears from that kind of information."

"We have the liaison team report." Kindervoort shuffled flimsies.

Mouse and benRabi had insisted on sending a few men ahead, weeks ago.

"I've seen it," Moyshe said. "They've given The Broken Wings the usual temporary free planet status. They've pledged an open auction. The city authorities are so nervous they've called up their police reserves and asked Marine MPs to help. They expect trouble. Nobody is saying why."

The coded reports said there were three hundred privately owned ships orbiting The Broken Wings. Each had brought a negotiating team hoping to carry off a supply of ambergris. Most of the vessels appeared to be armed.

All known space was, apparently, in the grip of an undirected war fervor. No one was behaving normally. The auction had a potential for becoming a wild brawl.

"Mouse, Moyshe," Kindervoort said, "I don't mind telling you, this thing has me scared. It's too big, and it looks like it could get bigger. Be very, very careful."

"It could get too big for anybody," Mouse said. His voice was soft and thoughtful. "It could roll us all under."

For two days *Danion* and her sisters drifted slowly toward The Broken Wings, watching and listening. They kept their presence secret longer than Moyshe expected. He and his compatriots obtained two days' worth of observations.

They provided no comfort. Angel City was hell incarnate. Armies of undercover people had materialized there. They were warring with one another with a fine disregard for reason and local tranquility.

The war scare had set off a chain reaction of insanity.

As a landing team leader benRabi now rated his own office and a part-time assistant. His wife filled the assistant's role.

Till this is over, at least, I'm important, he thought. He put little stock in Mouse's theory that they were being groomed to master a Starfisher secret service. He had been able to make no independent corroboration of the claim.

BenRabi's intercom buzzed. "BenRabi here."

"Jarl, Moyshe. I need you over here."

"Now?"

"Right. Final meeting."

"I'm on my way." He gathered his papers, donned fatalism like a cloak, and stalked toward Kindervoort's office. He met Mouse outside Kindervoort's door.

"Broomstick fly," Mouse said.

"No lie. Anybody with any sense would cancel the auction."

Mouse grinned. "Not the Seiners. You got to remember, this auction is part of their big picture."

"I think they'd go ahead even if it weren't."

"Come on in," Kindervoort called. A moment later he began introducing them to the Ships' Commanders and Chiefs of Security of the other harvestships of Payne's Fleet.

The gentlemen were present only as holo portrayals. Kindervoort, Storm, and benRabi would be aboard their vessels the same way. They and the holo equipment and technicians reduced Kindervoort's office to postage stamp size.

"You bring your final reports?" Kindervoort asked.

BenRabi nodded. Mouse said, "Right here. But you're not going to like them."

"Why not?"

"They're reality-based. Meaning they recommend that you cancel or postpone."

BenRabi added, "We can't handle security with what you've given us. Not under the conditions obtaining."

"We've been talking about that. How many more men would you need?"

"About a brigade of MPs," Mouse growled.

"Moyshe, you look surprised," Kindervoort said.

"Just thinking that this isn't like working for the Bureau. You ask the Admiral for more than he gives you, he takes half away and tells you to make do. I'd say another hundred men. And two more months to train them."

"Mr. Storm. Are those realistic figures?" one Ship's Commander asked.

"Minimum realistic. My partner is one of your incurable optimists. But there is an alternative. Cancel this shore leave plan. Don't send anybody down but members of the auction team. We can set up a compound…"

Danion's Commander interrupted. "Sorry. No can do, Mister Storm. We promised our people liberty. Mister benRabi, we'll give you as many men as you want. But the thing has got to be done now."

"You're going to lose people," benRabi protested. He was so irritated he stamped a foot. "Shore leave is stupid. The more people you let wander around down there, the fewer I'm going to be able to protect."

He had lost this argument several times before. The brass had promised everybody a chance to see what life on a planet was like. They would not go back on their word despite having learned that the Angel City situation was more deadly than expected.

Moyshe had begun to suspect that the complication was deliberate, and purely for the propaganda possibilities inherent in potential dead or injured tourists. If his guess was correct, then someone upstairs was as cold-blooded as his old boss, Admiral Beckhart.

"This's the way it's going to be, then," Moyshe said. "You'll have ten thousand tourists on the ground all the time. That's going to make the Angel City merchants happy and me miserable. I'll have half of a hundred fifty men if you give me the hundred I just asked for. That doesn't divide out too good, so the tourists will be on their own. If they get into trouble, tough. I'll cover auction people and VIPs. God can take care of the rest."

He surveyed his audience. He did not see any sympathy there. "You pushed me into this job," he growled. "Why not let me do the damned thing?"

Mouse backed him up. "The same goes for my shift, gents. That's the real world down there. The world of Confederation, espionage, and bad guys, I should say. Those people don't do things the Starfisher way. I've been led to believe that Moyshe and I were given our jobs because we know The Broken Wings and Confederation. And the intelligence viewpoint. I wish you'd accept our expertise. And quit trying to make other realities conform to your views about the way things ought to be."

Storm winked at Moyshe. They had taken the offensive. They had gotten in their licks.

Kindervoort said, "Let's calm down. This's no time for tempers. The job has got be be done, like it or not." Kindervoort's comm buzzed. "Security."

"James, Radio, sir. Is the Ship's Commander there?"

The Ship's Commander stepped to the comm. "What is it?"

"We've noticed an increase in coded traffic, sir. It could mean that we've been detected."

Within minutes several other departments reported similar suspicions. The interruptions kept Mouse and benRabi from arguing their case. The Ship's Commander excused himself, as did his Executive Officer. The holographic visitors faded away. The holo technicians started packing their equipment.

"Well, damned me," Moyshe grumbled.

"What do you think?" Kindervoort asked.

"It's hideous," Mouse snapped.

"Moyshe?"

BenRabi spread his hands in a fatalistic gesture. "What the hell? Nobody listens to anything I say."

"You think there's any chance they could lay hands on some-body who knows something worth their while?"

"Of course there's a chance. You've seen the damned situation reports. They mean business down there. I'm trying to do a job. If nobody will let me…"

"Moyshe, I'm not the Ship's Commander. Just between you and me, I think you're right. I argued your case harder than you think. The Ship's Commander just doesn't see the rest of the universe in anything but Seiner terms. He thinks Confederation is just like us, only working against us. He thinks this is some kind of competition between fleets. He's wrong, but he's in charge. If he wants shoreside liberty, that's what he gets. Do what you can, and grit your teeth if you lose a few. Just don't let them find out what's going on at Stars' End before we get hold of the weapons."

"That will mean fighting the Sangaree again, Jarl. Which means we won't get any back-up here if this show blows up in our faces."

"True. We're on our own. So we stall. We go slow. We keep the auction piddling along. With luck, Gruber will finish before we've lost our distraction value."

"That's candy," Mouse grumbled.

"From hunger," benRabi agreed. They had begun to slip into landside idiom again. "You're all hyper bent."

The public address system came to life. The Ship's Commander asked for volunteers willing to join the auction security effort down in Angel City.

People started showing up immediately. Amy was the first applicant.

"You're not going," Moyshe told her. "That's the final word."

She fought back. The argument became bitter.

"Lieutenant," Moyshe said, "you will remain aboard ship. That's an order. Jarl, will you support my directives?"

Kindervoort nodded.

"Damn you, Moyshe benRabi…"

"Honey, I'm not letting you get killed. Shut up and go back to work."

There were thousands of volunteers. Everyone wanted an extended vacation landside. No one believed there was any danger. Previous auctions were reputed to have been long, wonderful parties.

"You got your list?" Moyshe asked.

Storm nodded.

They had interviewed the candidates who had survived an initial screening. Each had noted the most likely names. They had agreed to take the first hundred names that appeared on both their lists.

Orbiting in to The Broken Wings, Moyshe found the recent past beginning to feel vacationlike in retrospect. He and Mouse would not make overnight soldiers of their volunteers. Even the old hands were terribly weak. Seiner lives revolved around space and ships and harvesting. They would make perfect Navy people. Groundpounders, never.

The toughest hurdle was to make them understand, on a gut level, that someone they could see could be an enemy. A given of Seiner life was that those you could see were friends. Their enemies always existed only as blips in display tanks.

"It's a hard lesson for landsmen," Mouse said. "That's why Marines stay in Basic so long. Our culture doesn't produce the hunter-killer naturally. We ought to build us a time machine so we can go recruit in the Middle Ages."

Moyshe chuckled. "They wouldn't understand what the fighting was about, Mouse. They'd laugh themselves sick."

Danion and her sisters went into geosynchronous orbit well above Angel City's horizon. The message was not lost on anyone. If there was too much foolishness downstairs, the fire could fall.

Moyshe, in spacesuit, wrestling a load of armaments, joined Storm for the journey to their departure station.

"Wish we had real combat gear," Mouse said. "These suits won't stand much punishment."

"Be nice."

"Get any sleep?"

"Couldn't. I kept watching the news from Angel City." Moyshe had been shaken by the reports.

"Me too. Something big is happening. There're too many undercurrents. Be careful, Moyshe. Let's don't get bent with it."

"You ever feel like an extra cog?"

"Since the first day I worked for Beckhart. There was always something on that I couldn't figure out. Here we are. And Jarl looks excited."

Kindervoort was overseeing the loading of the four lighters that would make the initial landings, in pairs at fifteen minute intervals. Storm and benRabi would command the teams aboard the lead pair.

"You're going overboard, Jarl," benRabi said as they approached Kindervoort.

"Why? The more we impress them now, the less trouble we'll have later."

"You won't impress them. Not when they have three squadrons here. Go take a look at what Operations has on those ships. Three Empire Class battlewagons, Jarl. The Second Coming wouldn't faze them."

"I smell Beckhart," Mouse said. "Something about the way things are going... He's back in the woods somewhere, poking holes in our plans before we know what they are ourselves."

Kindervoort said, "Make sure that..."

"I know! I know!" benRabi snapped. "We've been over everything fifty times. Just turn us loose, will you?"

"Go easy, Moyshe," Mouse said.

"You take it easy, Mouse," he replied, gently. Storm had begun shaking. He was thinking about the long fall to the planet's surface.

"I'll be all right when things start rolling. I'll go AM if I have to."

"Things are rolling now," Kindervoort said. "Get moving. Take your musters."

Work helped settle Moyshe's nerves. He mustered his men, checked their suits, made sure their weapons were ready, and that they had the first phase of the operation clearly in mind. He rehearsed it for himself. The lighter sealed off from *Danion*. Moyshe joined the pilot. He wanted to remain near the ship's radio.

"All go, Moyshe?" from Kindervoort.

"Landing party go."

"Pilot?"

"Ship's go."

"Stand by for release."

The pilot hit a switch. His visuals came up, presenting views of *Danion*'s hull, stars, and The Broken Wings in crescent. The planet was a huge, silvery scimitar. Its surface lay masked by perpetual cloud cover.

The Broken Wings was a very hot, very wet world, with a nasty atmosphere. Its handful of cities were all protected by huge glassteel domes.

"Dropping," Kindervoort said.

The magnetic grapples released the lighter. The pilot eased her away from the harvestship. Radar showed Mouse's boat, almost lost in the return from *Danion*, doing the same a hundred meters away.

They picked up their service ship escort and began the long plunge toward Angel City's spaceport.

Kindervoort would lead the second wave. Behind him would come armed lighters from other harvestships, ready to provide close air support if that proved necessary.

The planet grew in the viewscreens. On infrared it looked rather like Old Earth. Moyshe told his pilot, "The first survey teams thought this would be a paradise."

The pilot glanced at the screen. "It's not?"

"It's a honey trap."

A greenhouse effect made it a permanently springtime world. It was a riot with a roughly Permian level of life. Its continents lay low. Much of the so-called land area was swamp. Methane made the air unbreathable. The planet was on the verge of a mountain-building age. Three hundred kilometers north of Angel City lay a region locally dubbed the Land of A Million Volcanoes. It added a lung-searing touch of hydrogen-sulfide to the air.

The first wisps of atmosphere caressed the lighters. The escort braked preparatory to pulling out. The landing teams would be on their own the last 100,000 meters.

Mouse's boat screamed down less than a kilometer from benRabi's. Their pilots kept station almost as skillfully as Marine coxswains. They had handled atmosphere before, somewhere.

Moyshe became ever more tense, awaiting some sudden, unpleasant greeting from below. There was none. It was a picnic fly, except that it was a penetration run without thought to economy or comfort, just getting down with speed. Moyshe kept a close monitor on the radio chatter of the second wave, already in the slot and coming down.

The lighter rocked and shuddered, braking in. BenRabi staggered back to his men.

There was barely time for him to hit his couch before, with a bone-jarring smack, the ship set down. Moyshe sprang up and turned to the opening hatch, laserifle in hand. Behind him came two men with grenade-launchers, then the rest of the team.

Moyshe jumped out, dodged aside. Two hundred meters away Mouse hit tarmac at virtually the same instant. His pathfinders spread out to place the target markers for vessels yet to arrive.

The thing became anticlimactic. No one was home. The field was naked of ships and people.

Then a stiff-necked, thin old man in a bubble-top, The Broken Wings swamper's outsuit, stepped from a utility shed. "Beautiful landing, Thomas," he said on radio. "Ah. And Mouse, too. You've taught well, boys. But you had the best teachers yourselves."

"Beckhart!" Mouse gasped.

"You were expecting St. Nick, son?"

"You said you smelled him," benRabi snapped. "Mouse, raise *Danion*. Tell them to stand by on the main batteries. General alarm. Have Jarl come close circle with the air support."

"Thomas, Thomas, what are you doing?"

"The question is, what are *you* doing?" He covered Beckhart while Mouse handled the communications chores. Kindervoort came up on the suit frequency, chattering wildly. He wanted an explanation for the panic.

"I just came out to welcome you," Beckhart said. "I wanted to see my boys." All operatives were "son" or "my boys" to Beckhart. He treated them like family—when he was not trying to get them killed. BenRabi had strong love-hate feelings for the man.

He stifled his emotions. For the moment Beckhart had to be considered the most dangerous enemy around. His presence altered everything.

"What is all this?" the Admiral demanded. "An invasion? This is a free planet, Thomas."

BenRabi foresaw a sorry, sad old man act. The act that so often won the Admiral his way. One means of beating it was to throw him a hard slider. What the hell was his first name? Using it would rattle him.

"We heard there was some dust getting kicked up here," Mouse said. "Nicolas! Will you get those men deployed? What the hell do you think this is?" The Seiners were standing around gawking, stricken motionless by the sheer hugeness of the planet. How could you be military the first time you saw open spaces and an infinite sky? "We don't take chances, Admiral."

Beckhart chuckled. "There was a spot of trouble. I've got it under control."

"We heard something about martial law," benRabi said. "How does that fit with your standards of neutrality?"

"We pick on everyone separately but equally." Beckhart chuckled again. He glanced around at the Starfisher landing parties, then at the sky. "There's no violation in spirit, Thomas. I need what you're selling. You'll sell it in peace if I have to break every head on the planet. That's why I elected myself your welcoming committee. Now then, I think I've got everything ready for you. Why don't you ride in with me and tell me about your adventures?"

Mouse and benRabi exchanged glances. This was not what they had expected. It stank of Beckhart scheming. But... if the Old Man said things were under control, they were. He rarely lied, though he enjoyed razzle-dazzling you from the other room.

"Right," Moyshe said, making a snap decision. "Nicolas. Kiski. Pack up your weapons and get over here. Admiral, what's the transportation picture?" The spaceport, like any built with an eye to safety, was well removed from the city it served.

"Excellent. It should be arriving... Ah. Here it is."

A column of Marine personnel carriers rumbled onto the field.

"Did you bring the Guinness?" Mouse asked. "We might as well be sociable."

"A shipload," Beckhart replied. "And with any luck von Drachau will show up and share a few before we close up shop."

"Jupp?" benRabi asked. "Really?" He looked forward to that.

Jupp was still a friend, though he was on the other side now.

He and Mouse shuffled their men into the first few carriers, advised Kindervoort of the altered situation, and left for Angel City as the second wave began rumbling down the sky.

FOURTEEN: 3050 AD
The Main Sequence

Beckhart's word proved good. Angel City was quiet. Central Park, a recreational area at the city's heart, had been equipped with field tents, trailers, and miscellany the Admiral had borrowed from the Corps. Storm and benRabi set up for business before noon.

"Mouse," benRabi said, "you get the feeling we're being rushed?"

"It's not a feeling, Moyshe. It's a fact."

"How do we stall?"

Men with briefcases were lining up to obtain the little catalogs Moyshe's team had brought along. "Buy time," Jarl had said. It did not look like they would be given a chance. The various purchasing agents, impelled by the war scare, wanted the bidding to begin right away.

The Marines proved to be perfect policemen. They helped immeasurably. They showed favoritism only to Starfisher tourists. The Admiral seemed determined to avoid a significant incident, and to help the local shopkeepers relieve the Seiner sightseers of all their hard currency.

Storm lost his first tourist their second day on The Broken Wings. The man turned up again before Mouse learned that he had been taken. He was none the worse for wear. He was a mess cook from *Danion* who knew nothing anyone wanted to know.

"It's started," Mouse told benRabi when Moyshe relieved him. "Make sure everybody checks in before they wander off. Check their passes. The ones we have to watch have been given a red one."

"You know who grabbed the man?"

"No. I didn't try to find out. I just passed it to Beckhart. I figure we might as well let his people do it. We'll have more people to watch our criticals."

Moyshe lost several people on his shift. There was only one incident with anyone who mattered. His people handled it perfectly, and presented the would-be kidnapper to Beckhart's Marines.

The man turned out to be a frustrated newshawk trying to get around Seiner and Confederation censors. Beckhart booted him off planet.

Days ground by, producing no insoluble problems. The auction bidding was wild. Prime ambergris nodes repeatedly brought record prices. There were rumors that Confederation meant to get a stranglehold on the trade. Outsiders and private industry wanted to grab while the grabbing was good.

That rumor made Moyshe nervous. The way the Admiral shrugged it off, he suspected the Bureau had an angle.

The war scare, if not genuine, was convincing. Confederation and Ulantonid forces were marshaling on the boundaries of the March of Ulant. People were getting scared.

Did they mean to fight one another? Or some third party? The news people were wondering too. Luna Command had been leaking one line of news one week, another the next.

News snoops became Moyshe's biggest problem. They used every trick to capitalize on an opportunity to approach real Seiners. Moyshe did three interviews himself. Someone had tipped the media that he was a former Bureau agent.

He refused interviews after someone discovered that he and Mouse had been responsible for Jupp von Drachau's famous raid in the Hell Stars.

Then Seiners ceased to be newsworthy. The sword-rattling on the frontier faded away.

Luna Command had admitted that a secret research station and its entire solar system had been destroyed. The hitherto hypothetical nova bomb had been developed there, and proven in unfortunate circumstances.

Maybe there is a God, Moyshe thought. A loving God willing to turn an insane weapon on its creators.

There was a tape of the disaster. Navy claimed it had been shot by a supply vessel entering the system by happenstance. It got hours of air play.

It was awesome, but there was something odd about it. Moyshe could not shake the feeling that it had been faked.

Beckhart seemed to be amused by the whole thing. That was not his style. Not in the face of a genuine disaster.

Moyshe was using a free minute to try digesting sixteen months of back news when Amy walked into his trailer-office. "What the hell are you doing here?" he demanded.

"That's some greeting from a husband." She pouted. "I thought you'd be glad to see me." She pulled his rolling chair from behind his desk, spun him, and plopped into his lap.

"I'm not. It's too damned dangerous."

"You must've found yourself a girlfriend. Yeah. I know all about you Navy men."

"The danger… All right. I give up." He hugged her. "Let me knosh on your neck, woman."

There was a knock. "Up, girl. Enter."

A harassed and apologetic youth bustled in. "Messages and mail," he said. "Looks like some real excitement starting."

"How so?"

"Read. Read." The messenger folded his receipt and left.

The top flimsy was a copy of a terse communique from Gruber. He had sent a strong probing force toward Stars' End. It had been driven away by a combined force of Sangaree and McGraw pirates. "Amy! Read that."

She did. "What?"

"An alliance between the Sangaree and pirates?" He initialed the copy, flipped it into Mouse's In box.

The next flimsy was intriguing. Freehauler merchantmen off Carson's and Sierra reported that the Navy squadrons there had taken hyper. He passed the copy to Amy.

"All Naval personnel here have had their liberties cancelled. Two of the squadrons up top have been told to make ready to space. What do you think?"

"The war thing about to break?"

He shrugged.

The only other item was a magazine, Literati, with attached envelope hand-addressed to a Thomas McClennon, Captain, CN.

It baffled Moyshe.

"I see you've been promoted," Amy said. Suspicion edged her voice. He glanced at her, surprised. Anger and fear colored her face in turn.

"What the hell?" He set the envelope aside and turned to the magazine's contents page. Halfway down he encountered the title, "All Who Were Before Me in Jerusalem," followed by the promoted name. "No," murmured, and, "I don't understand this."

"What is it?" Amy looked over his shoulder. "Am I supposed to congratulate you? I don't understand what's happening."

"I don't either, love. Believe me, I don't." He slipped one arm around her waist, turned to the story.

It was the version he had written aboard *Danion*, before deciding to become a Seiner. How had the magazine obtained it?

He threw his thought train into reverse.

He had not packed the manuscript in any of the bags he had lost when his gear had gone back to Confederation without him. Though he had not seen the manuscript since then, he was sure it was in his cabin. He had not moved it. He was absolutely certain he had not.

"Amy, remember my story? The one you never could understand? You know what happened to the manuscript?"

"No. I figured you trashed it. I didn't ask because I thought you'd get mad. I never gave you any time to write, and I know you wanted to."

He made a call to Security aboard *Danion*. Fifteen minutes later he knew. The manuscript was not in his cabin.

Thinking it safely stowed away, he had not worried about it

before. He worried now.

Everything he and Mouse had learned about the Starfishers had been in that manuscript, penned between the lines and on the backs of sheets in invisible ink. If that had reached the Bureau...

"Amy, that business with the Sangaree failsafer... Come on. We've got to talk to Jarl." He grabbed her wrist and dragged her. He snatched the flimsies from Mouse's In tray.

"What are you mad about?" she asked. "Slow down, Moyshe. You're hurting me."

"Hurry up. This's important."

They found Kindervoort at a place called Pagliacci's. It was a dusky, scenty, park-facing restaurant where both Seiner and Confederation luminaries dined and amused themselves by pumping one another over pasta and wine. BenRabi pushed past the carabiniere doorman, overran a spiffy maître de, stalked across a darkly decorated main dining room, through garlicky smells, to a small, private room in the rear. Admiral Beckhart held court there these days.

He and Kindervoort were playing a game of fence-with-words. Kindervoort was losing. He was relieved by Moyshe's appearance.

Moyshe slapped the papers down in front of Kindervoort. "We've been had."

Kindervoort scanned the top flimsy. "Where're your ships headed?" he asked Beckhart.

The Admiral chuckled. "I don't ask you questions like that. But not to worry, my friends. It doesn't involve your people. Not directly." He chuckled again, like an old man remembering some prank of his youth.

Kindervoort read the second flimsy, then thumbed through the magazine. "I suppose you want me to congratulate you, Moyshe. So congratulations."

"Jarl, I didn't finish that story till a couple days before the landsmen went home. And I came into this mess graded Commander. Someone had to put the story on the ship to Carson's."

"And?"

"It wasn't me that did. I left it out of my stuff because it carried the notes I'd kept for *him.*"

"Ah. I see." Kindervoort considered Beckhart.

The Admiral smiled, asked, "This lovely lady your bride, Thomas?"

Amy favored him with an uncertain smile.

"Watch him, honey. He's another Mouse. He can charm a cobra."

Kindervoort stared and thought. Finally, he asked, "Did they get anything critical?"

"I can't remember. I think it was mostly social observations. Like that. Impressions. Guesswork."

"Sit down, Thomas," Beckhart said. "Mrs. McClennon. Drinks? Something to eat?"

"It's benRabi now. Moyshe benRabi," benRabi grumbled.

"I'm used to McClennon, you know. Surely you can't expect an old dog to learn new tricks." He rang for service. "Mrs. McClennon, you've caught yourself a pretty special man. I consider my men my boys. Like sons, so to speak. And Thomas and Mouse are two of my favorites." BenRabi frowned. What was the man up to? "So, though he defected and it hurts, I try to understand. I'm glad he finally found someone. He needs you, Missy, so be good to him."

Amy began to relax. Beckhart charmed her into giving him a genuine smile.

"There we go. There we go. I recommend the spaghetti, children. Astonishingly good for this far from nowhere." Jarl coughed, a none too subtle reminder that there was business to be discussed.

"All right," Beckhart said, turning to Kindervoort. "I'm exercising an old man's prerogative. I'm changing my mind. I'm going to spill the facts before there's a bad misunderstanding."

"Yes, do," benRabi snapped.

"Thomas, Thomas, don't be so damned hostile all the time." He sipped some wine. "First, let's swing back to the Ulantonid War. To their rationale for attacking Confederation.

"Our blue friends are obsessed with the long run. Us apes, the best we manage is a ten-year fleet modernization program, or a twenty-year colonial development project. They figure technological and sociological effects in terms of centuries. We'd save ourselves a lot of trouble if we'd take a page from their book. Thomas, sip your wine and be patient. I'm politely getting to the point.

"What I want you to understand is they roam pretty far afield in order to figure out what's coming up the day after next year."

"What's that got to do with whatever you're up to now?" Kindervoort asked.

"I'm getting there. I'm getting there. See. This right here is what's wrong with our species. We're always in such a damned hurry. We never look ahead. My point? Ulant does. When the war hates settled down and we let them build ships again, they resumed their deep probes."

"So?" Moyshe said. He was trying to fly easy, but for some reason he had a chill crawling his spine.

"Let an old man have his way, Thomas. It isn't every day I spout cosmic secrets in an Italian restaurant. Here it is, then. About thirty years ago Ulant made an alien contact. This was a long way in along The Arm. They eventually brought it to our attention.

"People, this race makes our friends the Sangaree look angelic. I've seen them in action myself. Really, words can't express it. What I mean to say is, I hope I don't have to see them again, here in our space. They're bad, people. Really bad. When they get done with a world there's nothing left bigger than a cockroach."

The Admiral paused for effect. His audience did not respond. He looked from face to face.

"That's a bit much to swallow," Moyshe said.

"It is. Of course. It took us a while to bite when the Blues brought it to us. By us I mean Luna Command. They knew better than to go to that dungheap called a Diet. For a good many years now, with the Minister the only civilian in the know, we've been working with Ulant to get ready."

BenRabi recalled his visit to Luna Command before drawing the Starfisher assignment. The place had gone completely weird. The tunnels had been filled with rumors of war, and crowded with military folk from a variety of races and scores of human planets beyond Confederation's pale. Even then there had been the smell of something big in the air.

"Then this confrontation with Ulant is a smoke screen? A light show cooked up with Prime Defender so she and you people could con bigger appropriations? Admiral, the first lesson pounded into me at Academy was that the Services don't make policy."

"Yep. And it's the first lesson an officer unlearns, Thomas. One of my staff boys quoted me a Roman soldier a while back. 'We are the Empire.' Thomas, the Services *are* Confederation. Those of us who have gotten old in our jobs take that to heart. We make policy. Me, I shape the whole Confederation outlook. I'm doing it right now, by talking about this. It's no big thing, though. The news is starting to break. So many people are in the know now, truth can't hide. In three months every citizen will have seen tapes documenting the murder of the world I visited… I can run that tape for you if you want. Just come over to headquarters sometime. Then you won't think I'm blowing smoke."

"I don't think it, I know it." But Moyshe was not sure. He had known the Admiral for a decade. He never had seen the man more excited, or more intense. He had assumed an aura, the way Mouse did when he talked about Sangaree. "You talk like a man who's found religion."

Beckhart nodded. "You're right. I'm getting carried away. But I've seen it. It doesn't make any sense, and that's why it's so damned scary. They hop from world to world, like galactic exterminators… I'm doing it again. Sorry."

"Why are you telling us now?" Kindervoort demanded.

"Trying to shed some light on what we're doing. We're going to make our first spoiling strike before the end of the year. We have just a couple of things left to straighten out before we move."

BenRabi had a sudden, intense feeling of danger. Startled, he glanced over his shoulder. There was no one behind him.

Beckhart's explanation, mad as it sounded, did tie the Bureau's frantic behavior into a neat ball. "What's still on your job list?" Moyshe asked. He glared at Beckhart, daring him to say something about Starfishers.

The original assignment now made military sense. Communications were the backbone of the fleet. Every ambergris node obtained would improve Navy's combat efficiency.

Beckhart surprised him again. "Sangaree, Thomas. The worms that gnaw from within."

Moyshe's mental alarms jangled. "You don't expect the Sangaree to be a long-term problem?"

"No. Thanks to Mouse."

"What?" Kindervoort and benRabi spoke together.

"Why were you sent to the Starfishers, Thomas?"

"To locate you a starfish herd. To get Navy a source of ambergris it wouldn't have to share."

"So you thought. So you thought. Actually, incorporation was a political goal, not military. It hasn't been important to Luna Command. We've known how to find Payne's Fleet for years. That's right, Captain Kindervoort. Starfishers can be recruited. I have agents aboard *Danion*. Thomas suspected as much when he charged in here with his magazine. But there was no pressing need to incorporate you. Grabbing a fleet might have started a fatal uproar. Nowadays... If I was a Starfisher who hoped for a future in my business, I'd polish up on my Confederation studies."

Kindervoort smiled a thin, wicked smile. "I don't think we need to worry, Admiral."

Beckhart winked at Moyshe, jerked his head to indicate Kindervoort. "Doesn't know me, does he? Thomas, the mission was aimed at the Sangaree. You should have known. That's all Mouse works. Don't interrupt your elders, boy."

BenRabi had intended to ask why he had been sent along.

"I thought the Starfishers, because they deal with the Freehaulers and McGraws, might have a line on Homeworld too. My guess was wrong, but my intuition was right."

You're lying, Moyshe thought. You're editing the past to fit the needs of the present. You knew, and controlled, more than you'll ever tell.

Beckhart said, "Mouse found what I needed. He got it out of the astrogational computer of a mind-burned raidship captured at Stars' End. He extracted the data and sent it out. Von Drachau was given the attack mission. Judging from the fleet alert, he pulled it off. He's probably on his way home now, likely with a mob chasing him. The pressure should ease for you at Stars'

End, Jarl. You might not have to fight your way in after all. You might say we've done you a favor."

Beckhart leaned back in his chair, grinning at Kindervoort's consternation. "You can't kid a kidder, boy. We guessed what you were up to before you got here. Our agents confirmed what we suspected."

"If you knew that," Moyshe said, "why haven't you given us any trouble? I'd think you'd jump on Stars' End like…"

Kindervoort kicked him under the table.

"Several reasons, Thomas. We're spread too thin already, guarding against their raidships if they get too excited. We've got no feud with you. And you can't do anything but get yourselves killed out there anyway. So why get excited?"

BenRabi studied the old man. Beckhart *was* excited. What else was up his sleeve? The theft of the Stars' End weaponry after the Seiners opened the planet?

Had Mouse reported their suspicion that the Seiners could manage it?

Why was the Admiral here, now, instead of in Luna Command? Stars' End would be a damned good reason.

It came down to Mouse. Had Mouse simply yielded to his hatreds and passed on the information about the Sangaree? Or was he still reporting?

Kindervoort asked, "If you're spread so thin, how could you mount a raid on Homeworld?"

"It wasn't a raid. It was a wipeout. Let's say the nova bomb disaster wasn't as complete as the news people have been led to believe. Let's suppose a couple of the weapons were taken out before the blowup. Let's take it a little further and speculate that a certain Jupp von Drachau tumbled one into Homeworld's sun."

BenRabi snapped up out of his chair, breaking Amy's sudden iron grip on his arm. He stared over Beckhart's head, into cruel vistas of self-condemnation.

A whole solar system destroyed!

"You're insane. You're all insane."

"I wish you could know how much soul-searching went into the decision, Thomas. I honestly do. And, despite the Four slash

Six memo, I don't think the decision would have been made had it not been for the centerward race. Thomas? Come and see those tapes before you judge us. All right?"

BenRabi ignored him. He was back to that failsafer day again. How did Mouse get the manuscript out to Beckhart? Kindervoort had watched them every second. Beckhart's Seiner agents must have handled it while Mouse was holding everyone's attention.

He remembered a Seiner known as Grumpy George. Old George was a coin collector. He and Moyshe had done business several times. George had had a superb collection. He had claimed to have made an outstandingly lucky "blind" purchase during an auction held on The Big Rock Candy Mountain, years ago.

Any truly devoted collector was vulnerable. And George was an obsessive.

This same George had come to Angel City with the first group of tourists. He had stopped by the office to ask about hobby shops. Moyshe had passed him on to Storm. Mouse had given him a list.

"How many hobby shops does the Bureau run, Admiral?"

Beckhart's eyebrows leapt upward. "Damn, Thomas. But you always were intuitive. Just one these days. Oddly enough, it's right here in Angel City."

"In other words, the place has served its purpose."

Beckhart leaned toward Kindervoort. "You see why he made Captain so young?"

Kindervoort simply looked baffled.

An ulcer that had not bothered Moyshe for a year took a sudden bite from his gut.

Someone pounded on the door. "Mr. benRabi, are you there?"

"Come in. What's up?"

"Someone just tried to kill Mister Storm."

"What? How?"

"It was a woman, sir. She just came up and started shooting."

"Is he all right?"

"Yes sir. He took off after her. She headed into Old Town."

Old Town was that part of Angel City which had lain under

the first settlers' dome. Today it was largely a warehouse district. It was the base of the city's small underworld.

"You think it's the Sangaree woman?" Kindervoort asked.

"Marya? A grudge like that is the only thing that would set Mouse off," benRabi replied.

"How could she be here?" Amy demanded.

"I'd better go dig him out," Moyshe said. "If it's all right with you, Jarl?"

"It's your shift. Do what you want."

"Amy, stay with Jarl." Moyshe told the messenger, "Find me six off-duty volunteers. Tell them to meet me outside my office. Armed."

"Yes sir."

Moyshe bent, kissed Amy. "In a little while, hon." He wished he could have been a more loving husband lately. Events had permitted them only the most brusque of relationships.

He caught Beckhart giving him an odd look. A baffled, questioning look.

What did that mean? Puzzled, he went to the door.

He paused there, glanced back. Kindervoort and Amy were sipping their drinks, lost within themselves. Poor Jarl. The pressures here were too much for him. He was becoming less and less active, more and more a figurehead. Was it cultural shock?

He would survive. He would make a comeback in his own milieu. He did not worry Moyshe.

His concern was the almost magical disappearance of the Admiral while his back was turned.

He hated to admit it. He loved that old man like a father. Their relationship had that attraction-repulsion of father-son tension. But he could not trust the man. They were of different tribes now.

He had to hurry if he meant to stay ahead of Beckhart.

He was a block from the restaurant when he encountered the first poster. It clung crookedly to the flank of a Marine personnel carrier. He trotted past before it registered. He stopped, spun around. His eyes widened.

Yes. The face of a woman, a meter high, smiled at him.

"Alyce..." he croaked.

Wham! Darkness slammed home. He no longer knew where or who he was. He staggered past the carrier, went down on one knee.

His head cleared. He was in Angel City... He looked behind him. There was a man following him... No. That was last time. Or was it?

For a moment he was not sure if he was Gundaker Niven or Moyshe benRabi. Somebody was trying to kill Gundaker Niven...

He shook his head violently. The mists cleared. Which name he wore did not matter. Niven. McClennon. Perchevski. BenRabi. Any of the others. The enemy remained the same.

He returned to the personnel carrier. The poster was gone. He circled the quiet machine. He could find no evidence one had existed.

"What the hell is happening to me?" he muttered. He resumed trotting toward his headquarters.

He encountered the second poster fewer than fifty meters from his office trailer. It clung to the side of one of the tents his people used for quarters. He reacted just as he had before. He came out of it clinging to a tree, gasping like a man who had almost drowned. The poster was gone.

Had it ever existed? he wondered.

The fragile stability he had constructed with Chub's help was fraying. Was he in for a bad fall?

He clambered into his trailer like a man carrying an extra fifty kilos, dropped into his swivel chair. His heart hammered. His ears pounded. He was scared. He closed his eyes and searched his mind for a clue to what was happening. He found nothing.

It had to be this contact with his past. The benRabi personality was not really him. It could not withstand the strain of the milieu of Thomas McClennon.

Then he noticed the envelope lying on his desk. The envelope that had been attached to the magazine *Literati*.

He stared as if it were poisonous. He tried to back away. One hand stole forward.

It was from Greta Helsung, the girl he had sponsored in Academy. His pseudo-daughter. It was a grateful, anxious, friendly missive, seven pages of tight script reviewing her progress in Academy, and her continual fears for his safety. She knew that he had been captured by enemies of Confederation. His friends had promised they would rescue him. They would get her letter to him. And this, and that, and she loved him, and all his friends in Luna Command were well and happy and pulling for him, and she hoped she would see him soon. There were several photographs of an attractive young blonde in Navy blacks. She looked happy.

There was also a note from an old girlfriend. Max expressed the same sentiments with more reserve.

What were they trying to do? Why couldn't yesterday let him be?

Greta had such a cute, winsome smile...

He sealed his eyes and fought to escape the conflicting emotions.

He began to feel very cold, then to shake. Then to be terribly afraid.

FIFTEEN: 3050 AD
The Contemporary Scene

There were fifty ships in the exploratory fleet. They had not seen a friend in two years. It was a big galaxy. They were 10,000 light-years from home, moving toward the galactic core, backtracking old destruction.

There had been eighty-one ships at the beginning. A few had been lost. Others had been left at regular intervals, to catch and relay instelled reports from the probe. Most of the ships were small and fast, equipped for survey and intelligence scanning.

The fleet was near its operational limit. Three months more, and the ships would have to swing around, the great questions still unanswered.

The advance coreward had been slow and methodical. Still, space was vast and only a fragmentary vision of enemy territory had been assembled.

The stars were densely packed here. The night around the fleet was jeweled far more heavily than farther out The Arm. The skies were alien and strange. The worlds were silent and barren.

Where were the centerward people building all their ships? Where did the killing hordes spring from?

The Ulantonid explorers had detected convoys heading rimward. They had seen a parade of dead worlds. But they had located nothing resembling a base, occupied world, or industrial operation. They had learned only that the enemy came from still farther toward the galaxy's heart.

Then, too, there had been the tagged asteroids in the dead solar systems. Huge metallic bodies three to five hundred kilometers long, all similar in composition. Eleven such rocks, marked with transponders, had been located. The Ulantonid specialists had been unable to conjecture the meaning of the tagging.

The probe fleet had established five tracks along which enemy ships advanced out The Arm. Each was a river of charged particles, ions, and free radicals.

Contact was carefully avoided. The mission was one of observation.

Remote surveillance of the charged paths showed not only the occasional outward passage of a fleet but the regular back and forth of courier vessels. That suggested the enemy had no instel capability. Which was an important deduction. The allies would obtain a tactical advantage by being able to coordinate their forces over far vaster distances.

The centerpiece of the Ulantonid fleet was its only true ship of war, a vessel which beggared the human Empire Class. It bore the name *Dance in Ruby Dawn.*

Humans named their warships for warriors, battles, cities, old provinces, lost empires, and fighting ships of the past. Ulant used the titles of poems and novels, symphonies and works of art. Each race found the other's naming system quaint.

Ruby Dawn carried the liaison team provided by Confederation's Bureau of Naval Intelligence. Those people had been away from home even longer than their Ulantonid shipmates.

Theirs was a grueling task. They had to survey all incoming data and isolate those bits which justified transmission to Luna Command. They had to be diplomatic with their hosts. It was too much for twelve people eleven thousand light-years from the nearest of their own kind.

An Ulantonid officer stepped into their working compartment. "Commander Russell? We're getting something that might interest you."

Russell was a short black man built like a tombstone. He almost responded, "We'll get it in a while, won't we? Where's the damned hurry?" He did not. The Blues were so courteous it made him ashamed to think of giving them a hard time.

"Important?" he asked. The Blues were showing strain too, though they were more accustomed to extended missions.

"*Song of Myrion* reported a strong neutrino source. It didn't look natural. On the other hand, it was two-thirds of a parsec from the nearest star. Control is moving probe ships in from several directions. It was felt that you would want to see the scans we're getting."

"Of course. Of course. Doris, you can get in touch through Group Voice Nomahradine. Lead on, Group Voice."

Russell did not expect anything. The Blues came up with something new twice a week. There was always a natural explanation. But someone always went along. It was part of the get-along policy. Never give the Blues offense. The squabbling and snarling had to be confined to liaison team quarters.

A communications officer greeted them with, "We might have something this time, Group Voice." He gestured. Russell surveyed the elaborate and only slightly alien equipment. One huge display pinpointed the probeships involved in the current exercise. They had taken positions on an arc one Ulantonid light-year from the neutrino source. Lines and arrows of colored light flickered in and out of existence.

Russell was astounded. The neutrino source was not a point. The lines indicated that it subtended a half second of arc, vertically and horizontally, from the point of view of each observer. He did some quick mental arithmetic. "Jesus," he murmured. "That's a globe... almost six times ten to the twelfth kilometers in diameter. That's five hundred times the diameter of the old Solar System."

The Group Voice was equally impressed. "Commander, that's one hell of an artifact."

Russell scanned the displays. There was enough mass in the region to slightly distort space! The stars behind did not show through.

"Could it be a dark nebula?"

"Too dense."

"You'll take a closer look?"

"When it's cleared up top."

"Whatever it is, it's moving. At a damned good clip."

"That's what makes us so interested, Commander."

Russell looked for a spare seat. There were none. The word was out. The place was filled with curious Blues. The Heart Of The Shield, or Fleet Admiral, made her entry. She spoke with her science officers, and included Russell as a courtesy. Russell simply listened. It was not his place to offer his thoughts.

It took three days to design a probe mission. A swarm of instrument packages would be placed in the great globe's path, well ahead, passive, hidden on old spatial debris. Care would be exercised so the ships placing the instruments would remain undetected.

It took three weeks to do the seeding. Another month passed before the globe reached the instruments. During that period scores of couriers were recorded moving to and from the neutrino source. Two convoys swarmed out toward the remote frontier.

Intense examination of space behind the Globular revealed it to be the focus of tremendous activity. Enemy ships swarmed through that trailing space. The Globular had a cometary tail of vessels falling away and catching up.

"It looks like the warfleets are clearing the way for this outfit," Russell told his compatriots.

"Aren't they working a little far ahead? I mean, it'll be thirty or forty thousand years before they reach Confederation."

"Maybe it's lag time in case the war fleets run into somebody stubborn."

"Stubborn? They could roll over anything. There're so many of them the numbers become meaningless."

"Still, there seems to be a gap in weapons and communications technology between them and us. I'd guess around two centuries. That means we'll kill a lot more of them than they'll kill of us. The Blues think they're frozen into a technological stasis. Their real weapon is their numbers. If they ran into somebody very far ahead of us, they'd suffer. They'd win, but it might take them generations. I'd guess they've been through it before, which would be why the Globular is so far behind the front."

Probes into star systems behind the Globular had shown, for the first time, the enemy actually living on planets. Billions of the little kangaroo people seemed to have been dumped, apparently to rework the worlds to certain specifications. The Ulantonid experts thought they would be taken off after the terraforming was complete.

Yet another puzzle.

More of the little creatures were occupied mining the asteroidal and cometary belts of numerous systems. Operating in hordes, they stripped whole systems of spatial debris.

The significance of the marked bodies had become apparent. The little folk were using that type asteroid as a portable world. The big bodies were mined hollow, given drives, and turned into immense spaceships. Given spin, they achieved centrifugal gravity. Built up in tiers inside, they could provide more living space than any planet. They could grow with their populations.

"They must breed like flies," someone suggested. "If they have to devour everything for living space."

"Question," Russell said. "The Blues say they leave the planets after terraforming them. Why?"

"Nothing about these things makes any sense," a woman replied. "I think we're wasting our time trying to figure them out. Let's concentrate on finding weaknesses."

Russell suggested, "Knowing why they're doing what they're doing might clue us how to stop them. Anybody think we can do that now?"

Ruby Dawn was a ship of despair. Hope had vanished. Its crew no longer believed their peoples would survive the coming onslaught.

"We need deeper probes," Russell said. "We have to get this far again past the Globular if we really want to know what they're doing. From here it looks like a million-year project to remodel the galaxy."

"But we can't probe that deep."

"No, we can't. Unfortunately. So we'll never know."

When the first remote instruments were activated by the Globular, everyone in the fleet made sure he or she could examine the incoming data.

Within hours the sight of lines of huge asteroid-ships, stacked tens of thousands high, wide, and deep, killed all interest.

What point to staring into the eyes of doom? Let the watching be done by machines that could not be intimidated.

The probe fleet turned toward home, pursuing the sorry knowledge it had sped ahead.

SIXTEEN: 3050 AD
The Main Sequence

Six of Moyshe's best men gathered outside his trailer. They had donned nighttime black. They were buttoning buttons and making sure their equipment was in order. Each bore weapons, carried a hand comm, gas mask, and any odd or end the individual thought might come in handy. To a man they were still trying to rub sleep from their eyes.

BenRabi leaned against the frame of the door to his office. He was still shaky. "You guys willing to get into a fight to save my friend Mouse?"

"You're on, Chief," someone muttered.

"He's just an immigrant, you know."

"We wouldn't be here if we weren't ready, Jack."

Another said, "We're ready, sir. He's one of us now. I never liked him much myself. He stole my girl. But we got to protect our own."

A third said, "Klaus, you're just spoiling for a fight,"

"So now I got an excuse, maybe."

"Okay, okay," benRabi said. "Keep it down. Here's the frosting for the cake. I think the Sangaree woman is involved."

"Yeah? Maybe this time we'll do the job right."

"I tried before. I didn't get a lot of support."

"Won't be nobody to feel sorry for her this time, Captain."

Moyshe started, looked the speaker in the eye. He saw no offense was meant. He and Mouse did have brevet-commissions as captains of police, with Kindervoort's regular captain's commission senior. Seiners seldom used their professional ranks and titles.

He grinned. "I think you're all fools," he said. "And I thank you for it. I'll be with you in a minute." He stepped back inside, scanned the current data on number of Seiners on-planet. The count was way down. People did not want to play tourist at night, when most everything was closed. He tapped out a red code to Traffic aboard *Danion*, meaning something was up and no one else was to be allowed down till further word. He guessed that within four hours there would be no Seiners on The Broken Wings who were not part of the security effort. He stepped outside. "Let's go."

They whooped like a bunch of rowdy boys.

They worried Moyshe. They thought this would be fun. He had to calm them down. They could get themselves hurt.

He led them aboard a Marine personnel carrier, took the control seat himself. The engine hummed first try. He roared toward Old Town, gears crashing and tracks whining. He was so excited that, for a few minutes, he forgot to cut in the mufflers.

Rumbling through empty night streets, he tried to anticipate Mouse. Where would Storm go? That would depend on his quarry. If Mouse lost her, the warehouse important to their first mission would seem to him a likely place to pick up the track again. The Sangaree, always nose-thumbingly bold, or stupid, might be using it again.

The warren of tall, crowded old brick buildings pressed in as Moyshe plunged ever deeper into the inky silence of Old Town. The wareshouse district was a nerve-taunting area. The smell of poverty and old evil reeked from every alley and doorway. BenRabi became jittery. He put on more speed. "Almost there, men."

He swung into the street leading past the warehouse he wanted, brought the carrier to a violent, shuddering stop.

A bright actinic flash, that left ghosts dancing behind his eyes, proclaimed nasty business afoot a half block beyond his goal. The old site had not been renovated. The Sangaree obviously were not using it.

"Stand by, men. Looks like we've found him." There was another flash. He eased the carrier over so it would not block the street. "Everybody out. Stand easy."

He used a pencil to scratch a diagram on the pavement. He was amazed at how easily the Old Town layout came back. It had been years... "Nick, you and Clair come in this way. Klaus, take Mike and Will and come in from over here. Kraft and I will go straight up the street. Test your comms. Okay. Move out."

Bright lase-weapons continued their ineffectual duel. BenRabi and Kraft stalked forward, clinging to shadow, till they spotted one of the duelists.

Moyshe studied the fire patterns.

Three gunmen were besieging a warehouse. One man was shooting back from inside. He had skill enough to keep the three pinned.

"They must have lost somebody already," Moyshe guessed. The besiegers seemed to be in the grip of a crisis of nerve.

"Maybe they're keeping him pinned for somebody else."

"Maybe."

The situation looked a little strange. The man in the warehouse was not behaving like Mouse. Mouse would not waste time sniping. He preferred the attack.

"What do you see?" Moyshe asked. His man was looking around with infrared nighteyes.

"There's just three of them. Funny. They look like pirates."

"What? Give me those." Moyshe took the glasses. Kraft was right. The besiegers wore McGraw jumpsuits. That made no sense. This was enemy territory for McGraws.

Could be Mouse inside, though—if they *were* pirates. They were working with the Sangaree now. Maybe Storm was hurt... Whispering to his handcomm, Moyshe moved teams into position behind each sniper. "Ready? Shoot on my mark. Shoot!"

It did not go well. The Seiners did not have what it took to do a man first hand, in cold blood. They allowed a vicious exchange of fire before dropping two of the men. The third escaped only after taking wounds no cosmetic surgeon would ever repair.

And still Moyshe worried. It seemed too easy.

He was changing. He was hardening into the paranoid hunter Bureau had made of him. He did not recognize the shift right away.

"All clear, Mouse," he called.

Ozone stench and the smell of hot brick assailed his nostrils. Sudden steam surrounded him, rising from a puddle left by the programmed rain of the dinner hour. A quick pair of lasebolts had missed him low and high. He scrambled for cover.

"What the hell is the matter with that bastard? Has he gone hyper-bent? Give me that stunner," he snapped at Kraft, who was too scared to move. "He must be hurt bad. Here. Take this." He shoved his own weapon into the Seiner's hands. "Come on. Get yourself together. You've got to help." To the other teams, via handcomm, he snarled, "Draw fire, you guys. And I mean give it to him. I'm going to stun him."

A stunning would not please Mouse, but benRabi considered the alternatives even less pleasant.

Beams on low setting tickled the ochre brick of the warehouse, bluing the night weirdly. The whole street crackled and flickered and came alive. Legions of shadows danced like spooks at midnight. The return fire became erratic and completely ineffective. Moyshe pinpointed the source, armed carefully, held his trigger stud down. "Get over there," he growled at Kraft.

The stunner's spine-tingling whine continued till several Seiners pushed through the warehouse's street door.

Minutes later, from the window, someone shouted, "You got her, Moyshe."

"Her? What the hell do you mean?"

"It's a woman. You got her clean. Don't look like there's any nerve damage."

A stunner sometimes played hell with its victim's nervous system. Death or permanent damage could result. It did not happen often.

"Is it Strehltsweiter?"

"No. Come on over. She's coming around."

"What about Mouse?"

"Ain't no sign of him."

A woman, he thought as he started walking. What the hell? There were only two women involved in this business. Amy and Marya. The man would have screamed if this were either of them.

The Sangaree woman was on The Broken Wings, though. Of that he was convinced.

The woman was leaning out the window, up-chucking, when Moyshe entered the room whence she had been shooting. Her shoulders slumped with defeat. Moyshe watched her from the doorway. She seemed vaguely familiar from behind.

"Chief's here, lady," one of his men said, his tone not unkind.

The woman pushed herself off the sill, turned.

"Alyce!"

The name came out a strangled toad croak.

"Thomas."

Hammers of darkness pounded his brain. Hands as light as the wings of moths tried to bear him up. A voice asked, "What's wrong, Moyshe?" from several light-years away.

Despite the additional impact of seeing the woman in the flesh, the episode ended in seconds. Cold, shaking, benRabi fought for self-control.

She deposited her behind on the filthy window sill. Her breath came in shallow, difficult gasps. Her face remained curiously immobile despite its obvious effort to portray a variety of emotions.

Shock? he wondered.

He looked inside himself.

He was shocked. Shivering, he tumbled into a dusty old chair, stared at this impossible ghost of a romance past. His thoughts swooped and whirled through a realm of chaos. His soul cried in torment as it had done so constantly during his ancient introduction to the Seiners. All the demons he had thought fettered with his starfish's help were now breaking their chains and howling up from their dungeons. The inexplicable mind-symbol he called the image of the gun flashed in and out of existence like some barbarous neon advertisement for mental disease.

He did not pass out again. Neither did he regain his emotional feet. He fought what was happening in his head, fending it while trying to analyze.

There was something a little changed about all those old spooks. They were not quite identical with their predecessors. Had time eroded them? Helped them grow older and more mellow? What?

"Moyshe? What the hell is wrong?" Klaus demanded. "Woman, what did you do to him?"

Moyshe heard. He did not respond. What could he do? What could he say? To Klaus or Alyce. He had not expected to see her again, ever, even in the tight social environment of Luna Command. Certainly not out here on the fringes of Confederation, a thousand lights from the scene of their passion and pain. It was too wildly implausible a coincidence... Yet there she sat, as agonizingly real as death itself.

He ground the heels of his hands into his temples, feeling the precursor pain of a savage headache. He gripped his stomach where his half-forgotten ulcer was coming to sudden, unpleasant life. His thoughts churned and sprayed like wild white water. His very brain seemed to be sliding on its foundations. Barriers came crashing down. Viewpoints shifted. If he did not grab *something* as he whipped past, his soul would be left a fanged wasteland as lovely and desolate as a bombed-out city.

He caught a glimmer of what was happening. He shied off like a whipped dog. He clamped down, shoving a hundred mental fingers into the sodden dikes. If he could just hold on till he found Mouse...

"How are you?" Alyce asked.

Her voice was different. It was older. Less musical. More hardened by life.

Her question had no meaning. It was just noise meant to break a fearful silence. He did not immediately respond. His men watched him with wonder and uncertainty, uncomfortably aware that they were on the brink of seeing a soul laid bare.

"I'm fine," Moyshe finally mumbled. "How're you?"

"Okay, now." But she was not. She was shaking violently. It

was a common reaction to stunner shock. She would be feeling as cold as he.

"Why were those men shooting at you?" he asked, trying to gain some stability by concentrating on business. "What're you doing here?"

"It was a girl, Thomas. With your hair and eyes."

"Shut her up!"

It began to twist and burn. Down deep inside, the dikes began to give. The demons howled and laughed. That insane image of the gun thing superimposed itself over Alyce's face. "Mike!" he gasped. "Take two men outside and keep an eye out for McGraws."

His second desperate attempt to achieve stability failed. The dikes were bulging inward. "Why're you here?" he squeaked.

"I thought it was all dead," she said. "I thought I'd forgotten it. But I can't, Thomas. Go away. Leave me alone."

Leave her alone? Yes. Fine. But how did he get her to leave him alone?

"Lady, the Chief asked a question," his man Nicolas growled. "Answer up."

"Easy, Nick. No rough stuff. This's personal, not business."

He spoke too late.

"Not business?" Snake-swift, the Seiner laid a hand alongside the woman's face. The blow hurled her to the floor. He caught her hair as she fell, yanked. She screamed, but her cry did not register with Moyshe.

What did was her hair, face, and throat coming away in Nicolas's hand. The Seiner raised his trophy like the shrunken, wrinkled head of a Cyclops. The unmasked woman seemed vaguely familiar, but she was not benRabi's old haunt.

"Moyshe, you done been set up."

BenRabi could not stifle a squeaky little laugh. "I done been, Nick."

Nicolas wheeled on the woman. "You start talking. What kind of game are you playing?"

"Don't bother, Nick. We won't get anything. We don't have the equipment." There were no tears in the woman's eyes now. She showed nothing but apprehension. Moyshe added, "I don't know if it would be worth the trouble anyway."

He did not need equipment. Despite the chaotic state of his mind, a strong suspicion blossomed. Someone was working on him. He had a good idea who, and why.

"Hey, Moyshe," another of the men called. "Mike says we got trouble. McGraws. A dozen or so. Out by the carrier."

He was regaining his composure. "It was a trap. But it didn't go according to plan." He turned to the woman. "The pirates weren't in the script, were they?"

To his surprise, she responded. She shook her head.

"You tell the Old Man to get him a better makeup crew. Nick, we've got to get out of here. See if you can get Kindervoort on Tac Two. Tell him I need a pickup squad. We'll let the Corps worry about their carrier."

He had cobbled together a false peace within him. He knew it would not last. He had to finish fast. He would begin crumbling again soon. The one straw too many had been thrown into the camel's back. From here on in each period of tranquility would be just one more frantic holding action doomed to eventual failure. The decay would accelerate whenever the survival pressure slackened.

He had seen it all before, in fellow agents. He was entering the initial stages of a spontaneous, uncontrolled, unsupervised personality program debriefing. It could get rough. There were so many identities in his background that he could lose his anchor to any of them.

"What about the woman?" Nicolas asked.

"Leave her. She's not the enemy."

"Moyshe," said another, "Jarl says to meet him by Jellyroll Jones. You know what he means?"

"Yeah. It's a statue in the old park. Pass the word to Mike. He knows the place. Nick, lead off. Keep close, guys." He turned to the woman. "Good-bye." He could not think of anything else to say.

She shrugged, but seemed relieved.

They slid out the back way, ran through a block of shadows. BenRabi began to worry about the time. He had been away from his job too long. How much longer? But it looked easy...

There was a shot and a shout.

A second slug ricocheted off brick near benRabi. Cobblestones became arrowheads piercing his chest as he tried to get closer to the soil.

Shades of his last visit to The Broken Wings, he thought.

His men returned the fire, their lasebeams scoring the brick of the walls of the buildings flanking the alley where the ambusher crouched.

"Come on!" benRabi snarled. "Shoot *at* him, dammit!" A fourth slug kicked chips of alley and lead into his face. He wiped at tiny pearls of blood, wondered why the assassin was concentrating on him. Was he Marya's man?

Where was Jarl? Where were Mike and his men?

"Dammit, you guys, don't you know this ain't a goddamned game?"

And where was Mouse, who had started this mess by disappearing? Emotion began to rage through him again, undirected and confused. He tried to control it, failed. His personality program resumed its dissolution. The only anchor left him was a hard, red hot anger.

A foot scraped cobblestone somewhere behind him. He rolled, shot, hit a leg. A man yelped, scrambled for cover.

The gunman with the antique firearm kept booming away. McClennon... benRabi took a second shot at his victim before he got out of sight.

Another shadow drifted into the shelter of a doorway.

Moyshe's program ceased its disintegration.

His perceptions reached a high usually stimulated only by drugs. He felt every point and angle of the cobblestones beneath him, seemed to become one with the dampness left by the programmed rain. He saw the grey and brownness of stone, the expanding sparks and yellows of another muzzle flash, heard the thud as a bullet smacked brick behind him. He smelled damp and sulfurousness of swamp the atmosphere systems could never completely overcome. He could even taste, it seemed, something salty.

Whoa! That was blood from a chip wound, dribbling into the corner of his mouth.

He edged sideways. Four meters and he would be in a position where the would-be assassin would have to expose himself to fire. He made it. The man shot. Moyshe shot back, heard a yelp. His men pursued him in his rush into that alley.

Moyshe kicked the revolver away from the would-be assassin. "This clown is as incompetent as you guys. Come on. Get your butts moving before I heat them up myself." He waved his stunner angrily.

There were shouts from the alley they had abandoned. He spun, dropped, fired quickly, followed his men. The sting of his flesh wounds drove him like a hunted beast.

Who am I now? he wondered. This isn't like me. I'm not a fighter. Gundaker Niven? Niven was supposed to be a hardcase.

The adrenaline had him on the verge of another case of the shakes. He had been through this kind of thing before, for the Bureau, but never had been able to achieve Mouse's calmness under fire. He always got scared, shaky, and constantly had to battle the impulse to flee.

Maybe that was why he had outlived several Mouselike partners.

But they, too, had been programmed to their roles.

He was doing well this time, he thought. He was showing flashes of case-hardened calm, and shooting when it was time to shoot. He had not thought himself capable of that.

Where the hell was that idiot Mouse?

After a dozen twists and turns along his journey he slowed, started trying to look like a tourist headed for the Jones monument. His men stalked along behind him.

The monument had not changed. It was the same tall bronze statue surrounded by the same small park, its boundary stockaded by imported pines and bushes. Between the trees and the statue there were a dozen lighted fountains where sea nymphs bathed in endlessly falling waters.

The park was the heart of an oasis in the desert of Old Town. Lining the streets facing it were several museums, the Opera, a library, and smart little shops which catered to the wealthy. Among them were homes belonging to some of Angel City's oldest families. The square was a tenacious place. It refused to admit that Old Town's glories had faded. Most decaying cities contained a few such pearls.

SEVENTEEN: 3050 AD
The Main Sequence

Jellyroll Jones, as great men went, was an accident. He never had been a hero. He came in near the foot of the list of space-age memorables. His most singular act had been that of arriving on The Broken Wings before anyone else. Native school children were taught to consider him a hero, in the mold of a space-faring Magellan, but his myths bore no relation to the truth. His discovery had been sheer happenstance, and against his will. His ship had crashed here because of damage the guns of a Palisarian Directorate police corvette had done his astrogational computer. He and his crew—the women represented by the fountain nymphs—had hidden here for a few months. Unable to take the heat, humidity, and stench any longer, they had radioed for help. The corvette had collected them. Old Jellyroll had died in prison.

Moyshe paused in a shadow. He studied the statue and the dancing tips of water columns visible above the trees.

"Jarl's on," his comm man told him.

Moyshe took the hand radio. "Jarl? Where are you? We've got people after us."

"Be there in five minutes, Moyshe."

BenRabi heard strange sounds behind Kindervoort's voice.

"What's going on, Jarl?"

"Roadblock. Trouble with the natives. We're talking them down."

"Don't take too long. We're only a jump ahead."

Nicolas, hand comm against his ear, shook his head. "Mike's three blocks from here. Says they might be pulling out. Maybe they read our signals."

"Jarl, we look okay for now. They're maybe running. We'll be waiting on the north side. You get anything on Mouse?"

"Not yet, Moyshe. Out."

"Out." BenRabi returned the hand comm, studied the park through nighteyes. It seemed peaceful enough. He started toward Jellyroll.

Flash.

"Shit. Not again." From the frying pan into the fire twice?

Maybe not. The shot had not been directed his way.

There were more shots. Someone was fighting in there. Mouse? It looked like a baby battle, a duel, two men moving between shots. One was armed with a stunner only.

"Nick, hold on here. I'll check it out." Moyshe trotted toward Jellyroll.

The action seemed to be among the fountains beyond the statue. BenRabi pushed through the trees. He tried to spot the duelists, but they had stopped shooting. Was it over? He slipped toward the statue. Jellyroll would make a good, high observation point.

The firing broke out again. The stunner seemed to be among the far trees. The lasegun was among the fountains. The lasegunner, illuminated by the fountain lights, was moving very carefully.

Moyshe climbed three meters up Jellyroll's pedestal, slithered into a prone position between the old bandit's feet. It did make a nice vantage point, but would be hell to get away from fast. He edged forward, trying to spot the duelists.

Though the farther man was in darkness, Moyshe found him first. The nearer remained veiled by the flying jewelry flung up against the ever-shifting colors of the fountain lights. The water susurrated hypnotically as it tumbled back into the pools.

A lasebolt crackled through the branches of a pine. The gentle breeze brought smoky resin scents redolent of evergreen forests. The farther duelist snapped a shot in reply. His face was visible for an instant.

Mouse.

No doubt about it this time.

Storm clutched his left arm as he dodged to a new position. What the hell? benRabi thought. What's the fool doing out here with nothing but a stunner?

Mouse's opponent shifted position.

"Ha!" benRabi gasped. "It is her."

The Sangaree woman had had cosmetic surgery, but her catlike, sensuous movements remained unchanged. She just could not hide that deadly animal grace.

He tried to draw a bead on her. "Welcome back, sweetheart," he murmured. He was not at all surprised to see her. This was another passage in her death-dance with Mouse and himself.

She did not know another dancer was about to cut in. He grinned. A fragment of an old personality returned. He became the hard half of Gundaker Niven again.

"Ha!" She was hurt too. Her left side sported a wet, hasty bandage. Mouse had gotten close once, but had missed his kill. Surprising. That was not like him.

It said something about how good the woman was.

BenRabi got a good bead. He had no trouble shooting. The woman yowled, jumped like a broken-backed cat, collapsed on the colored concrete. Her muscles jerked spastically, then she slowly stiffened into the almost-death typical of a solid stunner shot to the head.

Moyshe looked down at his weapon. "Good shooting, cowboy. Mouse!" He shouted to make himself heard over the fountains. "She's out."

"Moyshe?" Storm called back. "Is that you?"

"Yeah." Mouse sounded weak. "You hurt bad?"

"I'll live."

Storm came into the open, stumbling toward the statue. He thrust his wounded arm into his jumper for support, carried his stunner like a revolver. He paused beside Marya, stared down. "Checkmate. Finally." His gaze flicked to the statue, back down.

BenRabi shouted, "What the hell happened? I been running myself dead trying to find you."

"She sucked me in. Showed herself, took a shot, then ran. I lost my head. I ran right into it." He glanced up again, his expression odd. "But she made a bigger mistake, eh? Let her gut override her brain." Mouse smiled wickedly. His lips stretched in a ferocious duplicate of the woman's vampire grin. "You know the funny part, Moyshe? She was working with McGraws. That's scary when you think about it."

Mouse fell silent. He stared at the woman for a long time, as if loath to end the feud.

Though benRabi did not like it, time had proven the next move necessary. She had been given two chances. Twice she had come back for more. If Mouse did not end it here, they would have the hellsbitch on their trail again, all fangs and claws once more.

She and Mouse were two of a kind, Moyshe reflected. Only death would stop either of them.

"You've got to be realistic, Thomas... Moyshe," benRabi mumbled to himself. "What's got to be has got to be."

He waited. Mouse remained reluctant. Time stretched.

Personnel carriers rumbled in the street outside the park. Moyshe looked back, expecting to see Kindervoort.

Wrong. Marines. But just as good.

Back to Mouse. Was he stalling because he did not have a lethal weapon? He could use hers. Or his hands.

Then he understood. Mouse was thinking about his Holy Grail, the hatred that had driven him so long. He would not yet know about Homeworld, but killing Marya would be symbolic of the process he had initiated. Symbolic of attaining his lifelong goal. Jupp would be the weapon... Marya might be the last of the ancient enemy he would encounter.

The end of a road is always a disappointment, Moyshe reflected.

Poor Mouse. Down deep, where he lived, he knew that when Marya went there would be nothing left to hate. His Grail, for all its distant sparkle, was just another empty cup.

"Where do we go from here, Tommy?" he asked softly.

In the shadows between Jellyroll's legs, benRabi/McClennon could do nothing but shake his head. He did not know.

Moyshe/Thomas's mind was becoming pandemoniac. The outside pressure was off. There was nothing to hold the dissociation in check. He was this man for a moment, then that. Alyce crawled through his brain like a maggot through rotting flesh. Something within him kept shrieking *I want*, and not letting him know what. Sudden storms of emotion racked him, always without detectable cause. Anger. Hate. Love. Sorrow. Joy. Despair. A moment of each, whap! like the impact of a fist, then gone, as if some storehouse had been broken open and all the containers inside dumped at random.

He wrapped his arms around his head and moaned softly.

He croaked, "I don't know, Mouse," it seemed an hour after his partner asked his question. BenRabi wanted to say, "Stars' End, and back to the high rivers," but the other characters inside kept telling him he would never see a harvestship again, would never track another herd, would never again go into Contact, would never build that secret service for the Seiners.

That Alyce creature must have been a hypnotic key, he thought. She was supposed to unlock all the spooks hidden behind the barriers Chub had been unable to penetrate. But the key had not opened the lock all the way. No more than Mouse had back when, when he had tried before their scheduled return to Confederation.

Something had shorted out. Something was trying to take him back not just to Thomas McClennon before this mission, but all the way back, to a day when he had not as yet undergone any personality programming.

He did not want to make that journey. He wanted what he had found in the high rivers between the stars. He fought. Deep inside, he howled and clawed like a wild thing tangled in a hunter's net.

There were angry shouts in the street whence he had come. The Marines were disarming his men. Ordinary precaution, he supposed. His team had been operating outside its "reasonable jurisdiction."

Mouse made his decision. It favored discretion. He stooped to recover Marya's weapon…

"Don't!" The voice was soft enough not to be heard far, yet commanding. BenRabi/McClennon shrank into the shadows of Jellyroll's legs. His Amy Many-Names had appeared. She bore a nasty little pistol. Her features were as cold as Mouse's became when he went into assassin's mind.

Mouse looked at her, saw the absence of emotion, slowly straightened. He did not drop his stunner.

"Where's Moyshe?" she snapped. "The grubs will be after him. I've got to find him first. He's suddenly the key to everything. You two never really crossed over, did you?" The words tumbled out of her mouth almost faster than her lips could shape them.

Mouse did not answer. He just stared into Amy's eyes, holding them. He clutched his weapon and waited for her coldness to thaw.

Or was he waiting for McClennon? Thomas was not sure. Mouse might be turning his own peril into some kind of test.

McClennon was sure Amy's determination would not persist. She was not trained for it.

"Where's Moyshe?" she demanded again. Her voice rose, squeaked.

"Here, Love." He eased from the shadows. "Don't move. Please?"

Her gaze darted his way, noted his stunner.

Mouse raised his weapon.

"No, Mouse. Not my wife, you don't."

Mouse stopped. McClennon's tone halted him. He swung his head for a cautious look at his partner.

"Moyshe, why?" Amy asked plaintively. Her weapon did not waver a millimeter from dead center on Mouse's chest.

"Why what, honey?"

"This betrayal. We gave you everything…"

"What betrayal?"

He could hear the *I* she was saying inside. She had opened her fortress unvanquishable to him, and now his promises appeared false. He had come to her bearing banners of love, false banners, and had raped and plundered her soul.

He could hear her pain, but hadn't any idea what had brought it on. "What betrayal?" he demanded. "What's happened?"

"The Marines are arresting everybody. 'Interning them,' they call it. Your Beckhart sent Gruber an ultimatum. We open Stars' End for Navy or he nova bombs the Yards."

No, McClennon thought. There's something twisted here. Something not quite straight. Not that Beckhart would not make the threat. He would, and would follow through for the sake of the Stars' End weaponry. He was a man who believed in his mission. But the timing seemed askew.

Or was it? The Starfishers and Sangaree were inextricably entangled at Stars' End. Beckhart was free to move against the home ground of either. It was a remarkable opportunity. Earlier, he had gloated about having hit Homeworld's sun...

Damn! Damn! Damn! he thought.

The agent part of him, the old intuition, put together everything Beckhart had, and had not, said, and threw forth one incontrovertible answer. The Admiral had been after Stars' End from the beginning. From the moment he had summoned Cornelius Perchevski from his interlude with his quasi-daughter Greta...

As Moyshe benRabi it had been his mission to come up with leverage Beckhart could use to force the Seiners to open the fortress world to Luna Command.

He had been doing the Admiral's work even when he had thought he was working against the man. Damn! Damn! Damn!

And he did have the lever the Admiral needed. Beckhart had given that away in threatening Gruber.

The Admiral needed the location of the Seiner Yards. Mouse must have told the Old Man his partner could clue him in.

Gruber would yield to the threat. Not gracefully, but he would yield. No sane man would do otherwise once the fate of Homeworld became known.

Gruber would surrender. The single most commonly known fact about Beckhart was that he was a man of his word with a threat. He would use the bomb if refused.

But McClennon was sure the Old Man was running one colossal bluff right now. He could not have the coordinates of the Yards. Three Sky was huge, even if he knew to look there. Insofar as Thomas knew, there were just three people on The Broken Wings who could tell Beckhart what he had to know. Jarl and Amy would not talk.

He was in one hell of a tight place.

The Starfishers did not call their nebula Three Sky among themselves. McClennon doubted that one in a thousand knew that landside name, and not one in a hundred of those the coordinates for the Yards themselves. Mouse did not know. McClennon had acquired the information entirely by accident, while arguing with Amy.

"Where's Jarl?" he asked. He wondered how effectively his orders had been carried out after he had alerted the fleet. Well, probably. Amy was carrying on like they were the only red pass people left.

Tears rolled as she replied, "He's dead, Moyshe. He killed himself. Only about fifteen minutes ago. I got away while they were distracted."

"While who was distracted?"

"The military police."

So. That roadblock had been a setup. And Jarl, intuiting Beckhart's thrust, had gone the only way he could to avoid checkmate.

And Amy intended eliminating another information source. Him.

Where was the harvestfleet? Had Beckhart gotten his bluff in on Payne too?

Then what would Amy do about herself? Put a lasebolt through her own brain? She was capable. She seemed a bit self-destructive.

What if Beckhart's claims about a centerward race were valid? That meant the whole human race, as well as several neighboring races, were threatened with extinction.

It seemed a lot more than Seiner freedom lay on the line.

The weight of the decision he had to make seemed as heavy as that Atlas had borne. Heavier. Hundreds of worlds might depend upon his choice… Ambergris and the Stars' End weapons. They might make all the difference.

What to do?

He leaned against Jellyroll's leg and stared at the symbols of the sides of his conflict. Which should he betray? Which should he destroy?

It was in his hands alone now, and there was no evading the decision. He could not let it ride in hopes it would sort itself out. No god from a machine would swing down on a wire to relieve him of his burden.

He had always had a yearning to become a hero, even for the few shooting star moments Confederation culture allowed. He would become one to the trillions if he delivered Stars' End and its arsenal. He would stand beside Jupp von Drachau, destroyer of Sangaree... But that would make him Iscariot to millions of Starfishers.

His fingertips sensually caressed his weapon. There lay all solutions. In the gun. The final argument. In the words of ancient Mao, "All power comes from the mouth of a gun." War and violence, he thought. A certain breed claimed they solved nothing. Those folks ignored the fact that dead men seldom argued.

He remembered a small Ulantonid nun, seen in passing in the Blake City spaceport on Carson's an eon ago, while he and Mouse had been waiting to join the Starfishers. She had served a dead man...

He was vacillating. Avoiding decision. Riding a period of stability for all it was worth.

One squeeze of a trigger would settle a trillion fates. His friend? Or Amy, his love?

Those symbols remained as motionless as the man between whose legs McClennon stood. They waited too, aware that, for the moment, he was possessed of godlike power.

Mouse had, McClennon was sure, known the ramifications for some time. Perhaps since before the mission had begun. Mouse stared at Amy's weapon, half hypnotized by the death lying there. Death had never touched him...

He had been immune for so long...

Amy was pale and growing paler. She had had time to think, to see some of the possibilities, and to grow scared. Her gun hand quivered.

Mouse began moving, almost imperceptibly bringing his stunner a little farther forward.

"Wait!" McClennon snapped. "This is silly. There's a way out."

They looked at him, their faces grave and baffled.

His finger danced on his stunner's trigger. Amy squeaked as she fell. Mouse looked infinitely surprised. Shaking, McClennon peered into the street beyond the trees behind him. The Marines seemed uninterested in the park. Good. If the men just kept their mouths shut...

He scrambled down, collected weapons, stunned Marya again. Her breathing indicated she was partially recovered, and probably gathering herself for something.

He had to keep the three of them out of the way while he twisted the Admiral's tail. Maybe he could salvage something for everybody, though Beckhart would resent it all to hell.

But, dammit! It wasn't necessary to have big winners and losers. Everybody could lose a little and win a little and come out ahead in the end.

Beckhart would give in if he could not catch up fast enough. He had to have those coordinates soon, or see his whole intrigue blow up in his face.

McClennon laughed. He was going to get the best of the Old Man, and that was as rare as roc's eggs. Still chuckling, he threw Amy over his shoulder and headed for the tight darkness of Old Town.

She would come out of this hating him, but by doing it this way he would give her more than he ever could with love.

He searched his mind for signs of instability. All the gears were in place and working smoothly. Some sort of balance had been achieved. Not a natural one, but one that looked good for a while. He was now a little of everyone he had ever been, and a little more, too.

He hoped it would last long enough.

EIGHTEEN: 3050 AD
The Main Sequence

"What the hell is going on, Damon?" Beckhart's voice had a saw-toothed edge. "Storm and the Sangaree woman were in that park. Storm called to say he was going in after her. McClennon's men admit he went in. You chased the Seiner woman in there. Four people. Where the hell are they now?"

"I don't know, sir," the Major confessed. "We went in as soon as we knew where to look. They weren't there anymore."

"No shit? You're aware that three of those people are professionals, aren't you?"

"Yes sir. And two of them are ours, with no reason to run."

"One of them. I'm not sure what McClennon thinks he is. It's not his fault, but he has his head on backwards and it's falling apart. He probably doesn't know who he is or who he's working for half the time. He's the one I'm worried about. He needs psychiatric attention fast."

Beckhart massaged his forehead. He was growing a bitch of a headache. Just when it looked like he had it nailed down... He had to snag Thomas or his woman before Gruber called his bluff. He had to show at the Yards before the harvestfleets extricated themselves from the standoff at Stars' End. He had to move before the Sangaree raidfleet learned about Homeworld.

"Why the hell did that idiot Kindervoort have to go and kill himself?"

"He evidently had strong feelings."

"They're a stiff-necked mob. I've never figured them out. That damned Payne is still up there making nasty talk. With three squadrons sitting on his back."

"Just pride talking, sir."

"We screwed up, Damon. If we don't find those people, alive, we're had. *We.* Do I make myself clear?"

"Abundantly, Admiral. I've got all my men digging. The local police don't have any decent tracking gear, but it's still only a matter of time."

"The shorter the time, the better, Major. High Command is breathing down my neck. The CSN has a personal stake in what we're doing. He isn't very fond of me. So don't forget that water and horseshit both go downhill."

"Message received, Admiral."

"Good. Get out there and find them. And don't forget that they're professionals."

The Marines did not turn up a trace all night. Beckhart spent the time tossing, sharing his cot with a cruel dread.

He was afraid the Sangaree woman had gotten the drop on Storm and McClennon and had spirited them out of the city. She had gotten out once before.

Time trudged along. The tension built. He began snapping at everyone around him. "Like a mad dog," he overheard one of his technical ratings say.

That hit him like ice water. It made him count ten before speaking. He had an image of himself as a reasonable, fair, and fatherly superior. His pride demanded that he treat his subordinates well.

After thirty hours he locked himself in his tiny cubicle of an office. He drank coffee, gobbled aspirin, and wondered if he was too old to start praying.

"Admiral!" an excited voice called through the closed door. "Comm call. Field channel three. It's McClennon, sir."

Beckhart slapped his drab Navy comm unit, muffing the channel selection twice. "Come on, you bastard." A moment later, "Thomas? Where the hell are you, son? What's going on? Where's Mouse? You all right?"

"We're fine. Mouse is tied up at the moment." McClennon giggled. "All three of them are."

He's gone, Beckhart thought. Cracked completely. "Where are you, Thomas?"

"Around and about. Right now I'm here."

"McClennon... Report to me immediately. In person."

"No sir."

"What? Thomas, the whole damned thing is going down..." What was McClennon up to?

"Give me one little thing, Admiral. That's all I'm asking. One thing, and I give you Stars' End on a platter."

"What the hell do you think you're doing? When did Commanders start bargaining with Admirals?"

"Captain."

"That can be rectified. McClennon, I'm tired and I'm aggravated. Don't give me any shit. Tell me where you are so I can send somebody to pick you up."

"No sir. Not till I get what I want. I've got something you need. You give me something back. You want to talk about it?"

"I'll listen, Thomas. That's all." That's all. Had anyone had sense enough to try for a fix on McClennon's transceiver? Probably not. Too much to expect of these people.

"It's simple, Admiral. I'll give you the coordinates for the Yards after you execute some instrument guaranteeing the Starfishers' independence. Recognize them as an independent political entity. Offer to exchange embassies. Offer mutual non-aggression pacts. All those kinds of things that will make it hard for Luna Command to subjugate them without a big public outcry."

"Holy shit. You're out of your mind."

"I know it." Beckhart heard McClennon's pain and fear. The man was scared silly. He knew he was on the edge. "It's getting worse. I need help, Chief. But I've got to do this first."

"Thomas, the answer is no. You know damned well that I couldn't agree to something like that even if I wanted. Which I don't, I don't have the power."

"High Command does. I'll listen on this channel. You let me

know when the treaties are ready."

"Thomas, you're committing suicide. You're throwing your career away."

"Really? You mean you haven't used me up yet?"

"Thomas... You can't hide from me forever."

"I can try, Admiral. I can sure as hell try."

"Thomas, I'm going to have your balls for breakfast... Shit!" He was talking to himself. McClennon was gone.

He hurled a half-finished mug of coffee across his office. The brown liquid dribbled down the wall, onto a stack of memos that had accumulated while he worried.

Someone knocked.

"Enter."

Major Damon stepped in. "We triangulated the call, sir. No luck. He wired a standard Navy comm into a public box and made the call from a public box somewhere else."

"I told you we're dealing with professionals. But let's consider the bright side. It's a small city, and he has three prisoners to watch, feed, and keep clean. He'll make a mistake. Storm will jump him. Or we'll find him. Keep looking."

Damon left. Beckhart cleaned up his coffee mess, settled into his chair. He felt better. Almost relaxed. The worst possibilities were, for the moment, no more than ghosts of evil chance.

He made some elementary calculations. The lead time he had on the Seiners if he and they started for the Yards together. Stars' End was eight days rimward of The Broken Wings. The Yards were somewhere back toward the Inner Worlds. How long till a Sangaree courier reached Stars' End with the news about Homeworld?

The Sangaree had no known shipboard instel capacity. They communicated by courier exclusively. So his agents told him. So he hoped. The scheme depended on a long news lag and Starfisher stubbornness.

He smiled. If the fastest ship known had left Homeworld immediately after von Drachau's attack... He should have fourteen more days.

"Thomas, there's no way you can stay ahead of me for two weeks. Not in this burg."

Confidence soon yielded to doubt. High Command withdrew his Marines over his protest. The doubts grew stronger. On day seven the CSN personally called. Beckhart could conceal the truth no longer. He covered for McClennon by declining to name names.

He was loyal to his men. Thomas was no turncoat. He was a victim of his occupation and faulty technical preparation. Sooner or later every agent encountered the crisis. McClennon had had the misfortune to hit his at an historically inopportune moment.

Heads were going to roll among the Psych crew! On day eleven Beckhart came to the conclusion that the first head lost would be his own. The CSN kept making sounds like a happy executioner sharpening his axe.

"Come in, Major. I take it you're going to tell me the same old thing?"

"Unfortunately, sir. He's just not leaving any tracks. We did find a cellar this morning that someone had been using, but they were long gone when we broke in. We've covered sixty percent of the city now. We're reasonably sure he hasn't slipped back into what we've covered."

"Reasonably sure? Damon, I don't want reasonably sure. I want absodamnposilutely sure."

"And instead of sixty local police reservists, I want my battalion of Marine MPs."

"What could I do? They took them," he said into Beckhart's scowl. "I see it taking seven or eight days of searching with what we have, Major. We don't have that much time."

"The probability of contact is going up faster now, sir. He has less room to maneuver. The computers almost guarantee we'll find him within five days. The statistical profile is against him. I've had my people stop using the regular comm nets. He may have been monitoring our traffic."

"Of course he was. He's crazy, not stupid. All right. Carry on."

Beckhart leaned back, thought, Thomas, I've got to give you credit. You're good when you have to be. And, what the hell is wrong with Storm? He should have done something by now.

He knows McClennon better than anybody else. He's the best man I've got.

Was the little bastard in on it? The possibility had not occurred before. Mouse was the perfect agent. You did not suspect his loyalty.

But Storm's loyalty was to his dream of exterminating the Sangaree, of avenging his family. He had no motive but habit for taking a Bureau line in this. And he and McClennon had become close friends. They had done too many missions together...

They might have cooked this whole thing up with that Seiner bitch.

"Admiral. The CSN on instel, relay from *Assyrian.*"

"Oh, Christ. Again?"

"He sounds upset."

"He's always upset. Switch him through."

A moment later, "Good morning, sir."

"You found that man yet?"

"No sir. We're closing in. The computers say we'll have him any time now."

"I've got computers too, Beckhart. And a lot more input resources. I have the Sangaree raidmaster at Stars' End getting the word sometime day after tomorrow. We don't know what those people will do. Maybe go crazy. I've ordered the attack squadrons back off courier intercept. That's hopeless. They'll return to Carson's and Sierra. *Hittite* is moving up to Blackworld. Two Conqueror Class reserve attack squadrons are moving into the Twenty-First Transverse in case they break through the Twenty-Third. What concerns me more than the Sangaree, though, is what Gruber is going to do when he's free to deploy. I'd guess he'd head for the Yards. From what I've been told, if he gets there ahead of you, we lose. There's supposedly no way we can root them out, and no way to get close enough to deliver the threatened nova bomb. This isn't news to you. I repeat it in case you've lost sight of the facts. Your loyalty to your people is laudable, but..."

"I'm aware of the problem, sir. It was my intention to calculate a most probable quadrant and send von Drachau to wait there while I rooted this man out. That would give us a few extra days, added to the lead time we have because of the additional distance from Stars' End to the Yards."

"You're dealing with a stubborn man, Beckhart. You haven't found him yet, let alone gotten him to talk. You apparently know him. How long can he hold out after you take him?"

"I don't know, sir." Beckhart did not like admitting that. It was a question he had been trying to ignore. He had not come out equipped for mind probing. He had not begun to worry about possibly needing the equipment till lately.

"Why is he doing this?"

"You mean his motives? I don't know. Faulty Psych programming is what set him off. You might call it induced schizophrenia. Even he's not sure what he's doing, or why. Or even who he is a good part of the time."

"I suppose you still insist on protecting him?"

"Yes sir. I don't believe he's responsible for his own actions. I don't want him punished because of technical errors made by the people who prepared him for his mission."

"Okay, Beckhart. This is the word from High Command. Prepare to meet his demands. If you haven't got him in hand by noon Tuesday, Luna Command time, you give him what he wants."

"Sir!…"

"That's the word. We'd rather have Stars' End *and* the Seiners if we can, but Stars' End is for sure. We won't risk our shot at that weapon technology."

"Sir…"

"It's not subject to debate, Beckhart. It sounds spineless to me, too, and it's my idea. But that's the way it's going to be. If you get hold of him before deadline, we'll reevaluate our position. But only if you get hold of him."

Beckhart tried several arguments. None made any impression.

High Command's position was understandable. The very existence of the race was on the line. But still…

"Get me Major Damon," he ordered after the CSN secured. "Damon? Word from High Command. We find him by noon, Tuesday, their time. Or he gets what he wants. Do the best you can."

Beckhart leaned back, closed his eyes. He felt tired and old. He went over all the old ground. There must be a way of smoking Thomas out. He just had to look at it from the right angle.

But, oh, was it an elusive angle.

NINETEEN: 3050 AD
The Main Sequence

Mouse came around first. He saw McClennon sitting a meter away. Thomas wore a grave expression.

Mouse groaned. "Christ! My head. What the hell happened?"

"I shot you. Stunner."

"Why?" Storm tried to sit up. He could not. He was tied hand and foot.

"Aw, shit, Tommy. What the hell? Come on, cut me loose."

"I can't."

"What's wrong with you, man? I spent four months fixing it so we could get out. I could've left you behind… We bought the mission off, Moyshe. Tommy. With ten thousand percent interest… Damned! My head. Get me some aspirin."

McClennon had them in his hand. A plastic cup sat on the dirt floor between himself and Mouse. "Open your mouth. I gave you a little too much. All of you. I had to shoot fast. I don't have your finesse."

McClennon's face settled into tired lines. He had had no sleep. More water dribbled to the floor than passed Mouse's lips.

Mouse swallowed, but too late to avoid the aspirin's sour-bitter taste. He spat. "You'd better explain."

"I got backed into a corner, Mouse. I had to make a choice. You were on duty when the Old Man finally got around to laying the truth on the line."

"Beckhart? Our own fearless leader, who was born without a mouth?"

"Yes," McClennon repeated Beckhart's story about the center-ward peril word for word.

"Did you believe him?"

"He was convincing."

"He's always convincing. That doesn't make him any less a liar. And he's the worst ever born."

McClennon was surprised. He had thought that Mouse shared his belief in the Admiral's basic honesty.

"Still, that little fable would shed a lot of light on all the weird things that have been going on around Luna Command the last four or five years. I never did buy that crap about Ulant getting ready to hit us again. You sure he was telling the truth?"

"You should have seen his eyes when he described the Ulanto-nid intelligence tapes. But what really convinced me was when he said they're reactivating the Climbers."

"No lie?"

"That's straight."

"Wow. What do you know about that?" Mouse shook his head in amazement. It was a difficult task, lying on his side on that filthy floor. "You were going to explain why I'm lying here in this muck tied up so I can't even scratch my butt."

"It came to a choice, Mouse." McClennon's voice grew plaintive. "Between betraying Navy or the Starfishers. When I heard Jarl was dead."

"I don't follow you, Tommy. In fact, maybe you don't either. You don't look very stable. I think we'd better get you to a Psych center."

"I know. I can see what's happening to me. Mouse, I can't stop it!" He closed his eyes momentarily. "But I'm holding it off. I have to. Because when Jarl killed himself, that only left two people who could tell Beckhart where the Yards are. And he's trying to bluff Gruber by telling him he's going to hit the Yards if the Seiners don't pony up Stars' End and the harvestfleets. Me and Amy, and maybe you, are the only ones who can give him the coordinates."

"I can't, Tommy. That's one nobody let me in on. They didn't trust me the way they did you. They weren't supposed to."

"I didn't know for sure. I might've left you behind if I had. No. I couldn't have. You know too damned much about Angel City. You would've found me."

"Tell me what the hell you're doing."

"I'm going to trade Stars' End for the Starfishers."

"What?"

"I'm going to hide till he gets Luna Command to agree to let the Seiners be. In writing. In public. Then I'll tell him where the Yards are and he can hold them up for Stars' End. That way nobody loses but me."

"You're out of your head, Tommy. You won't pull it off. He's got too much time to find you. And he'll roast you alive when he catches you."

"No. He'll be damned nice to me. He's got to get me to talk. He doesn't have any psych probe gear with him, and he'll probably hold off getting physical for a while…"

McClennon had made his decision in an instant. Every second since he had been trying to justify it and find ways to make it work. He guessed that he would have to stay missing for a week.

He had decided he would not move during that time, except to do a few things that had to be done right away. No movement, no tracks for the hunters to pick up.

"I got to piss, Tommy. Bad." Mouse examined his surroundings. "Christ! This is the hole where the Sangaree used to hide the refined stardust."

"And it wasn't in our reports. What are you going to do, Mouse? Try to jump me first chance you get? Or will you wait it out?"

Mouse just looked at him. He had donned his poker face. McClennon wore a half smile when he cut the cords binding Mouse's ankles. "Take your leak in the corner."

"With no hands?"

"They're tied in front. Or hadn't you noticed?"

A tiny smile flickered across Mouse's lips. "You've been hanging around me too long. You're getting too cool."

"Go do your business."

"This place is going to get ripe."

"I don't doubt it."

It was an earthen-floored cellar, already rank and humid.

Mouse stumbled as he walked. "Damned legs are numb." He unzipped, leaned against the wall, panted as he urinated.

A stunner blast could leave a man debilitated for days.

Mouse finished. He turned. "That's a load off my mind."

McClennon let Storm take three steps before stunning him across the thighs.

"Ah, shit, Tommy. Why'd you have to go and do that?"

"Had to."

"You're getting hard, old friend."

"It's the company I keep." McClennon looked at the Sangaree woman. She was aware now, and watching with cold gunmetal eyes. He untied her ankles. "Your turn."

She rose and took care of it without a word. She did not complain or seem surprised when he stunned her too.

Mouse demanded, "What the hell is she doing here, anyway?"

"Let's say I'm keeping a card up my sleeve." She and Mouse did not know that Homeworld had been hit. She could be told and released. Her response might make a spectacular diversion.

Amy took forever recovering, and it was with her he had tried to be most gentle.

He was sorry as soon as she did come round.

Her he had not tied. He had thought it unnecessary.

He was playing chess with Mouse, using paper pieces on a board scratched into the earth. He did Mouse's moving for him. He was losing, as usual.

"Behind you," Mouse whispered.

Clothing rustled.

He hurled himself aside, rolled, grabbed his stunner, fired. Amy moaned, fell. She dropped the length of pipe she had been about to swing. It scattered the chessmen.

McClennon could barely tie her, so badly were his hands shaking. She remained conscious but refused to talk. Neither Mouse nor the Sangaree woman made any comment

Marya did smile a thin, hard smile.

The walls seemed to push in. For an instant he was not sure where he was or what he was doing. Then, for a moment, he relived part of his first visit to The Broken Wings. His name was Gundaker Niven and he and the Sangaree woman were bedmates again.

"Tommy?" Mouse said. "Tommy! Snap out of it!"

That did it, for a few seconds. Long enough for him to see all three captives trying to gain their feet, and Mouse dead last in the race.

Cold calm washed over him. He shot all three. In the head. It was dangerous, for them, but a lot less dangerous for him if he was going into one of his episodes.

He went. And became quietly crazy for a while.

He was a Starfisher named Moyshe benRabi... A Navy Gunner named Cornelius Perchevski... A naval attaché named Walter Clark... A sociologist named Gundaker Niven... Hamon Clausson... Credence Pardee... Thomas Aquinas McClennon... A boy wandering the cluttered light canyons of a city on Old Earth and getting a stiff neck looking up longingly at the stars.

Exhaustion overcame him. He fell asleep.

He wakened before his captives. His grasp on identity and reality had recovered, but all those other men were still there inside, clamoring to be released.

He wondered if he would be able to hang on.

He needed Psych attention bad.

His stomach churned and growled. He was hungry.

Food was the weak link in his plan. He had not yet obtained any. He would have to risk capture to do so.

He checked the time. Sixteen hours had elapsed since he had spirited the three out of the park. The Admiral would not have panicked yet, he reasoned. It would be awhile before the streets became too dangerous to risk.

He stepped down the stunner's output and gave his prisoners a few more hours worth of unconsciousness. Then he took Mouse's comm and went into the streets.

He made his first stop at a used clothing store, a marginal charitable operation a few blocks from his hiding place. He purchased worn, unstylish workman's garb. He changed in an alleyway. He repeated the process in a more stylish shop, and farther away still deposited his Seiner jumpsuit in a collection box belonging to the charitable organization. He worked hard to keep the surly Gundaker Niven personality in the forefront of his mind. When he was most successful he hunched slightly, spoke crudely, and looked too tough to mess with.

He purchased a collection of small tools, then a large woman's wig which he trimmed to a style favored by Angel City thugs. He placed a small bandage on one cheek and a pebble in his shoe.

He no longer looked or moved anything like any of the people the Marines were hunting.

Mobile patrols were everywhere, astounding the citizenry with their busy-ness, but he was not stopped or questioned. They were seeking a Starfisher.

They would get organized soon, he knew. It would be difficult to evade them then.

Whenever he was safely out of sight, he used Mouse's hand comm to eavesdrop on their radio traffic.

They were confused. They had four people to find, but did not know which was doing what to whom. Their interest of the moment was to make sure no one sneaked out of the city. After the boltholes were sealed they would launch their systematic search.

He wondered if he ought not to let Beckhart stew. The confusion would give him an edge. But no. The Admiral would need time to approach his superiors.

He stole an Out of Order sign off a public comm booth and carried it several blocks to a functional booth. He hung it and began making like a repairman.

The gimmicking took longer than he expected. The comm was of local manufacture. He had to figure out the color-coding of the circuitry. Then it became a classroom exercise. He installed Mouse's comm and closed the housing in minutes. He noted the terminal number and departed.

Finding groceries required imagination. Home cooking simply was not done. Rich and poor, Angel City's people ate out or had prepared meals delivered. Most food was artificial and recycled anyway. Only a few Terran tropical plants were adaptable to The Broken Wing's atmosphere and climate. No local was gourmet enough to have invested in the genetic engineering needed to adapt a wider range of food plants.

He ended up buying field rations from a swamp dredger's supply house. The saleswoman said he didn't look the type, but asked no questions. The underworld used the swamp for its own purposes. Curiosity could be harmful to a questioner's health.

He had no local money left when he returned to the cellar. He had Seiner cash and Conmarks, both of which were negotiable, but did not want to draw attention by spending outside currency. Conmarks were never rare, but still... He searched his prisoners and confiscated their limited wealth. Most of that was Confederation's interworld currency.

They submitted sullenly. No one was talking. He did not try starting a conversation. He gave them another taste of the stunner and returned to the streets.

He found a public comm and called the booth he had jiggered. The handcomm there broadcast what he had to say.

The Admiral was not pleased with him.

Finished, he patrolled around and rented two small apartments and an office, so he would have somewhere to run if the Marines closed in on his cellar. And, finally, he braved Central Park by night to steal an all-bands tactical transceiver/scanner from the inattentive MPs.

He used an old crate for a seat and the cellar wall for a backrest. He closed his eyes and listened as the tactrans scanned the bands. He heard a movement after a while. He opened one eye. Mouse was trying to sit up.

"Tommy, you can't keep doing that. You're going to hurt somebody."

McClennon turned the scanner down. "Sorry, Mouse. But I don't have a lot of choice." He leaned toward the transceiver. It was staying busy. His call had stirred Beckhart up good.

How long would he have to stay lost?

Days passed. He lost track. One moment it seemed only a few had gone by, the next it seemed a lot. Every hour was an eon trudging wearily off into eternity.

He thought he was doing well. He had kept three willful, angry prisoners hidden and controlled for days, Beckhart had not caught a trace of him. He had driven his mental problem into a straitjacket...

That jacket was not strong enough.

He was somewhere in Luna Command. A beautiful blonde, not more than seventeen, clung to his left arm. She whispered something into his ear. She called him Commander Perchevski. He was supposed to know her. He did not. He wanted to attack her.

Another woman took hold of his right arm. She insisted his name was Walter Clark. She wanted to take him away from the blonde morsel.

The females released him and assaulted one another. They fought over his name. He kept trying to tell them they were both wrong, that he was really Credence Pardee. Or was it Hamon Clausson? Wasn't he Hamon Clausson that time on Shakedowns? He forgot the women while he tried to locate his ID badge. It had fallen off his tunic.

There it was, beneath the edge of the carpet. He yanked it out. A kid with a somber, serious face stared off the card. The kid said, "Gundaker Niven," and grinned viciously.

He screamed.

There were men all around him. Some were a little shorter or a little taller, a little heavier or lighter, but each one had stolen his face. They pummeled one another mercilessly. Whenever one broke free and charged him, the others piled on from behind.

He jumped, closed his hands around the nearest throat. "I'll kill them," he gurgled. "I'll kill them all. Then they'll leave me alone."

He fought till he had no strength left. Weary, he fell to the floor. Darkness descended.

He wakened in a dank cellar on The Broken Wings. Three people watched with the cold, hungry eyes of vultures perched over a dying thing.

He glanced at his watch. He had been out ten hours. What? They had not jumped him? They were still here? He staggered to his feet, took a step, fell as vertigo hit him.

He shook his head hard. The cobwebs broke up. They drifted away. He looked around again.

Mouse quietly proffered the stunner.

Their eyes met. McClennon took the weapon. Mouse did not say a word. He crossed his wrists and offered to be tied again.

Thomas said nothing either. Nothing needed saying. He retied his friend and sat down to wait.

The hours groaned on,

He had not expected it to take so long. How long could the Old Man hold out? Why was he being so stubborn? Giving in would not cost him much. Confederation did not control the starfish herds anyway.

He supposed Beckhart was trying to save a political coup that would help overshadow the Homeworld abomination.

McClennon had to move only once to remain ahead of the search. Then the Admiral ran out of stall time.

Von Drachau returned from Homeworld. McClennon caught the news on his scanner. He guessed that it would not be long till the news reached Stars' End. That confrontation would dissolve. Gruber would rush to defend Three Sky.

That old traitor time had turned its coat again.

He was not surprised when his hand comm crackled and Beckhart came on. "Thomas, are you listening? This is Admiral Beckhart. Thomas, are you listening?"

"I'm here. Talk." That was all he said, for fear they would triangulate his position.

"Thomas, you've got what you want. Personally guaranteed by the Chief of Staff Navy." He paused for McClennon's reply. Thomas did not speak. "Thomas, are you there?"

"I'm listening, I said."

"You've got what you want. What're you going to do about it?"

He had not thought beyond forcing their acquiescence. How could he get it nailed down, on paper, publicly, without them dragging him into some back room and running him through a psychological grist mill?

"I'll call back."

He glanced at his prisoners. He had learned that he could not serve two masters and remain loved by the bondsmen of either. Amy's hatred tortured him mercilessly. And Mouse's anger... But Mouse was helping, if only by not doing anything when he had the chance. He had allowed friendship to obscure duty, had let it make him give the benefit of the doubt.

McClennon would not have made it otherwise.

But Amy... She refused to see what he was trying to do. She called him Judas.

Marya's sullen displeasure he could bear. He had had plenty of practice. Her sultry Sangaree face became a mild, passive, resigned reflection of everything he saw in his wife.

With Mouse he had no long-run worry. Mouse would get over his anger. He would forgive the treason. They were friends.

So, he thought. Time to face the Old Man. His wolves will be at the door the second I tell him where...

"Admiral? McClennon here."

"Thomas, I don't have much time. You're getting what you want. Can we speed things up?"

"I want someone from the Judge Advocate's there."

"What? You're not being arrested. You're not even being charged. I went to bat for you, son. Just give me the word. Where the hell are you?"

"I want him to witness, not to represent me."

"Christ. Thomas, you've got my word. That's all I can give you. It would take a week to get one of those space lawyers here. Now, pretty please, will you get organized?"

Okay, okay. Maybe Beckhart was right. He was wasting time. And the man *was* giving his word...

He told Beckhart where to pick him up.

TWENTY: 3050 AD
The Main Sequence

Four Angel City police officers came to the door, to escort Mc-Clennon to his commanding officer. He was puzzled, but did not ask why they were doing Corps work. He untied Mouse, Marya, and Amy, and said, "Let's go, gentlemen."

He had butterflies the size of owls. They were mating on the wing.

The streets were barren. Angel City had become half a ghost town. "Where is everybody?" he asked. He had heard nothing on monitor that would explain this emptiness.

"Drafted," one of the cops grumbled.

"What?"

"Almost everybody old enough was in the Reserves. It was a good way to pick up a few extra marks. They got called up."

"This war thing must be getting grim."

"Must be," the policeman admitted. "They called up everybody in the Transverse. Navy, Marines, Planetary Defense, whatever. Not only that, they took all the equipment that wasn't nailed down."

The officers were walking their charges to Beckhart's headquarters. McClennon saw very few vehicles. "What about the gang upstairs?" he asked, jerking a thumb skyward.

"The heavies? Still there. Let's hope they hold those Sangaree. You and your buddy here, and your Admiral and his crew, are the only military people left here."

"Guess we do have to take it serious," Mouse said. "The Old Man plays games, but they're not this expensive."

McClennon could not help being startled and disturbed. This general mobilization was a distressing indicator. It suggested that Confederation meant to hurl everything but the proverbial sink into the first passage of arms.

His thoughts strayed to his homeworld. Had Old Earth been stripped of men and equipment too? If so, he had to be glad he was in the Outworlds.

That madhouse planet would descend into an age of barbarism if the policing divisions vanished. Confederation did not interfere much, but did keep the violence level depressed,

A blowup had occurred during the Ulantonid War, and to a lesser degree several other times, when the Confederate presence was weak. After settling with Ulant, Luna Command had had to reconquer Earth.

When the mailed fist vanished, the cults and movements beat swords from plowshares, eager to settle old scores.

"Mouse," he said, "it's a strange world I call home."

Storm read him at a glance. "It won't be as bad this time, Tommy. I've seen some of the standing Mobe plans. They'll do some creative drafting. Something like the ancient press gangs. They'll grab anybody loose and ship them out all over Confederation. They'll scatter them so they don't cause much trouble."

"Sounds good. Break the whole mess up if they take enough of them."

"It would tap a big manpower pool. Old Earth didn't contribute a thing during the war with Ulant."

Amy, Marya, and the policemen all watched curiously.

Even Mouse did not understand Old Earth.

Earth was the land of the timid tailor, the world cramped with a people from whom all adventure had been bred. The pioneer genes had departed long ago. The stay-at-homes were, in the opinion of the rest of humanity, the culls of the species. Even McClennon willingly admitted that his fellow Old Earthers were determined to live up to their derelict image.

The average Old Earther would faint at the suggestion of going into space. And yet he could be astonishingly vicious with his fellows...

Savage decadence? That was the way McClennon saw his native culture.

"*Lo! thy dread empire, Chaos, is restored;*
Light dies before thy uncreating word..." he muttered.

"What?" Mouse asked.

"From a poem. By Pope."

Mouse grinned. "Welcome home, Tommy. You're acting like my old friend again."

McClennon grunted, grabbed his stomach.

His ulcer ripped at him with dragon's claws, like something trying to tear its way out. He nearly doubled over with the pain.

"Tommy?"

"Ulcer."

"We've got to get you to a doctor."

"A little while yet, A little while. I can hold out."

"What're you going to be like afterward?"

"I've got to see it through." Only after he had fulfilled his self-appointed mission would he dare concern himself with tuckpointing the mortar of body and soul.

The weeks of waiting had brought the ulcer back to life. The anticipation had been terrible. He had defied Beckhart before, but never in anything this important.

He was terrified. What would the man do? The Admiral was fair, but would not let fairness interfere with his carrying out his own orders.

McClennon tried to banish worrying by studying his surroundings. The few Angelinos in the street seemed subdued. Their auction excitement had been replaced by trepidation.

McClennon noted one odd, common piece of behavior. Every Angelino occasionally paused to glance upward. He mentioned it to Mouse.

"Maybe they're worried about the raidfleet."

He, too, glanced upward at times, but not in search of an alien doom. He told himself he was taking last fond looks at a sun.

The Cothen Zeven, the prison for military officers, lay almost a thousand kilometers below the surface of Old Earth's moon. Psychologically, it was as far removed from mainstream life as any medieval dungeon.

The self-delusion did not take. He was looking for something he had lost, something now so far beyond the sky he would never see it again. Payne's Fleet had taken hyper during the week. His Starfisher surrogate homeland was gone forever.

"In here," said the officer in charge of the police group. He led them through the entrance of a second-rate hotel.

Beckhart was tricked out full dress. He stood at a stiff parade rest as they entered. His face was corpse-like. Only an almost undetectable tightness of the eyes betrayed the anger pent within him. "Lock the women up," he said tonelessly, staring through McClennon.

Amy broke down. She exploded, mixing pleading, weeping, and outrage. Marya considered her with obvious disdain. Thomas wanted to hold her, to comfort her. He did not. Trying would only make things worse.

A bit of the true Beckhart slipped through the glacial shell. He took Amy's hands. "Be calm, Mrs. McClennon. You'll be headed home in a few days. Unless you'd rather stay with Thomas."

"Stay?" She laughed hysterically. She got hold of herself, sniffled, "I'll go home." Embarrassed by her outburst, she stared at the raggedly carpeted floor.

Past her, to Marya, Beckhart added, "I think we'll release you, too, madam." He smiled. It was that killer smile Thomas had come to know with Mouse. He saw it only when Marya's people had been done some special injury.

How we can be cruel, he thought. We're always willing to play petty torturers with our dull little knives.

Mouse understood that smile too. Von Drachau had scored! He seemed to glow. He assumed the mantle of Torquemada. He laughed. The sound of it was a little mad.

"He really did it? He broke through?" Storm spun toward Marya. "Let her live. By all means, let her live." He put on a big, cruel grin. Life for her would be crueler than death. She could look forward to nothing but flight and fear and utter lack of hope till a relentless, pitiless enemy finally ran her to ground.

Mouse told her, "Jupp von Drachau, our old friend from our younger days here, visited your Homeworld, dear."

Marya understood. Mouse had taunted her with his chance discovery during their captivity. He had mentioned the nova bomb.

She did not break. She did not give him an instant of pleasure. She simply smiled that hard, gunmetal smile, and promised with her eyes.

Nothing, ever, could more than lightly scar her outer defenses. Not after she had had to watch Mouse inject her children with the deadly drug that formed one of the foundation stones of Sangaree wealth.

The police removed the women. There was a long silence. Mouse and McClennon faced their commander. Thomas felt Mouse drawing away, closing up, becoming a Bureau man once again.

"Sit down, gentlemen," Beckhart said. "You'll have to bear with me. I'm a little edgy. The Broken Wings has been rough on me. Mouse, you go first. I want a detailed report."

McClennon's eyebrows rose. Beckhart was not going to press? What was he up to?

Mouse talked. McClennon retreated into introspection. He wrestled all the doubts he had held at bay since making his decision. The unanswerable *want* began insinuating sinister tentacles into his soul. He became increasingly confused.

"Thomas!" It was the third or fourth time his name had been called.

"What?"

"Your report on the last two weeks. I have to develop a position. You'd better think about what you'll say in your written statement, too. I tried to cover, but I couldn't. Not all the way. You'll have to stand a Board of Inquiry."

He began with Pagliacci's, lingered over the encounters with the Alyce-faces. He tried to make Beckhart understand that that deception had instigated his determination to scuttle Navy's plans for the Seiners.

"That was a mistake," Beckhart admitted. "I've made several

classics during this operation. The intent wasn't malign, Thomas. I meant it as a hypnotic trigger. Way back when, before you were supposed to return to Carson's, Mouse showed you a Chinese coin. That was supposed to be your cue. You didn't respond."

"That failsafer."

"He was ours. Yes. Another of my grand mistakes." Beckhart did not apologize for the murder attempt. They were professionals. They were supposed to understand. They were living chessmen playing a giant board. "Luckily, Mouse outguessed me on that one."

McClennon wandered through his tale, trying and failing to elucidate his behavior.

"Intellectually, I know what you're saying," Beckhart interjected. "Emotionally, I can't connect. Thomas, I'm one of those fools who actually believe in their work. It may be because that's all I have. Or maybe I never outgrew my idealism about Confederation. But that's neither here nor there. You haven't given me those coordinates."

"I haven't seen any guarantees."

"Thomas, I'll promise you anything. High Command has cleared it. They've published it. We'll make it stick. Even if it costs us a Senatorial Review. We can get around those. But that's something to worry about next month. Right now we need to get a hammerlock on Stars' End."

"And then what?"

"You just lost me, son."

"What happens to me?" Does it really matter? he wondered. Who cares?

"Technically, you're under arrest till you receive a Board ruling. You put yourself in a spot. You could end up the hero or the goat of this mess. Which one probably depends on how the first battle goes. I'd just as soon forget the whole thing myself. But it's too late. They know about you back at Luna Command."

"Look on the bright side, Tommy," Mouse said. "They can't legally make you work while you're under arrest. You'll get a vacation in spite of the Bureau."

Beckhart flashed Storm a daggers look. "Can the space-lawyer crap, son. The arrest will be strictly a paper technicality, Thomas.

In practice you'll be part of my staff till we sort out the Seiners and Stars' End. Mouse, you'll drag around with Thomas and me. As of now, you're his keeper."

McClennon caught a faint taste of life as he had known it before joining the Starfishers. He looked forward to the change. It might keep him too preoccupied to whine about his losses.

Poor Amy...

"First order of business, those coordinates. Then we get Thomas to a Psych team..."

A policeman came in. "*Marathon*'s stabilized orbit, Admiral. Her shuttle will be down shortly."

"Thank you."

"*Marathon?*" Mouse asked. "I thought she was in mothballs."

"She was when you left. Nothing is anymore. They're crewing the older ships with Reserves. They're replacing regular Fleet patrols. The initial battle will involve every first line ship we have."

"They sent one old cruiser to replace three heavy squadrons?" McClennon asked.

"Not exactly, *Marathon* is mine. Intelligence Admirals don't rate. Thomas, are you going to spill?" Beckhart turned to the policeman, who had remained near the door. "Officer, start moving our gear. Sergeant Bortle was supposed to scrounge up transport."

McClennon's immediate concern was that he had not had a bath. Sixteen days of grime, and he had to board a Navy ship?

"What's the program?" Mouse asked.

"First we bluff the Fishers. Then we move to Stars' End and ride herd on the scientists *Marathon* brought out. They'll supervise the Seiner teams. When I'm satisfied with progress, we space for Luna Command. After debriefing, you loaf till Thomas' Board is over. I imagine Thomas will get hung with a desk. He might even move back to the Line."

"How hard will they be on him?"

"The Board will clear him. On psychological grounds. There's precedent. But they'll want him off operations. Which makes sense, I guess. He could be burned out. He might still do commercial or diplomatic work. That wouldn't waste his training.

You I don't know about yet, Mouse."

McClennon looked inside himself and could find no remorse over his potential loss of job. He did not like his profession much.

"I might retire," Mouse mused. "Captain draws a good pension." Though he smiled, the coals of lost dreams lay banked behind his eyes. He had fulfilled his goals too early in life.

"Not till after the war, you won't," Beckhart said. "Nobody retires till then. Thomas? Are you going to give me what I need? Do I have to rub your nose in our intelligence tapes first?"

"All right. It's Three Sky Nebula. Inside the wedge and pointing toward galactic center, beginning about one a.u. inside. Give me a pen." He wrote a series of numbers on a memo sheet. "There're your jump-in coordinates. From there you go ahead in normspace. I can't give you the route through the junk. People who know it aren't allowed to leave."

"Three Sky? Really? I thought it would be way outside our usual sphere." Beckhart's stiffness began to fade. He became the Admiral of old. Smiles and friendship. And willingness to spend a man's life. "The purloined letter thing. That's why ships disappear there." After a pause, "I have things to do before we leave. Meet me in the lobby in half an hour. Ready for space."

"Ready for space?" McClennon asked.

"That was a subtle hint, son. Get cleaned up. I'll have a man bring you a uniform. And try to make peace with your woman."

"Thank you, sir."

He set a record for bathing, shaving, and shifting to the clean uniform. He had ten minutes left when he finished.

One minute later he entered the room Beckhart was using as a brig. It was just a hotel room without windows, with two guards posted outside its only door. Amy and Marya sat against opposite walls, ignoring one another.

"Amy?"

She refused to acknowledge his presence.

He grabbed her chin, forced her to face him. "Look at me, dammit!" For two weeks he had been trying to make her understand. She had refused. He wanted to beat it into her stubborn head. It took an effort to speak calmly. "We're leaving in a few minutes. If you want, you can come with us."

She glared.

"We'll end up at Stars' End. I thought you might want to join your research team there. Instead of being sent straight home."

Still she glared.

"If you go back with the internees, you'll end up at the Yards. With your mother. I thought maybe you'd want to go where you had a friend."

She would not say anything.

"All right. Be stubborn." He turned to the door. "Officer? I'm ready."

"Moyshe, wait. I… Yes. I'll go."

He sighed. Finally. The first yielding. "I'll clear it with the Admiral." A wan smile teased his lips as he left the room.

It would be a long journey. Maybe long enough for him to win his case.

Beckhart did not like his idea at first.

"Sir," McClennon explained, "she's best friends with one of the senior Fisher scientists. If we can tame her, she can help sell cooperation. You keep talking about Ulantonid intelligence tapes. Use them to persuade her. We don't really have to turn her, just to open her mind."

"Thomas… I can see right through you. You don't give a shit about… All right. It's another trade-off. Bring her. But you're responsible for her."

"Tell the guards to turn her over to me."

"Go get her, will you? You're wasting time."

An hour later, they were aboard the shuttle to *Marathon*. Mouse was shaking. Beckhart was lost in dispatches that had come out aboard the cruiser. Amy had her eyes closed. She was pale and grim.

McClennon stared at her and mentally roamed fields of might-have-beens and should-have-dones. He had gotten her to admit an intellectual understanding of his actions. And her inability to differentiate between personal and social allegiances.

She could not see his betrayal of her people as impersonal. She wanted his feelings for her to have been an agent's play-acting.

Somehow, that would absolve her of complicity.

She was a self-torturer.

Could he criticize her? Or anyone else? He lived his life in a self-inflicted Iron Maiden.

He and Amy had been doomed from the beginning. His program's instability had made him a natural victim for her inadequacies. They had been too much alike. And she too much like the Alyce creature programmed as one of his triggers. Maybe his ideal woman was a Marya, a cold, gunmetal woman armored at the pain points. A woman with whom it was unnecessary to exchange emotional hostages.

Had he changed during this mission? People did, but usually too slowly to notice. He did not trust the changes he saw. Too many might be artificial.

The Psychs would sort him out. A small team had come out aboard *Marathon*. Maybe when they finished he would know who he really was. He was not sure he wanted to know.

BOOK THREE
STARS' END

TWENTY-ONE: 3050 AD
The Main Sequence

The lights came on. McClennon, Mouse, and Amy sat in silence. The tapes had been grotesque. Storm finally squeaked, "Admiral... That's really what we're up against?"

McClennon peered at Amy. She met his gaze for an instant. "Moyshe," she whispered, "I think I'm going to be sick."

"It is," Beckhart promised Mouse. "It's tough to swallow. Even when you're there yourself. All that ruthlessness, for no discernible purpose, only makes it more frightening"

McClennon took Amy's hand. It was cool. She was shaking. "You need something?"

"I'll be all right. Just give me a minute."

McClennon turned, "Admiral. I've seen that kind of ship before."

"What? Where? How?" Beckhart came toward McClennon like a tiger stalking game. He seemed to have caught a sudden fever. A haze appeared on his upper lip. "Where?" he breathed.

"The Seiners have one at their xeno-archaeological research facility. You remember, Amy? I asked if it had been built by an intelligent slug? The one nobody wanted to work."

"That's right. You're right, Moyshe, It was exactly like the ships in the tape."

"Tell me about it," Beckhart said.

"There isn't much to tell," McClennon replied. "The Seiners found it in the Nebula. They considered it comparatively modern. They found it surrounded by ships left behind by the people they think built Stars' End. The same people who, I think, built the base Darkside. They assumed the ship had been attacked by accident during the Ulantonid War. I said its crew might have been studying the ships belonging to the Stars' End race. That's all."

Beckhart became thoughtful. "That isn't all, Thomas. There's always more. You just don't know it. Is there a connection? Think about it. Stars' End might be more than just a handy arsenal."

Beckhart was talking to himself, not his audience. McClennon smiled. The Admiral was making the sort of random connections that, when they paid off, caused him to be so effective.

"Thomas, I want you and Amy to talk to Doctor Chancellor's people. They came off the Lunar digs. There might be an angle."

"They should get together with Amy's friend, Consuela el-Sanga. She's more knowledgeable than we are."

"Fine. Fine. We'll arrange that. Meantime, get your brains boiling. Open them up to unexpected possibilities... Tell you what. We'll have another little get-together after dinner. With them included. *Marathon* brought me some new material. I'll lay it out then."

McClennon caught a bleak note. "Bad, eh?"

"Worse than you've seen."

Beckhart used the evening session to present the report from the Ulantonid deep probe. Afterward, he asked, "Any speculations, people?"

The science people were guarded. They wanted more data. McClennon asked, "Did Luna Command run that through the big brain?"

"Yes. And it asked for more data too. I think it has a human bias built in. It wouldn't accept the numbers. It suggested that Commander Russell be replaced by somebody less inclined to exaggerate."

"Looks to me like there's enough data to draw some first

approximation inferences. Like, the Globular and war fleets represent an effort to destroy any present and potential sentience. It looks like an effort to eliminate competition and remodel the galaxy for the comfort of one race."

A scientist protested, "You can't draw those inferences. They're anthropocentric. It could just as well be a religious crusade."

"What?" Mouse snarled. "Don't be ridiculous."

"Easy, Mouse," Beckhart said, "No idea is too bizarre right now. The truth is going to be something off the wall. Brainstorm, people. Come up with as many ideas as possible, then winnow them as we accumulate more data. We shouldn't use the facts to build something acceptable. The truth may not be."

The scientists were becoming restive. Beckhart continued, "One unpalatable fact that jumps right out is that they're going to try to destroy us. Add to that their incredible numbers. Add to that the fact that the Globular is forty thousand years away. People, I think we've found us a war that will last forever."

McClennon could not handle the numbers. Forty thousand years? Eight times as long as recorded history? That was one long-term operation.

The other side had been involved for the gods only knew how long already. Millions of years?

The oddities of the alien base on the moon's dark side, the abandoned ships in Three Sky, and Stars' End itself, seemed a little less strange when seen in that light. Presuming the mysterious builders had been enemies of the centerward race, their works might constitute a counter-operation of equally cosmic scale. He tried to tote up a picture based on known factors. It did not scan. There were too many questions. What was the role of the Sangaree? What had become of the builders?

Mouse leaned his way. "This is a little much for me, Tommy. I'm just a simple-minded soldier."

McClennon grinned. "I'll go along with the simple-minded." He had spent the afternoon with a Psych team. They had performed wonders. He felt content and optimistic.

Mouse was out of sorts. He had come off The Broken Wings moody and uncommunicative. The definitive proof was that the science team boasted several attractive women. None had yet been honored by the swoop of the eagle. Amy had mentioned it in one of her friendlier moments. McClennon had not noticed it himself.

"You going to be in the mood for a game after this?" McClennon asked. Mouse had not shown much interest in chess lately, either.

"I don't think so. What's going on?" A petty officer was whispering to the Admiral.

Beckhart announced, "The Sangaree just left Stars' End. They left the McGraws to the Starfishers." He smiled. "Looks like the incidence of piracy may fall off."

"What will they do?" McClennon asked.

"We don't know. Let's hope they give it a good think. I left Strehltsweiter with a message for her bosses. Maybe Homeworld will make them listen."

"What kind of message?" Mouse demanded.

"I told them to change their ways. I said I'm not interested in wiping them out, but I will if they don't shape up. I told them I could repeat the lesson at Osiris if they insist. I let her think we know where Osiris is, too."

"Do you?" Thomas asked.

"No. I lie a lot."

For the next week McClennon split his time between the Psych and scientific teams. The Psych sessions bled the pressure off his chaotic mind. Gradually one personality—McClennon—took hold. He suffered only one minor episode.

Marathon dropped hyper off Three Sky. Signals from von Drachau's *Lepanto* indicated that she and her escort had penetrated the Yards. There had been a few skirmishes, but nothing serious. The Starfishers were talking, but stalling.

The Admiral observed, "Gruber is trying to fox us. He's sitting tight at Stars' End. Know what he's doing? Betting to an inside straight. He's thinking, if he can pull some of those weapons out quick enough, he can turn the tables on us."

Beckhart thereupon demonstrated his proconsular power. He contacted the Seiner leadership, told them the time. He designated it as launch minus twenty-five hours. He ordered the channel kept open and the countdown broadcast at five-minute intervals. Incoming traffic was to be recorded and otherwise ignored. Requests for delays and further negotiations consequently fell on deaf ears.

At launch minus two hours twelve minutes the Seiners of Three Sky surrendered unconditionally. Fleet Marines began occupying key installations immediately.

Beckhart summoned McClennon. "Thomas, we've finished twisting their arms here. Find your lady and ask her if she's going or staying. We space for Stars' End in one hour."

"Yes sir. Sir, I just came through Communications. The Sangaree raidfleet is still headed for Homeworld."

"Good. We'll be able to release a few squadrons, then." His eyes went glassy. "The big strike is getting closer. The Blues have picked their spot. We're waiting till the other side walks into it. Find your lady."

Amy was easily found. She would not leave her cabin unless dragged. He knocked. "It's McClennon," he said. "The Admiral sent me."

She seldom talked to him unless under pretext of business.

"What does he want?"

"We're spacing for Stars' End. You want to stay here, or go along?"

"They gave up?"

"They didn't have much choice."

She sighed. "Moyshe, I try hard to understand what's happening. But I can't. Do you think he'll keep his word?"

"I don't know. I really don't. We'll find out the hard way. He'll leave people here to establish the new order. I wish I could find out what their instructions are. What are you going to do? You have to decide quick. We're ready to leave."

"I'm going to Stars' End. Consuela is out there. They made her head of the whole team."

"Well, good for her." He did not depart immediately. She refused the opportunity he offered.

It keeps right on hurting, he thought as he stalked along the passageway. She won't even try to understand.

After relaying Amy's decision, he went looking for his partner.

He found Mouse in the wardroom, staring mindlessly into a

holovision cube. He sat, "What's the matter, old buddy? Want to talk?"

Reluctantly, Mouse killed the holoshow. "Not yet, Tommy. I'm not ready."

"All right. You noticed that little blonde Lieutenant from Weapons? Tanni Something."

"From B Missiles? Primo stuff. Looks like she'd turn a man every way but loose. There's something about the little ones…"

"They say she's a Scorpio."

Mouse laughed. "You didn't fix me up, did you?" Mouse had been known to opine that Scorpio women were the hottest in the known universe. McClennon could not get him to elucidate the workings of a geocentric astrology transferred to Outworlds skies.

"Not exactly. I asked a few questions. I figured the answers might pique your interest."

"I'm interested. That little bomb is ready to go off. You can tell just by the way she moves. Blow in her ear and you're liable to start something five guys couldn't handle. But I'm also not interested. If you know what I mean."

"No. I don't. You've been celibate for a month. I thought I'd see entropy shift into reverse first."

"I got things to work out, Tommy. Can we drop it?"

"If you want. We're heading for Stars' End." As if to back him up, the ship's hyper alarm sounded

"I heard they finally gave in."

"Now all we've got to do is impress Gruber."

"The Old Man will find a way."

"He always does, doesn't he?"

"Tommy, what do you think our chances are?"

"What?"

"Our chances of coming through this thing with these centerward creatures."

"We'll never know, Mouse. It's going to go on for a long time. Our great-grandchildren's great-grandchildren are going to be fighting this war. And it's a sad thing."

"Sad? How so?"

"It may destroy us. As a race. I don't mean destroy like wipe us out. I mean put an end to what makes us what we are. I've been thinking about it a lot. You know how I get."

"You think too much." Mouse smiled.

"The human race is crazy, see. No two of us are alike. And when we form up in mobs, no two mobs are alike. We're always flying off in a skillion different directions. Everybody doing their own thing. Every culture, too. And that's a survival trait, I think. There's almost a Darwinian thing with cultures. Some die out, and others come to life. There're always some on the way out and some on the way in. The thing is, there're always a lot of different ones around. When one goes down, there's always another there to take its place."

"I'm not following you," Mouse said in a slightly amused tone. "What's that got to do with anything?"

"Look, this centerward race… To fight it we're going to have to pull together. Generation after generation. Like an anthill. We're going to turn into a warfare race. Our whole focus will be the struggle. Kids will be born to a system that will turn them into the best soldiers possible. If they're survivors, they'll work their way up and get old in harness. They'll have kids of their own, who will follow in their footsteps. After a few generations nobody will know there's any other way of life. And then, in a way, we'll be just like the things we're fighting. The diversity will be gone. And we'll be trapped in a dead end. Because every culture is a dead end eventually. I mean, what does a warfare society do after it polishes off its last enemy? Turn on itself?"

Mouse looked at him askance. "You do worry yourself about some strange things, my friend."

"I think it's a valid concern. I think we should start taking the long view now and try to retain all the diversity we can."

"So write a report suggesting a study."

"I think I will."

"It won't matter much when they wipe us out, Tommy. And from where I sit, that looks inevitable. All we can do is delay it. That'll be like trying to keep the river from getting to the sea by bailing it with a teacup."

"Maybe. Maybe."

The ship shuddered. It seemed to twist away around them.

Marathon was on her way to Stars' End, that legendary, inviolable, virgin goddess of a fortress world that had intrigued a half dozen races for countless centuries.

TWENTY-TWO: 3050 AD
The Main Sequence

Marathon dropped hyper ten days after departing Three Sky. She cruised norm thirty hours before being joined by the heavy squadrons from The Broken Wings. Beckhart was afraid Gruber might still need convincing.

"There're a hundred harvestships there," Amy protested. "You know how big they are, Moyshe. Plus all the service ships. What makes anybody think a few dozen Navy ships could whip them? The whole Sangaree raidfleet couldn't."

"I hope you don't have to find out."

Mouse explained, "These ships were built for that kind of thing, Amy. All they can do is destroy. Especially the Empire Class. Other ships. Orbital fortresses. Cities on the ground. They were built to chew them up. What you Starfishers have is a bunch of ships built to do other things. Their guns were hung on them as an afterthought. Your harvestships were put together in jumbles, just growing, never designed for any special purpose."

"I still think you're all overconfident."

Both Thomas and Mouse shrugged. McClennon said, "You could be right. We're supposed to believe we're invincible." He glanced at Mouse. "Maybe that's why this centerward thing is so oppressive. It shakes our faith."

They were in *Marathon*'s wardroom. Most of the science team were there too. The countdown to hyper drop had declined past the ten-minute mark. People with no duty assignment had gathered to look at what McClennon called a thirty-first-century war god.

An untouchable world. A dead metal machine voice that shrieked against the big night, threatening anyone who came near. Stars' End. The arsenal of yesterday, more securely defended than the virtue of any medieval virgin.

"You don't need to worry," McClennon said. "If there were any chance of trouble, we wouldn't be sitting around here. We'd be on battle stations."

"The Weapons people aren't on alert," Mouse said. He was staring at a small blonde woman wearing Weapons insignia over her Lieutenant's stripes. "Watch how she moves, Tommy."

McClennon smiled. "I think he's coming around. The tomcat is coming through."

Mouse reddened slightly.

"Jesus," McClennon said softly. "You? Embarrassed?"

"I don't know, Tommy. It seems like I've changed a little. I don't understand myself."

"One minute to hyper drop," a remote voice announced. It drowned in the chatter of the wardroom.

Beckhart and the chiefs of the science team stalked in and took seats near the holo globe that had been set up at the compartment's center.

"Looks smug, don't he?" McClennon said.

The wardroom fell silent. *Marathon* dropped hyper. In moments a featureless ball filled the holo globe. Surrounding details appeared as the ship's sensors picked them up. First came the escort vessels, then the harvestfleets, then vistas of lifeless wreckage left by the fighting with Sangaree and McGraws. The planet, though, showed no changes.

McClennon had seen it before. He was not amazed. The builder race had removed any topography Stars' End may have had. It was a world machined smooth.

"Like a big-ass cue ball," Mouse murmured.

"It doesn't look so friendly when it opens up," Thomas said.

He shuddered, remembering. "It gets what looks like a sudden case of acne…"

Someone sat down beside him, At the same moment he saw a Communications messenger whisper to Beckhart and pass a flimsy. What was it? he wondered.

"Commander McClennon?"

He glanced to the side and found himself face to face with the little blonde Weapons officer. "Yes," he gulped, taken aback.

"Hi, I'm Tanni Lowenthal. Weapons." She wriggled her diminutive derriere a centimeter closer.

Mouse chuckled. Thomas turned. Storm's attention seemed inalterably fixed on the holo globe. As was Amy's, though color was climbing her throat.

"What can I do for you?" Thomas asked.

"Nothing. I just wanted to meet you. Someone said you were you, so I thought I would introduce myself. You're famous, you know." She laid a hand on his. It was small and hot and felt strong. He nearly jerked away.

Mouse made a small sound again.

"It's really strange, isn't it?" the woman asked. "Stars' End, I mean."

"Very. Especially when it's in a bad mood."

"Oh. That's right. You were here before, weren't you? When you were with the Starfishers."

The conversation lasted only a few minutes. The woman abruptly said, "That's my cue. Off to the salt mines. Bye." She squeezed his hand and looked him directly in the eye for a second.

"Bye." Baffled, he looked around to see what had happened during his distraction.

Beckhart, apparently, had announced something. He had missed it. "What was that, Mouse?"

"The Seiners have it open already. We can send our people down right away." Storm was fighting laughter. He nodded toward Tanni's departing figure. "That's what you get for asking questions, Tommy. The word gets back."

Amy glared into the globe. Her jaw was tight. Her face was red. Smoke seemed about to pour from her ears. "How did that half-witted sex machine ever earn a commission?" she demanded.

Still grinning, Mouse said, "She's probably quite competent at what she does."

"I don't doubt it a bit. She looks the type."

Mouse made a little wave signal to tell McClennon to make himself scarce. Amy was ready for a scene. A scene she had no right to make, inasmuch as she had declared her relationship with McClennon void.

McClennon rose and moved nearer the Admiral. When he had a chance, he asked, "Will I be able to go down? Just to poke around?"

Beckhart looked thoughtful. "I suppose. It seems safe. They've been down for a week and nothing's happened. But wait till the science people are all down. Ask Amy to see me in my office later, will you? I think I've got a liaison job for her."

"Yes sir." He wandered back to Mouse and Amy. Storm had calmed her down. He was still grinning.

"Tommy, I think I'll take you up on that game you've been talking about. You see a table?" The new was wearing off. Ship's crew were drifting out.

"Over there. Amy, the boss wants you to come to his office when you get a chance."

He and Mouse pushed through the crowd and seized a pair of table seats. Mouse produced his portable chess set.

"I wish you'd wipe that smirk off your face. Makes you look like an idiot."

"I can't help it, Tommy. It's really funny, the way she zeroed in. Isn't she something?"

"No doubt about that. I'm wondering what."

"I couldn't decide if you were going to attack her right there or have a stroke. You can find out what, you know. She told you who she was and where to find her. Now it's your move."

Science team people began descending to the planet next working day. The afternoon of the same day witnessed the arrival aboard of a company of stone-faced Seiner dignitaries. Mouse and McClennon were assigned to make them welcome. Amy turned out to help.

Mouse asked, "What's that you're wearing?"

"My dress uniform."

"What dress uniform?"

"My police uniform. Your Admiral had it flown over during the night."

McClennon observed, "I didn't know you had one. I've known you a year and a half and never saw you wear it."

"That's where we went wrong, Moyshe. We spent all that time hiding."

He expected a difficult, delicate afternoon. He did not argue. "You may be right." He scanned a list on a clipboard. "How many of these people do you know?"

She scanned it too. "Only a few, by reputation. Gruber. Payne. They're all Fleet and Ship's Commanders."

Over a hundred names were on the list. "Mouse, we can't give them all honors." He glanced at the sideboys waiting to pipe the visitors aboard.

"No shit. It'd be tomorrow before we finished."

Amy had seen enough of the back and forth of senior Navy officers to know what they were talking about. "Don't bother," she suggested. "We don't do that kind of thing. They wouldn't know what it was. Just be polite."

Mouse went to talk it over with the chief petty officer in charge of the sideboys. McClennon stood with Amy, studying his list in order to avoid eye contact.

"You look good in that uniform," she said softly. "All those medals…"

"Beckhart likes to hand them out."

"You'll get another for this business?"

"Probably."

"Moyshe… Something I should tell you. When I said we were hiding from each other… I was hiding from you. And fooling myself. The reason I was so eager to throw a net on you…"

He glanced at her. She was showing a lot of color. "Yes?"

"It's embarrassing. I don't like myself very much when I think about it."

"Well? I don't like the things I've done, either."

"I was the Ship's Commander's special agent. I was supposed

to keep an eye on you and report to him. Because he wanted to make you into the head of a Starfisher secret service. That meant you were going to be important. I wasn't important. I wasn't ever going to be. The only way I could have gone any higher was if Jarl died or left *Danion*."

McClennon saw what she was trying to say. "It's all right. I understand. And now I know why you did so many things I thought were strange."

"Moyshe…"

"Forget it. We've got pain enough. Don't drag up any old stuff."

A red light came on over the lock housing. The ship-wide address system announced the arrival of the visitors' shuttle. It admonished all hands to remain courteous and helpful in every circumstance. The lock cycled. A great burly bear of a man stepped inside. He looked around as if expecting to be assaulted by the legions of the damned.

"Gruber," Amy whispered.

"Get him, Mouse," Thomas said.

"Me?"

"You got more balls and more suave than me." Mouse introduced himself as Captain Storm of Admiral Beckhart's staff. He introduced Thomas and Amy, then asked the Fishers to follow them.

The sideboys stood at superb, perfectly matched attention while the Seiners disembarked.

The Marine sentries at the wardroom door were military perfectionists too. They snapped to present arms.

Admiral Beckhart was waiting inside. He wasted little time introducing himself, or excusing himself for having assembled them virtually at gunpoint. He presented the Ulantonid tapes. While they ran, Mouse and McClennon passed out copies of the known data on the centerward threat. Amy distributed copies of the tapes.

The lights came up. Beckhart said, "Gentlemen, you've just seen the reason for our unfriendly behavior. I'll now answer any questions. Doctor Chancellor, Captain McClennon, Captain Storm, and your own Lieutenant Coleridge will also speak with anyone who likes."

McClennon was amazed by the reserve of the Seiner leaders. Even the worst tape scenes caused no stir. They remained obstinately uncommunicative.

Danion's Ship Commander isolated Amy. They fell into heated discussion. The others asked only a few questions while Amy's interrogator worked, then conferred with Payne and Gruber.

The Fishers ignored Storm and McClennon completely.

Replying to a Gruber query, Beckhart said, "We'll be completely open with the available data. In accordance with High Command directives, you've received copies of almost everything. The centerward race threatens all of us."

McClennon told Mouse, "Ever notice the Old Man's split personality? He's three different people, depending on who he's talking to."

Mouse smiled. "We all are. More than three, usually. He's just obvious."

"Think they're buying it?"

"Payne's people are. Most of the others aren't. Gruber looks like he'll give us the benefit of the doubt." He picked lint off his dress black tunic. "We're victims of our reputation. They can't believe we're being straight."

Gruber proved willing to listen. That willingness extended the session for hours. Stewards came in, set up tables, served a meal.

Gruber finally seemed satisfied. His sub-chieftains began filing out, following Mouse to the lock.

Amy walked with McClennon. Starting at the desk, she said, "I'm going back to *Danion* now."

"Okay."

"Moyshe… I'm sorry."

"I am too, Amy. About everything. I never wanted to hurt you."

"Stay happy, Moyshe."

"You too."

She was the last Seiner into the lock. Mouse turned to McClennon. Thomas nodded.

Mouse ordered the lock cycled.

"Think it went over?" McClennon asked.

"I don't know, Tommy. I don't… Tommy? What's the matter? Chief, help me here. Stretcher. Somebody get a stretcher."

The episode was McClennon's worst yet. It took the Psych team three days to bring him out.

It had surprised him completely.

TWENTY-THREE:
3050 AD
The Main Sequence

"I don't think you should go, Thomas," the Admiral said. "Let Mouse handle it. Suppose you had one of your attacks?"

"I'll be all right. Look. Ask Lieutenant Corley. She says it'll take a week to reach another crisis point."

"Mouse?"

"Somebody has to look over their shoulders, right? Otherwise we won't know if they're getting anywhere. That's just the way those people are. They're not going to say anything till they're sure nobody can shoot them down. Scientists would rather be dragged through the streets naked than be wrong. If Tommy goes, we'll have twice as many eyes."

"All right. Thomas, you know the woman who heads the Seiner team. Talk to her. Take a recorder. I want to hear what she says."

Twelve hours later McClennon and Storm, accompanied by a pair of Marine sergeants, entered the cold metal halls of Stars' End. The dock ring of their landing bay was a good twenty kilometers below the featureless planetary surface. The plunge down the long, dark shaft had been harrowing. Mouse had lost his supper.

The Marines began horsing an electric truck off the shuttle.

Mouse walked along a steel passageway, away from the dock ring. He peered into what had to have been Ground Control in an age gone by. "Tommy, come take a look in here."

McClennon had to stoop beneath the passageway ceiling. He joined Storm. "What?" He saw nothing but a Marine sentry.

"By that console thing."

"Oh. A skeleton."

The reports said bones could be found throughout the fortress. Thousands of skeletons had been encountered.

"We're ready, sir," one of the Marines said.

McClennon snapped a picture of the bones. "All right. Mouse, let's hit Research Central first."

"Right. We'll probably get everything there anyway."

"Be charming. Consuela el-Sanga looks vulnerable."

"Am I ever anything else?"

The little truck streaked through the endless halls, down ramps, around perilous turns, ever deeper into the metal world. The Marine driver fled on as if being pursued by the shades of the builders. He shuddered visibly each time they encountered one of the skeletons. They passed through one chamber where a score of the builder folk had died.

"The bones that have touched and shaped our lives," Thomas said. "From afar, like virgin princesses."

"You getting poetic again?"

"I do when I'm depressed." He glanced at the Marines. They stared forward impassively. "And this place is depressing." The soldiers seemed to have come out of a robot factory. They had shown no reaction to the Admiral's tapes.

The driver's suicidal rush was the only evidence that either man was disturbed.

The truck swooped into a level with ceilings vaulting a hundred meters high. Brobdingnagian machines crowded it, rising like the buildings of an alien city. There was life here, and light, but it was all machine.

"I wonder what they are."

"Accumulators for the energy weapons," Mouse guessed.

"Some of them. Some of them must be doing something with the air."

"Look!" Mouse squealed. "Sergeant, stop. Back up. Back up. A little more. Look up there, Tommy. On the fourth catwalk up."

McClennon spotted the androgynous little machine. It was busy working on the flank of one of the towering structures. "A maintenance robot."

"Yeah. All right, Sergeant. Go ahead."

They descended more levels, some as high-ceilinged as that of the robot. They saw more of the mobile machines, built in a dozen different designs.

Obviously, only the builders had perished. Their fortress was very much alive and healthy. Storm and McClennon saw no evidence of breakdown.

"It's like walking through a graveyard," Mouse said, after their driver had had to wend his way across a vast, open floor where hundreds of skeletons lay in neat rows. "Chilling."

"Know what, Mouse? I think this is really a pyramid. It's not a fortress at all."

"You're not serious."

"Why not? Think about it. Can you think of any strategic reason for putting a world fort out here?"

"Sure."

"Such as?"

"Right over there are the Magellanic Clouds. Sic somebody on me willing to spend a few hundred millennia conquering the galaxy and chasing me, and I'd build me an all-time fort across my line of retreat before I jump off for a friendlier star-swarm."

"Now who's getting romantic?"

"Romantic, hell."

"They could just go around it, Mouse."

"That centerward mob don't go around anything. They'd just stay here till they cracked it open."

"Maybe you're right, but I'm going to stick to my theory."

They reached the research center a few minutes later. McClennon located Consuela el-Sanga almost immediately, and found her completely free of animosity. He was surprised.

"Why?" she asked. "I'm no Seiner. I'm just one of their captive scientists."

"I didn't know." He introduced Mouse. He wondered if Consuela had heard from Amy.

"Moyshe… That wouldn't be right, would it?"

"McClennon. Thomas. But call me whatever's comfortable."

"Thomas, this is the most exciting time of my life. We can finally compare notes with your people… It's like opening up a whole new universe. Come on. Let me show you what we're doing." Her walk had a youthful bounce despite the higher than Seiner-normal gravity.

Mouse's eyebrows rose questionably. McClennon shrugged. "Come on. Before she changes her mind."

A horde of people were at work in a nearby chamber, where hundreds of folding tables had been arrayed in long rows. Most were burdened with artifacts, papers, or the tools of the scientists and their helpers. To one side technicians were busy with communicators and a vast, waist-level computer interface.

Consuela explained, "The people at the tables are examining and cataloging artifacts. We brought along several thousand laymen to help explore. Whenever they make a find, they notify comm center. We send an expert to examine the site. The confab over there is an ongoing exchange with your Lunar dig people. The people at the console are trying to reprogram Stars' End's master brain so it can deal directly with human input."

"You found a key to the builder language?" Thomas asked.

"No. That will come after we can talk to the computer."

"You just lost me. That sounds backwards."

"It works like this: The starfish commune with the machine. They relay to our mindtechs. The mindtechs relay to our computer people. They build parallel test programs. Communications send them down. Our computer people here try to feed it back to the master brain. The starfish read the response and feed it to the mindtechs again. And round the circle. The idea is to help the computers develop a common language. So far we've only managed a pidgin level of communication. We think we're on the brink of breakthrough, though."

"Math ought to be a snap," Mouse said. "It's got to be the

same all over the universe. But I can see how you'd have trouble working toward more abstract concepts."

"Unfortunately, we're using a non-mathematical interface," Consuela replied. "The starfish aren't mathematically minded. Their conscious concept of number is one-two-three-many."

"Thought you said they were smart, Tommy."

Consuela said, "They are. But theirs is an intuitive rather than empirical intelligence. But we're making headway. When our computers can link..."

"Be careful," McClennon admonished. "Be very, very careful."

"Why?"

"This is the boss machine, right?"

"So the fish say."

"Okay. That makes it big and powerful. It might be playing games with you. It's insane."

"Come on," Mouse protested. "How can a machine go crazy?"

"I don't know. I do know I was in Contact during the first battle. I got a little direct touch. It was plain out of its micro-electronic mind. I'd be afraid it could use its capacity to seize control of my own command computers."

"He's right, Captain. Thomas, we know. It's a real problem. Most of the starfish are riding herd on its psyche. Only a few are helping communicate. It seems to have several psychological problems. Loneliness. A god complex. A deeply programmed xenophobia and bellicosity... It is, after all, the directing intelligence of a weapons system."

"A defensive weapon," McClennon suggested. "Mouse laughed at this. But think about it. Is Stars' End a pyramid?"

"I don't understand."

"I'm going to wander around," Mouse said. "Don't run off without me, Tommy,"

"I won't. By pyramid I mean it serves the same function as Old Earth's Egyptian pyramids."

"A tomb? I don't think so. The idea isn't new, but it's been mostly a metaphor."

"Assume the builders knew... You don't have all the data." He explained about the centerward race and his suspicion that the builder race had been fleeing it. "Okay. They come to the end of the road. There's nowhere to run, unless they jump off for the Magellanic Clouds. I think they gave up. I think they stopped, built themselves a pyramid, put their treasures inside, and died out."

Miss el-Sanga smiled. "A romantic theory that fits the known facts. And a few you've conjured up, I think. Ingenious, Thomas. I suppose we'll be able to answer you when we complete contact with the master control."

A boyhood incident came to mind. He had discovered—independently, so far as he could discern later—that A squared plus B squared equaled C squared. He had been excited till he had explained it to a friend. The friend had laughed and told him that Pythagoras had crossed the finish line thirty-five hundred years ahead of him.

He felt the same deflation now.

"I hear you and Amy broke up."

"Yes. I didn't realize you knew."

"She called yesterday. She was very depressed about it."

"She took something personal that wasn't."

"That was the feeling I got. Her story was one-sided, but I got the impression you were trying to do what was right for everybody."

"I tried. I don't know how successful I was."

"You two shouldn't have gotten involved in the first place. Landsmen and Seiners don't speak the same language. I've been with them thirty-six years and I still have problems."

"We were both looking for something. We were too eager to grab it."

"I've been through that, too."

"Help her, will you? I never meant to hurt her."

"I will. And don't feel so guilty. She's more resilient than she pretends. She likes the attention."

"I thought you were friends."

"She was a lot more than a friend for a while, Captain. Till she met Heinrich Cortez."

"Oh."

"Hey, Tommy!" Mouse bore down on them like a mini-juggernaut. "Come here." He about-turned and steamed a reverse course.

"Excuse me, Consuela." He chased Mouse down. "What?"

Mouse stopped. "I just talked to a gal who's doing the same thing for the Fishers that we're doing for Beckhart. She was pissed. These clowns, some of them, have been here for ten days. The Fishers have eight thousand people down already. And they haven't even started looking at weapons systems. They don't even care. All they want to do is collect broken toothbrushes and sort old bones."

"They'll get to it, Mouse. You've got to give them a chance to let the new wear off. And they've got to get a dialogue going with the master control. If they manage that, it'll save time. In the long run. The machine can redesign the weapons for us. That would save ripping the old ones out of here, orbiting them, then building ships around them."

Mouse calmed himself. "Okay. Maybe you're right. But I still don't like to see *everybody* doing something else when weapons are the reason we're all here."

"What if the weapons technology requires other preexisting technologies?"

"What do you mean?"

"Go back a hundred years. Build me a pulse-graser with the technology available then. You couldn't do it. You'd have to create the technology to create the technology to construct the pulse accumulators. Right?"

"Sometimes I don't like you a whole lot, Tommy." Mouse grinned. "I'll tell the Seiner lady to be patient."

"If the Captains will excuse me?" The senior of their Marine custodians approached them.

"Yes, Sergeant?" Thomas asked.

"The Admiral's compliments, sirs, and he needs you back aboard ship immediately."

"What is it?"

"He didn't say, sir. He said to tell you it's critical."

Mouse looked puzzled. McClennon was very much so.

The news hit the busy chamber before they departed.

The starfish had had a brief skirmish with sharks. Hordes of the predators had appeared. A continuous stream were still arriving.

"Holy shit!" Thomas said. "I'd forgotten about them."

"They didn't forget us," Mouse grumbled. "Damnation!"

People swirled this way and that. The mood approached panic. Doctor Chancellor rushed over. "I heard you're going up. Take this to the Admiral, just in case." He shoved a folder into McClennon's hands. "Thank you." He dashed toward the team working at the computer. They were trying to prepare an instantaneous shutdown of the round-robin should the sharks attack.

"They should tell the idiot box to scrub the problem for them," Mouse said as they pulled away. "What did he give you?"

"His notes. They look like a cross between a journal and regular scientific notation."

"Give me some of those."

Their driver flew around worse than he had coming the other direction.

"Here's an interesting one," Mouse said. "No furniture."

"What?"

"The exploration teams haven't found any furniture. There goes your pyramid theory."

"He's right. I didn't see anything but machinery. The bodies are all laid out on the floor."

"Maybe they're invaders too?"

McClennon shrugged. "Here's one that will grab you. How big do you think Stars' End is?"

"Uhm... Venus size?"

"Close. Earth minus two percent. But the planetary part is smaller than Mars. The rest is edifice."

"What?"

"His word. I'll give you the question. Since most of the structural volume would be hollow, how come the place has so much gravity? It's a couple points over Earth normal."

Mouse sneered. "Come on, Tommy. Maybe it's the machines."

"Nope. You're going to love it. According to this, the builders, before they started building, took a little planet and polished it smooth. Then they plated it with a layer of neutronium. The fortress structure floats around on the neutronium, which may be a cushion against tectonic activity."

"Whoa!" Mouse clung to the truck as its driver made a violent turn. "How did they stabilize the neutronium?"

"Figure that out, and how they mined it in the first place, and you and me will get rich."

"What's the kicker?"

"He doesn't have one here. I think it's implied. I didn't see anything at the Lunar digs or Three Sky that would suggest that level of technology."

"So the little people *are* interlopers. Just like us."

"Maybe." McClennon had an image of Bronze Age barbarians camped in the street of a space age city.

"Keep talking. I don't want to think about the fly up."

A Navy Lieutenant awaited them at *Marathon*'s ingress lock. "If you'll follow me, sirs?"

The Admiral awaited them on the bridge. "Ah. Thomas. I was beginning to wonder."

"Is it critical, sir? We haven't slept for ages."

"It's critical. But the Seiners say it doesn't look like it'll break right away. Rest up good before you go over."

"Over?"

"I'm sending you to *Danion*. I want you to go into link and give *Assyrian* and *Prussian* a fire control realtime."

"You have got to be kidding."

"Why? My calculations show them capable of cleaning up that little mess out there. It's a chance to show Gruber what can happen if he gets tricky."

"Point. Sir, you're over-optimistic. Sharks are super deadly. They throw anti-hydrogen when they get mad. Second point. Why me? A Seiner mindtech could do the job, and probably better. They're better trained."

"I want you. I don't want some Seiner who'll adjust the data to make us look bad."

"I have to go?"

"It's an order."

"Then make it another ship. I'm liable to get lynched aboard *Danion*."

"*Danion* is Gruber's choice. That's the ship we know. He has secrets too."

"Thanks a lot. Sir."

Mouse stage-whispered, "The ship's Legal Officer would back you if you want to refuse. You don't have to work when you're under arrest."

"I got troubles enough without getting the Old Man mad at me. Madder at me."

Beckhart glared at Mouse. "You're going with him, son. Head bodyguard. Take your two Marines. Tommy, if it will make you more comfortable, stay with the Psych people till time to go."

"I will."

Danion had not changed—except there were no friendly faces aboard now. Amy met them at the ingress lock. A squad of grim-faced Security people accompanied her. She installed the party aboard a convoy of small vehicles.

People spat and cursed as they passed.

"Tell me something," Mouse said. "How come everybody knows we're here?"

"This isn't Navy," Amy replied curtly.

"You keep on and I won't make love to you anymore." Mouse laughed when she turned to glare at him.

"Easy, boy," McClennon said. "We've got to get out of here alive."

Something thrown whipped over their heads.

"Did you see that?" Mouse croaked. "That was Candy... She wanted to marry me."

"Amy, have you shown people those tapes?"

"What tapes?"

"The centerward..."

Mouse nudged him. "I smell a little political skulduggery, old friend. A little crafty censorship. Old Gruber is afraid he can't keep people cranked up if they find out what's really going on."

"You're not to discuss that," Amy said.

Mouse grinned. "Oh! The Saints forfend! Never, my dear. What are you going to do about it if I do?"

"I saw Consuela yesterday," McClennon said, heading them off.

Amy softened. "How was she?"

"Twenty years younger. Happy as a kid loose in a candy store. She's hoping you'll come down."

"You went?"

"Yesterday. It's interesting. But I don't think we'll get as many answers as questions."

The convoy entered Operations Sector. A huge door closed behind them, isolating them from the rest of the ship. Mouse wondered aloud why. No one answered him. McClennon's former tech team, Hans and Clara, awaited him. Their faces were not friendly, but were less inimical than any he had seen outside Operations. Clara even managed a smile.

"Welcome back, Moyshe. You even get your old couch."

"Clara, I want you to meet somebody before we start. You never got the chance. This is Amy."

Clara extended a hand. "Amy. I heard so much about you when Moyshe was with us."

McClennon removed his tunic, handed it to Mouse. The Marine sergeants considered the couch and its technical stations, posted themselves to either side, out of the way.

The Contact room had fallen silent. People stared. Obviously, no one had been warned that Contact expected visitors.

Thomas settled onto the couch. "Clara, I'm not sure I can do this anymore."

"You don't forget. Hans."

Hans said, "You let your hair grow, Moyshe. I'll have to gum it up good."

"Haven't had time for a haircut since we hit The Broken Wings." He shuddered as Hans began rubbing greasy matter into his scalp, and again when the youth slipped the hairnet device into place. A moment later the helmet devoured his head.

"There's a fish waiting, Moyshe," Clara said. "Just go on out. And good luck."

TSD took him. Then he was in the starfish universe.

Stars' End was a vast, milky globe surrounded by countless

golden footballs and needles. The three Empire Class warships became creeping vortices of color. They were at full battle stations already, with their heaviest screens up. Golden dragons slid across the distance, orbiting well beyond the ships.

And beyond the dragons, against the galaxy... "My God!" he thought.

He saw great shoals and thunderheads of red obscuring the jeweled kirtle of the galaxy. The sharks were so numerous and excited that he could not discern individuals.

"Yes, Moyshe man-friend. Will attack soon," a voice said inside his mind.

"Chub!"

"Hello. Welcome home. I see by your mind many more adventures lived, Moyshe man-friend. I see doors opened where once shadows lay."

"What in heaven... You've changed, Chub. You've become poetic."

Windchime laughter tinkled through his mind. "Have been so lucky, Moyshe man-friend. First a spy linker who taught jokes, then a she linker filled with poetry."

McClennon felt the starfish reaching deep within him, ferreting through the hidden places, examining all the secrets and fears it had not been able to reach before. "You remember fast, Moyshe man-friend."

On cue, an outside voice said, "Linker, Communications. We have an open channel to *Assyrian* and *Prussian* Fire Control. Please inform us when you're ready to begin."

Fear stalked through McClennon. The starfish reached in and calmed him. "I'm ready now," he replied.

He listened in as *Danion*'s communications people closed their nets and linked with the dreadnoughts. He heard the chatter as the Navy and Seiner fleets went on battle alert. From his outside viewpoint he watched screens develop around the Navy ships. The two giant warships began creeping toward the shark storm.

The sharks sensed the attack before it arrived. Suddenly, they were flashing everywhere, trying to reach their attackers and the ships behind them.

McClennon felt the flow from Chub go through his mind into *Danion*. He saw the response of *Assyrian* and *Prussian*. Their weapons ripped the very fabric of space. Sharks by the hundred died.

And by dozens and scores they slipped past and hurled themselves at the massed ships around Stars' End.

In ten minutes space was aglow from the energies being expended. And ten minutes later still McClennon began to feel bleak, to despair. When he recognized the mood's source, he asked, "Chub, what's the matter?"

"Too many sharks, Moyshe man-friend. Attacking was mistake. Even the great ships-that-kill of your people will not be able to endure."

McClennon studied the situation. Space was scarlet, yes, but he saw no sure indicators of defeat.

Still, starfish could intuit developments before even the swiftest human-created computer.

He began to see it fifteen minutes later. Whole packs of sharks were suiciding in the warships' screens, gradually overloading them. They were doing it to every ship. Near Stars' End at least a dozen vessels were aflame with the fire that could burn anywhere, as anti-matter gasses slowly annihilated the metal of their hulls.

It got worse.

"Moyshe?" Clara's voice seemed to come from half a galaxy away. "You've been in a long time. Want to come out?"

"No. I'm doing fine."

"You're thrashing around a lot."

"It's all right. It's grim out here."

A driblet of fear was getting past Chub's sentinel effort. The starfish himself was in a state of agitation. His kind were being slaughtered.

It got worse.

Prussian was compelled to withdraw. The sharks redoubled their assault upon *Assyrian*. *Hapsburg* picked up the realtime link and replaced *Prussian*.

The Navy squadrons fared better than did the Starfisher harvestfleets. Their fire patterns were virtually impenetrable.

From somewhere, a voice screamed, "Breakthrough! Break-through!"

McClennon did not understand till much later. At the moment he thought it meant the sharks had managed their victory. It was not till Chub began exulting that he realized the tide had turned.

The sharks were turning on themselves, pairing off and fighting to the death in ponderous, savage duels. Winners searched for new victims. Here and there, a few began to flee.

Within half an hour the only red to be seen was that fading from fragments of dead shark. Space was aboil with the activity of the scavenger things that followed the sharks. Chub kept giggling like a teenager at a dirty joke. "We do it one more time, Moyshe man-friend. This time when impossible. And in grand style. Grandest style possible. Will make bet. Herd and harvestfleet will have no trouble from sharks again for age of man. So many died here…"

"Moyshe?" Clara said. "Still okay? I think we should bring you out. You've been under a long time."

A sadness came over McClennon. For an instant he could not identify its cause. Then he knew. Chub was sorry to see him go. The starfish knew that this time it would be forever.

"I don't know what to say, Chub. I already said good-bye once."

Chub tried a feeble joke. McClennon forced a charity laugh.

"Not so good?"

"Not so good. Remember me, Chub."

"Always. The spy man from the hard matter worlds will remain immortal in the memory of the herd. Stay happy, Moyshe man-friend. Remember, there is hope gainst the world-slayers too. The Old Ones tell me to tell you so. They are remembered from other galaxies. They have been stopped before."

"Other galaxies?"

"They come to all galaxies eventually, Moyshe man-friend. They are the tools of the First Race, the hard matter folk of the beginning. They do not grow old and die. They are not born as you, but in machine wombs from pieces of adults. They are created things. They do not reason as you. They know only their task."

McClennon felt the starfish struggling with concepts alien to the starfish mind. There was an aura of the extremely ancient in what the creature was trying to tell him. Chub seemed to be translating very old mood lore into the relative precision of modern human thought.

"They scourge the worlds that they might be prepared for the First Race, Moyshe man-friend. But the First Race is gone, and not there to take the worlds, nor to end the work of their tools. They were gone before the birth of your home star."

"Who built Stars' End? Do you know?"

"The little hard matter people, as you thought. Those whose bones you found. They were enemies of the First Race. They won that struggle, but still run from the tools of their foes."

"But..."

Chub knew his questions before he thought them. "They are old, too, Moyshe man-friend. They flee, and the killers-of-worlds pursue. This is not the first time they have passed through our galaxy. You do not know Stars' End. It is old, Moyshe man-friend. Older than the stones of Earth. The enemies of the world-slayers are but a ghost of what once was. They perish in flight, and decline, and always they leave their trail of traps for their foes. The herd knew them of old, Moyshe man-friend, in other ages, when the galaxies were young and closer together and our fathers swam the streams arching between them."

"You're getting poetic."

"The moods mesh, Moyshe man-friend. The moods mesh."

"Moyshe? You'd better not stay much longer." Clara's voice was more remote than ever. He began to feel her urgency.

"Linker? Communications. We're breaking lock."

"Linker, aye. Chub, I..."

"Coming to you, Moyshe man-friend. You will remember."

The starfish's message puzzled McClennon. He would remember what?

Something hit his mind. It was an overpowering wave. Panicking, he yanked upward on his escape switch. "Chub... My friend..." were his last screaming thoughts before the darkness took him.

Pain!

Overwhelming pain, worse than any migraine. His head was pulling itself apart.

He screamed.

"Hold him!" someone yelled.

He writhed against restraining arms. Something pierced his flesh. Warm relaxation radiated from that point: The pain began to lessen. Soon he could open his eyes and endure the light.

"Get back!" Clara snapped at someone. "Moyshe, how do you feel?"

"Like death warmed over. Over."

Though she looked relieved, she growled, "I told you to come out. Why didn't you?"

"Chub was telling me about Stars' End. End. About who built it, and about the centerward race. Race. It was important. Important."

"You pushed it too far."

"Give me another shot. Shot. I'll be all right. Right. How's the battle coming? Coming? What happened, anyway? Anyway?"

Hans held his arm while Clara gave him the second injection. The pain receded. It became a slight irritation over his eyes, like a sinus infection.

"They made the breakthrough with the Stars' End master control, Moyshe," Hans said. There wasn't the slightest animosity in the youth now. "You held them long enough. Once it found the key, it broke our language in seconds. It saw our problem. It did whatever it did about the sharks."

"What did it do? Do?"

Mouse stepped around where he could look into McClennon's eyes. "We were hoping you could tell us. You were out there."

"I didn't know what was happening. Happening. One minute we had no hope. Hope. The next minute the sharks sharks had been hit by a hurricane or something. Or something."

"The Empires didn't do so hot, eh?"

"They did magnificently. Better than all of Payne's Fleet Payne's Fleet did during the first battle. Battle. I think Gruber Gruber will be properly impressed. Impressed. There was just more there there than anybody expected. Expected."

Mouse frowned at him. He asked Clara, "Why is he doing that?"

"I don't know. I've never seen it before."

"Why am I doing what? What?"

"Echoing yourself."

"What do you mean? Mean?"

"How soon can we move him?" Mouse asked.

"Any time," Clara told him. "But he should stay here. Our medical people know how to handle mindtech problems."

"No. The Admiral wants him right back. Come on, Thomas. Feet on the floor. Let's see if you can stand."

"No problem. Problem." He was weak, but he could get around. Why were they all looking at him that way?

He began to remember.

"He told me I would remember. Remember."

"Who told you?" Mouse asked as he guided McClennon toward the door and conveyances waiting outside.

"Chub. The starfish. Fish. I'm beginning to. To. Mouse, I've got to see the Admiral. Admiral. I'm remembering everything the fish know about the centerward race and their enemies. Enemies." He turned. "Clara. It was good to see you again. Again. Hans. Be a good fellow. Mind your grandmother. Mother." He reached with his right hand. Surprised, Hans shook it.

"Of course, Moyshe. Good luck." He glanced at Clara.

The woman said, "Good luck, Moyshe. Maybe you'll surprise us again."

McClennon smiled weakly. "I hope not. Not. No more battles, anyway. Way. Mouse. Let's go. Go."

He was driven by anxiety. He wanted to report what he had learned before the memories slipped away.

Mouse stopped to talk to Amy before he boarded the shuttle. "Take care of yourself," he told her. "And be happy. What's happened wasn't your fault. You could say it was fate."

"I know, Mouse. But that doesn't make it hurt any less." She smiled wanly. "Greater destinies? It's probably for the best. Sorry I was such a bitch."

Mouse shrugged. "No problem. Take care."

"Take care of Moyshe." Mouse looked at her strangely.

"He's your friend, but he's the husband I'm going to remember." She leaned close, whispered, "Promise not to tell him till he's past the worst part. We've got a baby on the way."

"It's a promise. He doesn't need that on his mind too." Storm backed through the hatchway, waved, turned, found a seat. For a time he was too amazed to be disturbed by the fly.

McClennon sat opposite him, beside one of the Marines, writing furiously.

TWENTY-FOUR: 3051 AD
The Contemporary Scene

The Defender Prime of Ulant gave the order. The Climbers left their mother ships. Pursuit destroyers moved to positions in reserve-and-chase, ready to pounce on any courier or fugitive fleeing the battle. The Empires and Conquerors and their Ulantonid, Toke, Khar'mehl, and aChyfNth equivalents began to move. The cruisers, frigates, and bombards formed their holding screen. A gnatlike swarm of singleships put on inherent velocity preparatory to a lightning pass through the enemy, spewing energy and torpedoes and collecting to-the-minute intelligence for the Defender's master battle computers.

The centerward people were unsuspecting. Even the folk they were attacking had no idea that help had come.

Years of Ulantonid staff planning had gone into this action. It was their game. For the first time ever Confederation personnel were accepting orders from outside commanders. Even the Warriors of Toke set aside their pride and accepted direction from leaders more knowledgeable than they.

Twelve sovereign governments of five races were represented in the Allied fleet.

The Climbers materialized amid the enemy force. They expended their munitions stocks before their foes could react.

They returned to their mothers to rearm.

Seconds later the singleships dropped hyper.

It took a special breed to fight the one-man scout ships. Egoists, solipsists, men convinced of their own invulnerability. Men who could not be intimidated by the knowledge that they had virtually no defense but speed and violent maneuverability.

The singleships streaked through the centerward war-fleet, spewing their hunter missiles and flailing with their lone nose-mounted energy beams. For some speed proved a liability. There were so many enemy vessels, shifting in confusion, that there were collisions.

Data flowed to the computers of the Allied fleet. The size, disposition, orientation, vectors, and velocities of enemy units began to appear in the huge displays of the Defender's command and back-up command vessels. Ships and installations belonging to the race under attack were identified and tagged friendly. Enemy command ships were identified and targeted for special attention by the next Climber sortie.

The General Staff of Ulant had planned thoroughly and well. There were no unpleasant surprises.

The heavies closed and began pounding a technologically inferior enemy.

The advantages were all to the Allies. All but one.

They were outnumbered a hundred to one.

They were a single-minded folk, those centerward creatures. When unable to fight a ship any longer, they took to their shuttlecraft and tried to land on the planet. The handful who reached the surface looked for something to kill, and kept at it till something killed them. Aboard ship and on the ground they had only a limited concept of tactics.

Tactics were unnecessary when the only strategy needed was the application of overwhelming numbers.

They seemed unacquainted with fear, and constitutionally unable to retreat. They simply fought and died and let someone else take their place.

The only ships to leave the battle were couriers departing at ten-hour intervals.

The pursuit destroyers handled them, as well as couriers

coming in.

One by one, Allied warships were destroyed or injured beyond any capacity to continue fighting.

At hour forty of an action originally projected to endure about one hundred hours the Defender Prime instelled Ulant. She expressed her fear that her command was insufficient to fulfill its mission. Effective losses: twenty-four percent of commitment. Current estimated active ratios: 70-1 in the enemy's favor.

Her figures did not take into account displacements. Her ships were concentrating on the more important and dangerous enemy vessels. A significant percentage of the remaining ships were lightly armed troop transports.

The centerward people stubbornly insisted on devoting strength to their assault on the planet.

The Defender's pessimism was not unwarranted. Her one-hundred-hour report showed the Allied fleet over fifty percent neutralized. All missile stores had been expended. Breakdowns were claiming the energy weapons. She had lost the use of the last of her Climbers. Her crews were drained by exhaustion.

She disengaged.

The enemy ignored her departure. They closed ranks and continued their disrupted planetary assault.

The Defender received instructions to stand off and observe. Confederation was sending reinforcements. Convoys bearing munitions and repair spares were in space.

In the end, after a month of brutal fighting, the last centerward warship was annihilated. The Allied fleet returned home, to lick its wounds and reflect on the savagery of the encounter. The Defender departed without contacting the planets she had saved. She wanted no replacement enemy fleet finding any information on the mysterious rescuers.

A great victory, by numbers. A huge slaughter. But a Pyrrhic affair. The carefully husbanded and prepared strength of the Allies had been decimated.

At least four more warfleets were moving out The Arm. Nothing, really, had been won, except the knowledge that such a monster force could be overcome. The victory did not fill the several high commands with joy.

It simply unleashed an even more grim foreboding of things to come.

TWENTY-FIVE:
3050-3052 AD
The Main Sequence

McClennon had been relating his memories for months. "Christ, Mouse. I'm sick of it. Why can't people be satisfied with the deposition tapes?"

Mouse moved a pawn, trying to initiate a trade. "Because it's so damned fascinating. It's like meeting somebody who can wiggle his ears. You want to see him do his trick. I can't help it either. I wish I could get inside your head. Man, remembering what the galaxy looked like before Old Sol was formed…"

McClennon refused the trade. He moved a knight to support his own pawn, glanced at the time. "Four hours. I'm beginning to dread it. They'll do the whole debriefing routine. For two years of mission. And they'll stay on me about my starfish memories till they know the whole physical history of the universe."

Mouse glanced at the clock too. *Marathon* would be dropping hyper soon, preparatory to decelerating in to Luna Command. "Debriefing doesn't excite me either. On the other hand, we'll get to see a lot of people we haven't seen for a long time. They'll all be changed."

"Maybe too much. Maybe we won't know them anymore."

McClennon tried to focus on his friends in Luna Command. Max would be older. Greta would be a different animal. He might not recognize her now.

His thoughts kept fleeing to the memories. He found something new each time he checked them. They were intriguing, but he could not shed the disheartening parts.

There were not just five warfleets coming out The Arm. There were eighteen. And the galaxy was infested by not one, but four Globulars. He could not console himself with the starfish view that, in the long run, the enemy was never entirely successful. He did not care that this was their third scourging of the Milky Way, that life always survived, and that sometime between the grim passages, over the eons, new intelligence arose to contest the world-slayers' efforts. He could not be consoled by the knowledge that the enemy would not reach Confederation in his lifetime.

If there was a God, He was cruel. To have allowed the creation of such all-powerful, enduring monstrousness...

"Chub thought he was giving me a gift," McClennon said. "He knew I was curious about the past. And he knew his species had information we wanted. It was a gift of despair. It just showed us how hopeless the whole thing really is."

"I wouldn't say that. You're down too far."

"Why do you say that?"

"You told me the fish said they can be stopped. That it had been done before. The Stars' End people were working on it when the plague got them."

"They were working on us, Mouse. Trying to breed some kind of killer race of their own."

Mouse shrugged. "Hi, Tanni."

McClennon glanced up into laughing green eyes.

Mouse suggested, "Why don't you take my friend for a walk? He's down again."

The woman laughed. "That's what I had in mind. Or would you rather play chess, Tom?"

McClennon grinned. "Let's flip a coin... Ouch! No fair pinching."

"Come on, you. I've got to go on station in an hour." She undulated out of the wardroom.

"Wait till Max gets a look at that," Mouse said.

"Hey. She better not. Not ever. Hear? The fireworks would make the nova bomb look pitiful."

Mouse laughed. "I'm looking forward to it, old buddy. I can't forgive you for snagging that before I did."

"You can't win them all, Mouse." He hurried after Tanni Lowenthal, Stars' End, the mission, starfish, and centerward enemies forgotten.

He spent a month in the bowels of Old Earth's moon. The mind-butchers demolished his soul and on its foundations rebuilt to saner specifications. The first three weeks were horror incarnate. He was forced to face himself by mind mechanics who showed no more compassion than a Marine motor pool man for a recalcitrant personnel carrier.

They did not accept excuses. They did not permit stalling. And even while he slept they continued debriefing him, tapping the incredible store of memories given him by Chub. They were merciless.

And they were effectve.

His sojourn among the Seiners had mellowed his memories of the cold determination of his Navy compatriots. He had come in unprepared. He was less ready to fight the reconstruction.

It went more quickly than his doctors anticipated.

When he was past crisis they opened him up and repaired his ulcerated plumbing.

He was permitted visitors on day twenty-nine.

"Two at a time," his nurse protested. "Just two of you can go in."

"Disappear," Mouse told her.

"Yes sir. Captain. Sir."

Mouse was nearly trampled by two women. He dropped his portable chess set. Chessmen scattered across the floor. "Oh, damn!"

Greta plopped her behind on the edge of the bed, flung herself forward, hugged McClennon. "I'm glad you're back. I've been calling every day since I heard. They wouldn't let me come before."

And Max, the old girlfriend, "Christ, Walter. What the hell did they do to you? You look like death on a stick."

"That's why I love you, Max. You've always got a pleasant word." He squeezed Greta's hand. "How are you, honey? How's Academy?"

She started babbling. Max got on about some new stamps she had at her hobby shop. She had been saving them for him.

Mouse recovered his chessmen, deposited the set on the nightstand, took a chair. He crossed right leg over left, steepled his fingers before his mouth, and watched with a small smile.

McClennon turned his head, trying to hide his eyes.

Softly, Max said, "Walter. You're crying."

McClennon hid behind his hand. "Max... It was a rough one. A long one and a rough one. I was lost for a long time. I forgot... I forgot I had friends. I was alone out there."

"Mouse was there, wasn't he?"

"Mouse was there. Without him... He brought me through. Mouse. Come here." He took Storm's hand. "Thanks, Mouse. I mean it. Let's don't let it get away again."

For a moment Storm stopped hiding behind the masks and poses. He nodded.

Greta resumed babbling. McClennon hugged her again. "I'm having trouble believing it. I thought you'd have forgotten me by now."

"How could I?"

"What am I? A sentimental fool who helped a pretty girl in trouble. We never knew each other."

She hugged him a third time. She whispered, "I knew you. You cared. That's what matters. When you were gone, your friends were always there to help." She buried her head in his shoulder and blubbered.

McClennon frowned a question at Max, who said, "Your Bureau took care of her like family. She's got to be the most pampered Midshipman in Academy."

"And you?"

Max shrugged. "I did what I could." She seemed embarrassed. "Well, how else was I going to keep track of you? I don't have connections."

"I'm glad you're going to be all right," Greta murmured.

"Dad?"

More tears escaped McClennon's eyes.

"Did I do wrong? I didn't mean…"

"It's all right, honey. It's all right. I wasn't ready for that." He squeezed the wind out of her.

"Just get the hell out of my way, woman!" someone thundered in the passageway outside. Beckhart kicked the door open. "See if you can't find a bedpan over around Tycho Crater, eh? Go on. Get scarce."

The nurse beat her second retreat.

The Admiral surveyed the room.

McClennon stared at his professional paterfamilias.

"Looks like everything's under control," Beckhart observed.

"Place is drawing a crowd," McClennon said. "Must be my animal magnetism."

Beckhart smiled with one side of his mouth. "That's one crime they won't convict you of, son. Lay out that board, Mouse. I'll beat you a game while we wait for the females."

The game had hardly started, and McClennon had hardly gotten Greta's eyes dried. The door swung inward again. The nurse watched with a look of despair.

Tanni Lowenthal's face rippled with emotions. It selected an amused smile. "Tom. I thought I'd get here first. I guess you don't run as fast when you've got short legs." She crossed gazes with Max. The metallic *scrang* of ladies' rapiers meeting momentarily tortured the air. Then Max smiled and introduced herself. She and Tanni got past the rocky part in minutes.

Beckhart checked his watch. "Damn it, they're late. I'm going to have somebody's…"

The harried nurse stepped in. She carried a portable remote comm. "Call for you, Captain McClennon."

"Let me have that," the Admiral said. He seized the comm. "Jones? You find her? Got her on the line? All right. Thomas, your mother." He handed the comm to McClennon and returned to his game.

McClennon did not know what to do or say. He and his mother were estranged. She was Old Earther born and bred, and they had battled fiercely ever since his enlistment. Their last meeting, just before the Seiner mission, had ended bitterly.

"Mother?"

"Tommy? Is it really you?"

"Yes."

"I thought you'd been killed. When they came to the apartment... God. They say you were mixed up in this war business that's got the whole world turned upside down. The spikes are everywhere. They're grabbing people off the streets."

"I was in it a little." She had not changed. He hardly had a chance to get in a word of his own.

"They said you got married. Is she a nice girl?"

"It didn't work out. But yes, she was. You would have liked her." He checked his audience. Only the Admiral seemed to know his mother's half of the conversation.

They did not talk long. There had been little to say since he had gone his separate way. It was enough that, for all their differences, they could show one another they still cared.

McClennon handed the comm to the Admiral when he finished. "Thank you, sir."

"I owe you, Thomas. One mission and another, I put you through hell for four years. I won't apologize. You're the best. They demanded the best. But I can try to make it up a little now. I can try to show you that I didn't take it all away..." Beckhart seemed unable to say what he meant.

"Thank you, sir."

A baffled, resigned nurse opened the door. A youth in Midshipman blacks stepped in. "Uncle Tom?"

"Horst-Johann! Jesus, boy. I hardly recognize you. You're half a meter taller."

Jupp von Drachau's son joined the crowd. The boy had been closer to McClennon than his father since his parents had split. The boy was in his father's custody, and resented him for being absent so much. Thomas did not understand the reasoning behind the feeling. The boy saw Jupp more often than him... He thought of his mother and reflected that children applied a special logic to that species of adult called a parent.

He lay back on the bed and surveyed the gathering. Not a big circle, he thought, but all good friends. Surprisingly good friends, considering what he had been through the past few years... Friends whom, most of the time, he had not known he had.

He really had been way out there, lost in the wildernesses of his mind, hadn't he?

The universe now seemed bright and new, specially made for him. Even his starfish memories and his knowledge of the doom approaching from centerward could not take the gleam off.

Horst-Johann was first to leave, after a promise to visit again come the weekend. Then Mouse, who had to return to his own extended debriefing. Then Tanni, who had to get back for her watch aboard *Marathon*. She departed after a whispered promise that left him in no doubt that his masculinity had survived the hospital weeks.

Beckhart sat his chair silently and waited with the patience of a statue of Ramses.

A half hour after Tanni's departure, Max announced, "We have to leave, Walter. Greta has to get back for morning muster. You be good. And try not to collect any more little blondes."

McClennon grinned self-consciously. "You coming back?"

"For sure. I'm keeping an eye on you. You're not sneaking off on me again... It's been a long time, Walter."

Greta blushed.

"Thanks for coming. And Greta. Thank you. Come here." He hugged her, whispered, "I'm there when you need me."

"I know."

"It's important to have somebody who needs you."

"I know. I'll be back Saturday."

After the women left, Beckhart sat in silence for several minutes. McClennon finally asked, "Aren't they going to miss you at the office?"

"I'm not as indispensable as I thought, Thomas. I come back after six months in the field and find them caught up and not a problem in sight."

"What's on your mind?"

"I really said it before, about as well as I can. That I'm sorry I had to do what I did."

"Sorry, but you'd do it again."

"If something comes up. I don't think it will. Things are

damned quiet now. The war has everybody's attention."

"Will we be able to do anything with Stars' End? Or what I learned from the starfish?"

"About the fish info I don't know. It does prove there's a hope. Stars' End... Our Seiner friends have gotten it straightened out. The place is almost a high-technology weapons museum. Some of the simpler systems will be available when next we engage."

"The gods are dead. Long live the gods," McClennon murmured.

"What?"

"Nothing. Nothing at all."

"A long time ago, in another life, I promised you a vacation. I sent you to Payne's Fleet instead. This time I'm sending you home. I've already sent word to Refuge to get your house ready. Take Mouse along."

"Mouse?"

"Mouse took care of you when it got tough. It's your turn. He's slipping. The Sangaree are gone. That hate kept him glued together since he was a kid."

"All right. I understand."

A mountain of paperwork was needed to close out the mission and put the Board of Inquiry into motion. The latter would be handled entirely by deposition. Thomas rolled through it. Nothing daunted him. The Psychs seemed to have rebuilt him better than original issue. He worked like a slave, and had energy left to flit from friend to friend evenings and weekends. He reminded himself of Mouse in days gone by, when Storm had been everywhere at once, pursuing a hundred interests and projects.

Mouse was the opposite. He could not finish anything.

Then it was all done. *Marathon* took them aboard and spaced for the quiet Cygnian world called Refuge, which was home for millions of retired civil servants and senior Service personnel.

But for Tanni Lowenthal the journey might have been depressing.

Going home. His showing for the mission some money, some stamps and coins for his collections, some new and old memories, and an armistice with himself. Somehow, it did not seem enough.

But he had found his friends, the people he had thought missing so long. So why was he disappointed?

There had been one soul-scar the Psychs had not been able to heal completely.

He could not forget Amy.

They had never really finished. They had not said *the end*. They had just gone separate ways.

He liked things wrapped up neatly.

Time passed. Cygnian summer faded into autumn. Fall segued into winter. Mouse and McClennon played chess, and waited, growing closer, till Mouse revealed the whole story of his past, of the origins of his hatred for the Sangaree. Gently, McClennon kept his friend's spirit from sliding away completely. Gently, he began to bring Mouse back.

The report of the Board of Inquiry, delayed repeatedly, drew no closer.

From Cygnus it did not seem there *was* a war. Luna Command had expanded its forces six-fold, and had begun building new weapons and ships, but otherwise Confederation seemed to be going on as before.

Tanni visited occasionally. Max and Greta kept in touch.

And yet...

Some nights, when the dark winter skies were terribly clear, McClennon would put aside his stamp collection, coins, or the novel he had begun writing, and would go out on the terrace. Shivering, he would stare up at stars burning palely in unearthly constellations and picture huge ships like flying iron jungles. He would think of swarms of gold dragons, and a million-year-old beast he had taught to tell a joke.

He never loved her more than he did now that she was lost forever. Mouse had told him... She might use his name to frighten his own child. She would not hate him now. She would understand. But there would be appearances to be maintained, and social winds with which to sail...

Life never worked out the way you wanted. Everyone was victimized by social equivalents of the theories of that dirty old man, Heisenberg.

The comm buzzed. McClennon answered. A moment later,

he called, "Mouse, Jupp's coming in to spend a few days." He returned to the terrace. The ship burned down the sky, toward where the city's lighted towers made fairy spires that soared above distant woods. McClennon pretended it was a shooting star. He made a wish. "Want to play a game while we're waiting?"

Mouse grinned. "You're on."

"Stop smirking. I'm going to whip you this time, old buddy." And he did. He finally did.

Glen Cook is the author of dozens of novels of fantasy and science fiction, including *The Black Company*, *The Garret Files*, Instrumentalities of the Night, and the Dread Empire series. Cook was born in 1944 in New York City. He attended the Clarion Writers' Workshop in 1970, where he met his wife, Carol. "Unlike most writers, I have not had strange jobs like chicken plucking and swamping out health bars. Only full-time employer I've ever had is General Motors." He currently makes his home in St. Louis, Missouri.